The Letter

The Chateau Series Book 1

EMMA SHARP

ISBN: 9798685837639

DEDICATION

To my Family.

Other Books by Emma Sharp

Sweet Pea – Chateau trilogy book 2

Secrets and Surprises – Chateau trilogy book 3

Nellie, The Diary of a French Bulldog Puppy

Coming soon – Innocence in Provence

ACKNOWLEDGMENTS

Editor - Lynn Worton

Cover design - Sarah Jane Design

Web - www.emma-sharp-author.com

Email - info@emma-sharp-author.com

1

The view through the window gradually begins to change, deserted countryside now becoming quaint sleepy villages, and it's not long before the train slows then comes to a halt. I'm the only person left in the carriage, checking my travel documents for the umpteenth time I can see that the next village is the end of the line; and my destination.

I still feel the need to pinch myself, check that

I'm not dreaming, just like the day that I received the letter; the one that appears to be changing the course of my life.

It was just over four weeks ago now; I remember it as though it was yesterday, it's playing on a loop inside my head, and as the empty train sets off again so does the memory...

“Morning, did you have a good shift? Oh, the post has just arrived, something important by the looks of it, I had to sign for it," Jenny, one of the girls that I share the house with says.

“I’m shattered and my feet are killing me, is the kettle on?” I reply with a yawn, “anyway, why are you up so early; I thought it was your day off?"

"It is, damn postie woke me up hammering on the door," she says, handing me the letter and insisting that I open it.

Taking it from her I examine the thick, sturdy envelope, before carefully tearing the top off. Flopping down into the worn armchair behind me, sinking into its comforting cushions after my long night shift, I begin to read...

Dear Miss Mackley,

I am acting for the administrator of the estate of the late Miss Mary Whitehead, who died on 14th February in France. Miss Whitehead had no spouse, children or siblings and her parents died during her lifetime. I believe that you are her great niece and only relative. Therefore, I would appreciate if you could contact the office on the telephone number provided to make an appointment to discuss her estate. If you require any further information, then please do not hesitate to contact me.

Yours sincerely

Peter Armstrong

"You look like you've just seen a ghost," Jenny says, handing me a cup of tea.

Shocked, I look back at her, "I think I actually might have!" before making my way to the small, untidy kitchen in search of much-needed sugar for my cuppa.

On my return I find her jumping up and down with the letter in her hand squealing, "Oh-my-god! Oh-my-God! Oh-my-God!" Running towards me, she almost knocks the hot drink out of my hand as she envelops me in a big hug, squeezing what little life I have left out of me. "What are you going to do?" She asks, as she begins to calm down a little.

"Well, after breakfast, or is it supper? I'm going to bed to sleep…"

Jenny doesn't let me finish, "You can't be serious! You could be a millionairess! You've got to ring them. It's eight forty-five am, they'll be open in fifteen minutes!"

Looking at the clock I shrug, "It's probably a case of mistaken identity, I don't have a single relative that I'm aware of since my gran died... or even worse, it could be a scam."

I polish off two slices of jam on toast while I wait for the fifteen minutes to pass, might as well get this over with so I can have a restful sleep before going back to work tonight.

I get through to the solicitor's office, who confirms that I am the correct person they are seeking. They won't give me any more information over the phone but ask to meet with me the following day; I will need my birth certificate, and my parents and grandmother's death certificates.

I'm brought back down to planet Earth as the train once more comes to a halt.

"End of the line!" Shouts a short, stout man in broken English, poking his head through the carriage door.

Fighting with my luggage, I exit the train to find myself standing alone on a tiny platform in the middle of nowhere. Looking around, I locate a small building and make my way towards it. The little ticket office, to my disappointment, is closed. My eyes land on a picket fence in need of attention, with a gate leading to a narrow lane. Proceeding through, I jump as the voice of a well-spoken gentleman interrupts my thoughts.

"Mademoiselle Mackley, I'm Monsieur

Bertrand. Pleased to make your acquaintance," he says, taking my hand to his lips for the briefest kiss.

Momentarily startled by his actions, I pull myself together and nod, trying to form a smile on my face. "Monsieur Bertrand, thank you for meeting me."

"Let me take your bags," he says pulling my case towards a large black car, the only car in the rough car park. Opening the door, he ushers me into its cool interior before getting into the driver's seat and bumping out onto the lane. "We have quite a journey ahead of us," he informs me, looking in the mirror.

Watching the umbrella pines slowly thin out and give way to fields of giant sunflowers, I find I can no longer keep my eyes open, and sleep overtakes me. The words, "Nearly there now Mademoiselle..." filter through my slumber. Opening my gritty eyes, I get my first glimpse of the Chateau at the top of the hill. My Chateau. The photos don't do it justice; it looks resplendent in the bright sunshine. We enter through the imposing giant gate posts and into the tree-lined drive, the green canopy turning it into an ethereal tunnel, a welcome respite from the fierce afternoon sun. I feel lost. A few weeks ago, I was a newly qualified, penniless nurse, sharing a rented house in Yorkshire, and now I appear to own a Chateau in France.

2

The trees end abruptly, forcing me to squint through the harsh light at the building before me. Locating my sunglasses, I put them back on before stepping out of the now open car door, to be met by a ruddy-faced, rotund man in shabby clothes. Monsieur Bertrand introduces him as Pedro, a local man who has been acting as caretaker in the absence of an owner.

"Pedro speaks very little English," Monsieur

Bertrand informs me.

Pedro, looking pleased with himself holds out his calloused hand, "ello."

Smiling, I respond in school girl French, "Bonjour Pedro."

The two men converse between themselves in French before inviting me inside, giving me very little time to take in the crumbling exterior of the building. Entering through the large oak doors, I'm immediately startled to be met by two suits of armour festooned with cobwebs, standing guard at the bottom of a once-grand staircase. Smiling and nodding, Pedro gesticulates towards a door on the far side of the hallway. Cautiously following him, I find myself in a humungous kitchen, which looks like it belongs in the pages of a historical novel. There is not a fitted unit in sight; dominated by an oversized fireplace, complete with fire grate, and accompanying blackened side oven, with a once shiny copper kettle boiling merrily on top.

"Tea? You must be weary after travelling so

far, "Monsieur Bertrand says, as Pedro proceeds to hunt in an old oak dresser producing three dusty mugs, which he wipes on his shirt. Nodding, I continue to look around the room, expecting a camera man to pop out of one of the numerous alcoves shouting, "You've been framed!"

Looking back at Monsieur I stutter, "Erm, is, erm, this for real?"

Smiling sympathetically, he shows me into a smaller side room off the kitchen, about eight feet square; a scullery, which would also now be considered a museum piece, probably fitted in the late sixties. It consists of an old ceramic sink, a turquoise refrigerator with rounded corners, and wall to wall Formica. My eyes focus on a dated electric oven in the corner, "Does that actually work?" After a short conversation with Pedro, he assures me that yes, the oven and fridge do function. "Well, that makes everything just perfect," I respond sarcastically, but my sarcasm is lost on them.

"I'll show you around the main areas of the

Chateau then leave you to unpack and settle in," Monsieur Bertrand says. The reality begins to kick in, and my state of panic must show on my face as he puts his hand on my shoulder and continues, "Pedro will show you how to work the boiler, so that you will have hot water. His wife did a little shopping for you and has filled the fridge, enough to last you a few days, until you find your way around."

While staring at him open-mouthed, he smiles and ushers me down a set of well-worn stone steps into a large open space with stone floors and a vaulted ceiling containing an ancient machine with rollers fitted to the top of it, next to an old brown sink, "That's not a boiler," I say, confused.

"No, it's your washing machine, the boiler is through the arch at the far side." Gingerly following the two men, I finally see a huge rusty contraption which wouldn't look out of place on the Titanic.

"Voila!" Pedro says, pointing to it enthusiastically.

"You expect me to operate that!" I say aghast. Nodding, Pedro rattles out a list of instructions which Monsieur Bertrand translates for me. Even in English it sounds incomprehensible.

"You will soon get the hang of it; I will write it all down for you... The oil tank is around the back of the house. The inventory says it's half full, so keep an eye on it. - Now, let's continue with our tour," he says, looking at his watch.

The rest of the afternoon passes by in a blur. A tour of the drawing room, sitting room, study, library and cloakroom - all in a similar state of disrepair is next, before being rushed around upstairs to see six bedrooms, one with a tiny en-suite in mustard yellow and two bathrooms, quite unlike anything I've ever been in before.

"I can see you've had enough for today; I'll leave you my number. Also, you can ring Pedro if you have any problems, his daughter speaks fluent English," Monsieur Bertrand says as he hands me the details.

Pulling my phone out of my pocket to store the numbers in my contacts list, I realise that I don't have a signal. Looking back at them in horror, Pedro offers a Gaelic shrug, and Monsieur Bertrand points to an old-fashioned telephone positioned on a desk in the hall. "How am I going to manage? Is there any internet?" I ask, trying to quell my impending panic attack.

"No, but there's a fax machine somewhere," he says, making his escape out of the front door and getting back into his car, waving as he leaves. Pedro turns to face me, kissing me on both cheeks before climbing on his antique bicycle and cycling off down the drive, leaving me all alone.

"Come back!" I shout to his disappearing form, but he only turns and waves.

3

Lowering myself slowly to the ground, I sit cross-legged on the cobbled drive, close my eyes and put my head in my hands. What am I going to do? I can't stay here! Forty-eight hours ago, I left the UK; each day of my journey was like a slow walk back in time, and now, here I am firmly stuck in history. What started out feeling like I'd won the lottery now feels like a bad dream - and I want to wake up. I'm brought back to reality by the chiming of a clock. Looking around I can see the large clock sat above an outbuilding to the left of the Chateau, six o' clock. Standing on shaking legs, I walk towards it. As I get nearer to the outbuilding, I see it was once rather grand, with three large symmetrical arched doors across its facade, but now it stands dilapidated.

I notice movement as I grow closer to the

building, a flash of black and white as a startled creature rushes inside, squeezing through a hole at the bottom of a rotten door. Turning the metal handle, I find it's locked, and I have no idea where to find the key. That's when I realise. I don't even have a key to the Chateau. Resigned, I turn around and retrace my steps, to find an oversized key inside the Chateau door. Then, I'm greeted with my first dilemma when I step inside. Do I lock myself in? The key is way too big to carry around with me. Do I leave it in the lock? Am I even safe here? What am I going to do? Well, I'm here for tonight at least, I'd better pull myself together. In the morning I will phone Monsieur Bertrand and instruct him to sell the Chateau on my behalf. With my decision made, I now feel a little lighter.

Back in the kitchen, as if on auto pilot I read the instructions for the boiler that Pedro had left on the table. Plucking up the courage I enter its dingy cave, and after several failed attempts to ignite it, I manage to wake the slumbering beast. It groans and creaks slowly into life, and before long the water pipes start to rattle and vibrate as warm water begins to circulate through the arteries of the Chateau. Feeling pleased with my achievement, I take the stone steps back up to the hallway and head for the kitchen, wondering if I'm going in the right direction and wonder whether perhaps I ought to leave a trail of breadcrumbs like Hansel and Gretel.

Thinking of breadcrumbs my tummy starts to rumble, reminding me that I've eaten very little since leaving the Auberege after breakfast this morning, now I can't help thinking that I wish I had stayed there! Opening the old fridge with trepidation, I can smell its contents before I see them. On closer examination I narrow the culprit down to a small round box woven out of some type of raffia. Lifting the lid makes my eyes water, as the pungent smell permeates my nostrils. Replacing it quickly I read the label: Camembert. I don't think that will be on tonight's menu, a slice of Cheddar or Cheshire would have been more like it! Unable to locate a bin, I struggle to open the sticking kitchen window, and place it on the windowsill outside. My next find is a tub of foie gras - I don't think so! I allow it to remain in the fridge though, as its odour isn't quite as disagreeable. Well, I can't ring Dominos Pizzas for a takeaway delivery, so I'd better continue with my quest.

Ten minutes later, and I have located some sliced cooked ham, a basin of eggs and various salad items, still covered in soil; - I'll make an omelette! Setting about my task, I wash the salad, beat the eggs, and chop some ham. My next obstacle is the cooker, If I can breathe life into the old boiler, then I can handle the stove - I tell myself, while I fiddle with the controls, trying to turn on one of the old coiled rings. I assume I've succeeded when an unpleasant singeing smell meets my nostrils, and it's not long before it starts to glow red. Ceramic hobs obviously weren't standard in the seventeenth century. Now all I need is some oil and a frying pan. Searching through the sea of Formica I find both, and soon have quite an edible meal. Needing a drink, I continue my exploration of the cupboards but can't locate any bottled water.

Turning on the cold tap, I question whether it's drinkable. Pouring myself a glass of water and looking at it, I say out loud "Eau portable," as I remember some more schoolgirl French. It looks and smells okay, and to my surprise it tastes okay; just plain water. Refilling my glass, I quench my thirst while sitting at the large table in the big kitchen, sorting my way through the pile of paperwork left for my attention. Some of it is in English, but most of it is written in French, I will have to wait for someone to assist me with this task. How frustrating!

4

Feeling better after eating, I decide to explore my new abode in greater detail, starting with the ground floor. There are bound to be other entrances into the building, and for safety reasons I need to locate them and see if they're secured. The first one I find easily enough, it's off the 'big' kitchen into a rear porch; obviously a later addition, it is furnished with an old sea chest, a long church pew, and a collection of Victorian-era coat stands. A smaller door nestles between two windows, too dirty to see out from. Turning the key in the door, I'm surprised to find that it opens easily onto a yard area. Stepping out, I realise I am now standing outside the back of the Chateau, where I can see several more outbuildings. One of them is an out-of-place, pebble-dashed garage, probably built in the nineteen seventies. Stood next to that is what I think is the afore-mentioned oil tank. Okay, nothing too scary out here, I tell myself, and leave the outbuildings for another day, locking the door behind me as I carry on with my task.

Retracing my steps back through the 'big' kitchen and out into the entrance hall, I decide to start with the first door to my left, which turns out to be the formal dining room. I step off the cool tiled floor and onto a worn, dusty carpet, embellished with red and gold flowers. The room contains a large, dark wood table, with twelve mismatching chairs and an enormous sideboard, nothing like the one my gran had in our modest dining room. A smile forms on my face as I remember her fondly. If she's looking down on me now, I wonder what she would make of my new-found situation? "Pull yourself together lass and get on with it," was a phrase I often heard her say to me in the dark days after my parent's accident, along with "You're a strong girl, you can do it." A warm tingling sensation travels down my spine as I look around the room, to see the evening sun streaming through the large bay window, reflecting off the sparkling dust particles dancing around me, lifting my mood a little.

The large bay window is wearing a pair of substantial velvet curtains that look as though they were once a vibrant red, but now aged and faded to a dirty pink. Matching worn cushions adorn the window seat, beckoning the weary to rest and admire the view. An ornately carved marble fire surround dominates one wall, now covered in dust and cobwebs, but it still manages to retain its beauty and elegance. Something compels me to close my eyes and imagine the table surrounded by smartly dressed, 'well-to-do' people, making polite conversation over a bottle or two of local wine. I can almost hear their happy chatter.

Returning from my daydream, I leave the dining room after checking the windows are closed and cross the hall into the once impressive drawing room, a spacious area, where a grand piano immediately grabs my attention. It must have been here on my earlier brief tour, but I'd completely missed it. Even though I've never played before, I'm drawn to sit on its rickety stool and try the keys, thrilled to hear that they still work, probably out of tune - but I wouldn't know. Scanning the rest of the sparsely furnished room, I note tattered leather chairs and sofas, and an empty drinks cabinet. Next, a pair of French doors catches my eye; these appear not to have been opened for decades, sealed shut by overgrown climbing roses. The sharp thorns more of a deterrent than any key, no need to worry about security in here then, just a dashing young prince trying to hack his way through to rescue his princess. If only!

By contrast, the library is a smaller, darker room with no large windows. Most of its light filters through a glass panel leading into the hall. Rows of dusty books line the walls, some of them weighty tomes, not my idea of bedtime reading. A door in the corner invites me into the smaller, cosy sitting room. That's more like it! The old oak panels, which adorn the walls of the ground floor, have at some time been washed a chalky white in here. They are now peeling and scratched, which adds character. Apparently, Chintz was clearly in vogue when this room had its last refurbishment. The curtains, sofa and chairs, light shades and cushions all match, but perhaps not quite the look Laura Ashley aims for today. At least this room is usable, lacking dust and cobwebs; someone must have cleaned it for my arrival, - along with 'Formica kitchen'.

That only leaves the cloakroom, which

confuses the life out of me. That is until I open what I think is the lid of an old chest, to find a porcelain toilet bowl inside! There are two of them, each in a little cabinet with closing door. Do they even work? Fixed to the opposite wall are two old sinks, side by side, that appear to be supported by metal legs. Carefully, I turn on a tap, and water gurgles out with much banging and popping. It's even hot! Some of it splashes onto the dull black and white tiled floor, revealing a shine beneath the dust. Stepping back out into the hall, I see the evening light is fading, like me. Enough for one day. I think I will make a cup of tea, and decide which bedroom to fall asleep in.

My bags are in a neat pile at the top of the stairs on the galleried landing. I don't remember bringing them up; it must have been Pedro. Placing my cup of tea on a table nearby, I look down with caution onto the hall below. It's quite a drop, good job I don't suffer from vertigo. I have a choice of six bedrooms, which should I choose? With my eyelids already drooping, I enter the first door to find an old metal framed double bed, complete with sheets and blankets, looking lost in the vast room. On the opposite wall is a grand fireplace, as wide as the bed. Approaching with caution, I pull back the bedding to inspect its suitability, it will have to do. Retrieving my luggage, I find the basics, and use the small en-suite shower room, containing an old toilet, tacky shower cubicle and the tiniest of sinks. At least they function despite the sickly colour! I will have to remember to leave a pair of sunglasses in here.

Sitting up in the lumpy bed with my now cold tea, I take note of my surroundings. A chalky-white dressing table with ornate mirror sits against the wall between the fire and the window, a seventies teak chest of draws is in the opposite corner, and a large, carved oak wardrobe occupies the wall to my right. A thread bare basket chair in the corner completes the ensemble. It's very eclectic, the room perhaps containing something from every century. Finishing my drink, I lay down, the old bed springs moaning in protest. I need to get some sleep. The creaks and groans around me are very unfamiliar, the sounds of an old Chateau, earlier bathed in the mid day sun, now cooling down and going to sleep, like me. I hope.

A muffled thudding noise breaks through my slumber and rouses me. Sitting up in the half-light, waiting for my eyes to adjust, I remember where I am.

Thud. Thud. Thud.

There it is again! It sounds to be coming from above me. Is it something in the attic? Well, it can't be intruders, not above me. Evaluating the situation, I decide it's nothing to be alarmed about and look at my watch; it tells me it's a little past two in the morning. Glancing out of the vast window to my left, I can see a myriad of stars lighting up the inky black sky, no light pollution here, and no need to draw the curtains, as I'm without neighbours. Settling back down in the uncomfortable bed, I close my eyes, and try to shut out the thudding noise. I'll investigate the attic tomorrow.

Tossing and turning, sleep eludes me. The bathroom calls. Flicking the light on in the tiny en-suite, reveals several large cockroaches scurrying for the shadows, I let out a shriek and jump back into the bedroom. As I calm down, I consider my options. I could try to locate the bathrooms on the other side of the galleried landing, but would they be any better? Probably not, I pop my head back into their abode, my eyes scan the floor, gone. No doubt they are hiding in a crevice watching me relieve myself. Note to self, don't walk around barefoot in the bedrooms! Then unpleasant thoughts pop into my head. Are they in the bedroom? In my bed? What do they eat? Am I on their menu? As if trying to catch them off guard, I tip-toe back to the bed and pull the covers off swiftly. To my relief, I don't come across any more. This time. Perhaps they're under the bed, waiting for me to go back to sleep. Bending down, I peer under the bed into the gloom. Something's under there! Grabbing my useless phone, I use it as a torch to peer into the blackness. A chamber pot! Perhaps I will make use of it instead of the cockroach infested toilet!

A little unsettled, I climb back into bed and try again to get some sleep, though it's not long before I think I can hear faint scurrying noises. Is that the blighters coming back out to feast? Pulling the covers over my head and screwing my eyes tight shut always defended me from the imaginary monsters when I was little, perhaps that will work now. I give it a try and eventually drift off.

An eerie screech interrupts me next. Sitting back up and locating my phone, I note that it's only an hour later. Assuming it came from outside, I tell myself that it's probably an owl or some such creature, nothing to worry about, perhaps it even eats cockroaches! Lying back down again, I try to quell my nerves. I am, after all, a qualified nurse, used to working night shifts and dealing with pain and death, so this should be a walk in the park by comparison.

5

The next time I open my eyes, it's daylight. Wondering where I am, I quickly come to my senses and realise there's some commotion outside. Looking at my phone, I see the time is seven-fifteen am, who could be here at this time? Pulling on a robe I stare out of the giant window to see an old truck pulling a trailer, which appears to contain some animals. Following on behind it is a young boy on a bike, about ten or eleven, with a large black and tan dog running behind, and they are herding several goats down the drive with them. What on earth are they doing on my land? I remember the cockroaches just in time and locate my shoes, checking inside them before slipping them on, and charging down the stairs, wrestling with the heavy front door.

"Hey! What are you doing on my land with those animals?" I shout as a man roughly thirty-five years of age pulls his truck to a stop and slowly gets out. I repeat my question a little louder.

The man shrugs his shoulders, folds his arms, and leans lazily back against his vehicle. He slowly replies in broken English, "I 'erd you ze first time, I'm not deaf!" Looking at me, he slowly shakes his head and smiles, as if laughing at some joke I'm not a party to.

"Can I help you, are you lost?" I ask, not taking my eyes off the dog.

Slowly uncrossing his arms and standing up straight, he looks into my eyes, "No it is not me zat is lost, and it is me zat has been 'elpin' you."

Frustrated, I put my hands on my hips and stare at him. "I don't understand."

The young boy arrives at his side and dismounts, instructs the fierce looking dog to sit, and hands me a grubby piece of paper. Perplexed, I take it from him, trying to keep as much distance as possible between myself and the dog, then read it. It's a bill, stating that I owe Xavier Besnard from Ferme Du Bois 500 Euros, for seven goats, two donkeys and fifteen hens.

"What do you mean?" I ask shocked.

"Zeez are your animals, I' av kept zem for you," he replies, as he disappears to the rear of his trailer and begins to open it. That's when I hear the excited braying of a donkey.

"Wait a minute! My animals?" I shout as I rush over to him. He only nods his head slowly and carries on. "Stop!" I shout over the increasing noise of the animals, hens clucking, goats bleating and the noisiest donkey I've ever heard, not that I've had much contact with donkeys before. My gran had asthma, and was allergic to fur, so I've never even had a guinea pig.

"Where do you want zem?" He asks casually.

Thinking on my feet, I hastily form a plan. "Err, why don't you keep them... for free... and we'll forget about the bill."

After more shrugging, he shakes his head. "I

'av no need for zem. Zay are a pest, escaping and eating my crops. I should bill you for ze damage zey have done!" Cringing, I weigh up my options and sadly conclude that I don't have any. As I look around, feeling lost and deflated, his face softens, and he points to the left of the Chateau. "Zere are stables and paddocks round ze back, we will take zem zere," he says.

"Can you wait while I get dressed? I'll come with you." I reply, rushing inside for some clothes when he nods.

Wearing jeans and t-shirt with my hair looking like a bird's nest, I climb into the cumbersome truck, and sit by his side. Clearly not interested in what I look like, he signals to the young boy, who gets back on his bike, and like a sketch from Monty Python, we continue at a snail's pace around the back of the Chateau. I am now in unknown territory, scanning the undulating land around me, I can see no boundaries. How much of this do I own? Reality check! I know nothing of caring for animals, a cute kitten I could probably manage but donkeys! I clearly need to do some research, but with no internet, and no phone signal, how am I supposed to proceed?

After what feels like an hour, but in all probability is only about ten minutes, we come to a halt in an area that resembles a small farmyard.

"Voila," the farmer says, pointing to a stable block with barns and numerous other outbuildings, some in better condition than others. He wastes no time in jumping out and striding over to the stable. Opening the door, he inspects the gloomy interior. "Zis will do," he says, then sets about the task of transferring the two, now restless donkeys from his trailer to their new abode. Attaching a short rope to their head collars, he leads them out of the smelly trailer, then passes me their cords.

I look back at him clueless, and he tries to hide his amusement, "Just lead zem into ze stable and don't stand behind zem, zey might kick!"

That's enough to scare the living daylights out of me, so I drop their ropes and jump back out of the way. The two donkeys take this unexpected opportunity and break free, trotting and bucking their way to the other side of the yard.

Quickly, I scurry back into the truck to get out of the way of the fearsome beasts, preferring its smelly interior to the possibility of being trampled to death by the wayward creatures. Composing myself, I then peer out of the dirty window to see the young boy walk over to them, take hold of the ropes, and lead them inside with no effort. I risk joining them only when the stable door has firmly closed.

Feeling a little foolish, I saunter back over, "They don't seem to like me."

The farmer and his son both laugh and shake their heads, "Zey know you are afraid of zem. You 'av to be ze boss!"

The hens make their way out of the trailer and disperse, clucking and pecking their way around the yard as if nothing had happened.

The final two seem to be larger and are bickering with each other as they go their separate ways into the undergrowth.

"Where do you want ze goats?" Asks the farmer, looking at me for an answer.

Hopeful of his guidance, I shrug my tense shoulders, "Erm, where do you suggest?"

Shaking his head and laughing again, he talks to the boy in French, who also laughs before securing them in two separate paddocks.

"Zees are boys, and zees are girls," he gestures to both paddocks, then goes on to explain when I look at him in confusion, "Unless you want babies, zey need to be apart. But zat boy will get out I zink" he adds, pointing to the largest one.

"I don't know anything about caring for animals," I admit in a small voice.

"You will learn quickly. Zey need food, water, and mucking out daily. And ze lady goats need milking," he says, doing the actions as he speaks. Sensing my panic, he continues,

"Okay, for no extra cost I will do it wiv you today, zen you will know."

Lifting a sizeable stone and locating a key, he opens a small shed and brings out a sack of feed, which he divides into two buckets and puts in with the donkeys along with two buckets full of water. "Tomorrow you can let zem in ze paddock, zey will 'av settled down." Next, he puts the feed into several small pans, before retrieving a stainless-steel bucket and small wooden stool, then enters the lady goats' paddock. To my astonishment, the goat's queue in an orderly line as the boy then takes over from his father. He sets down a pan of food in front of the goats, sits at the side of the first goat and starts to milk it. I watch this from the relative safety of the yard, but it's not long before I am beckoned in and told it's now my turn.

Leaving my comfort zone behind me, I enter the paddock with trepidation.

"Come, sit," The boy says, as he tries to explain the method to me. His English is better than his father's; at least I can converse with someone, even if he's only ten. Tentatively sitting on the wobbly stool, I hold the teats as instructed - they feel soft and warm - the boy encourages me, and all seems to be well until I do something to cause the poor animal discomfort. It bleats loudly and kicks the bucket over, spilling the white frothy liquid on the ground, and my feet. The boy makes quiet, reassuring noises, and the poor goat settles and stands still again.

"See? I can't do it!" I protest, jumping up.

Shrugging again, the farmer replies, "Yes you can. It takes practice, and patience."

The boy finishes the first goat. It scampers off, seeming to have forgiven me, and another moves forward to take its place. One down, five to go! Standing back, the boy insists I do the rest. By the time I get to number five I seem to have got the hang of it, they skip off happily to eat the long grass. I, on the other hand, have wet sticky feet and a bucket of goat's milk that I don't know what to do with. Pleased with my efforts, I hand the boy the bucket of warm frothy milk.

"Yours," he says, turning away to put the equipment back in the shed.

"What do I do with it?" I ask awkwardly.

"What do you think?" They reply in unison.

Okay, I asked for that. "Is it nice?" I ask but, get no reply as the boy and his father gather their possessions. The bike is loaded into the back of the trailer, along with the animal excrement.

"I will come back for ze 500 Euros anozer day," the farmer shouts through the window, as he turns his vehicle around and leaves me in the yard with the animals. My animals! A memory flashes through my head; I'm a little girl sat on my mother's knee in the garden singing 'Old McDonald had a farm, E-I-E-I-O'. If only she could see me now!

6

Watching them leave the farmyard and disappear makes me realise how isolated I am. When will I see another person? Sure, I have the animals for company now, along with the cockroaches, but I can't ask them for advice, they're more of a liability. And how am I going to pay the farmer 500 Euros? My distant relative left some money for me but not enough to live off and maintain this stately crumbling pile! Looking around for inspiration, I notice a lane that leads away from me and appears to continue up a hill. Perhaps I should explore in that direction, but not now, I need to get back inside to cool down. I must remember to wear a sun hat! Turning around, I trip over the bucket of milk, some of it sloshes out onto the stone floor of the yard. I suppose I ought to take this back to the kitchen and get it in the fridge before the sun sets about turning it into cheese.

Walking back to the house with the bucket, I turn back to see a small black and white cat lapping up the milk off the floor. I can't help wondering if it's now my cat. Do I need to feed it? It must have survived by itself for the last few months, probably keeping the mouse population in check. Well, at least I have found a use for some of the goat's milk.

Back in the kitchen, my stomach reminds me that I've not had breakfast and it's already mid-morning. With no cornflakes in sight, I settle for boiled eggs and some bread, which is now a little dry. The coffee on the other hand, is freshly ground, not a jar of the instant stuff I'm used to drinking; I must admit it's tastier, just the smell of it is uplifting. Note to self, when feeling down smell the coffee, not the roses!

My first job this morning had been to ring Monsieur Bertrand and instruct him to put this place up for sale, but my farming lesson hijacked that. Locating my phone reminds me that I don't have a signal, so I will have to use the museum piece in the hall. I pick up the handset and fumble with the older style dial. After waiting impatiently for the call to connect, but it goes instantly to voice mail.

I leave a short message then, realising I don't know the land line number, I hang up. I locate the address and phone number on the documents in the kitchen and ring back, leaving him another message with the number. So, now what? I can't sit here in the hall waiting for him to call back. Does technology this old have a voice mail? I very much doubt it!

I would quite like a shower to wash the goat smell off my legs, but don't fancy running the gauntlet of the cockroach infested en-suite. Perhaps the other bathrooms are better.

Five minutes later and I'm in one of them, it had obviously been fitted at the same time as the Formica kitchen. The bath, toilet and basin are the colour of mushy peas, and the tiles look like an explosion in a paint factory! In the bottom of the tub are several dead insects in varying states of decay. The water in the toilet is a muddy brown colour. Holding my breath, I flush it; thankfully, it appears to work. Trying all the taps, in turn, I discover that the hot tap on the bath has ceased, there doesn't seem to be a shower here either. Okay, on to the next one.

The second bathroom looks cleaner but is way older. The bath is huge and has a strange arrangement at the end, a tall curved wall made of some type of ceramic, with old pipes lining its interior, and a giant showerhead fixed above it. Is this the world's oldest shower? Does it work? Turning on a large, heavy lever sends water spluttering and bubbling slowly at first, then faster, out of the pipes and eventually the shower head. Yes, it seems to work, what a strange contraption. I'm in luck. First though, I feel the need to clean it and the rest of the bathroom. I locate a bottle of pine-smelling liquid and a cloth in the corner under the window. Half an hour later, it smells better and passes for use. In no time I've gathered my things, and I'm enjoying the luxury of a hot shower, with jets spraying my aching body. Bliss!

Climbing out of the shower I can hear a shrill noise; it sounds to be coming from downstairs. Wondering what it is, I grab my robe and step out into the hall. The sharp sound continues, is it an alarm? Half-way down the stairs, I realise it's the phone. As I'm about to reach the bottom step, it stops. Damn! It's probably Monsieur Bertrand. I find his number and ring him back, but it still goes to voicemail. I leave him another message asking him to ring back. I stay put, standing in a puddle of water from my shower for what feels like ten minutes before going to get dressed. I'll have to try again later.

Dressed and feeling fresher, I find myself aimlessly rattling around the Chateau, not quite knowing what to do next. What would my gran do? I know the answer straight away, make a list! She always had 'to-do' lists on the go. Finding a pen and note pad next to the phone, I sit at the desk in the hall and start my list. First, contact Monsieur Bertrand to get the Chateau on the market. Second…

Tapping the pen on the desk, I can't think of

anything. Perhaps I ought to find the local village; I'm going to need provisions. Yes, that's number two.

How will I get there, is it far? I realise I know nothing and no one, apart from the farmer, whom I owe 500 Euros. Maybe I ought to avoid him. Monsieur Bertrand said that Pedro has a daughter who speaks English, I'll ring them, she should be able to help me. I dial the number, and I'm delighted to hear the voice of the female who answers.

"Hello, I'm Laura at the Chateau. Sorry to bother you but-"

I'm interrupted by a fast-talking lady speaking entirely in French, most definitely not Pedro's daughter. Disappointed, I manage, "Au revoir," and once again hang up without achieving anything. Why is this so difficult? I'll go for a walk, and check on the animals, it might lift this melancholy feeling.

All seems to be as I left it up at the farmyard, the donkeys appear to be napping, and the goats are happily eating the long grass, making more milk for me to collect in the morning. The hens are pecking happily. Do I have to catch them and lock them up for the night? Will there be foxes here? I'll worry about that later; it won't be dark for hours yet.

Continuing up the path that I saw earlier, now wearing my oversized straw hat, I slowly meander through sparse woodland before coming out at the top of a small hill into open grassland, containing very long grass, now brown and in need of water. A few brightly coloured flowers remain amongst the frothy seed heads of long-faded blooms. It's very serene, listening to the wind gently blowing over its surface, which gives it an almost fluid-like quality. I'm momentarily distracted when my pocket vibrates and my phone springs to life. Oh-my-God! I have a signal! Looking at my phone, I do a happy dance on the spot. I have six texts from Jenny and several missed calls, feeling guilty for not contacting her, I sit and read them in order.

How're things, have you arrived yet? X

You must be there by now! X

Going to work, hope everything's ok. X

Getting worried. X

LAURA! X

OK, this is silly, should I ring Interpol? X

I ring her number, but it goes to voicemail. I suppose I deserve that, she's probably at work.

"Hi, I'm okay, sorry for not getting in touch; no signal in the Chateau, had to come out and walk up a hill, have a landline, will ring you this evening. I can't even begin to describe what this place is like. Speak soon. Miss you."

Well, that's progress. I try accessing the internet, but the signal isn't strong enough, perhaps it will be in the village, but how do I get there? Yes, that has to be the next mission, finding the village.

7

Arriving back at the Chateau and ready for lunch, I stop in my tracks. There's a bicycle leaned up against the entrance, looking around I can't see anyone. On closer inspection, the bike resembles the bone shaker that Pedro had been riding on. Calling through the open door, I shout, "Hello... bonjour!" A young woman pops her head out of the kitchen door.

"Hello, I'm Sylvie, Pedro's daughter. Sorry to intrude, I thought you might not have heard me knocking."

I rush up to her and hug her like a long-lost friend, her brow furrows a little, probably confused by my actions. Not perturbed, she embraces me.

"I am so pleased to see you!" I blurt out and make myself stop and think before my mind goes into overdrive with the long list of questions I have.

"I brought fresh bread," she says, pointing to a baguette on the table, as she puts the kettle on the stove.

Trying to slow my mind I take a deep breath, "Thank you so much for coming, I rang your number earlier, but the lady that answered was only speaking French."

Shrugging in imitation of her father, she replies, "Yes it was Mama, she doesn't speak English, sorry."

Washing my hands, then slicing the bread, I continue, "Please don't apologise, I'm so grateful that you're here. I need to find the local shops, and I wondered if you could show me where they are, if you've got time."

Pulling the meagre contents out of the fridge, I manage to make a ham salad, as we chat and get to know each other. Sylvie is twenty-four and works three days a week at the local primary school, the other two days she helps her parents with jobs. They too have goats, hens, and a few cows; it appears to be the norm around here, as well as olive trees and an orchard. I start to relax a little now I have someone to ask for advice. I recount the experience of my first farming lesson, which she finds amusing.

"You need to make cheese from your milk," I look back at her aghast. "It's not difficult, I'll teach you! And, you'll need transport to get to the village."

Looking back at her vacantly, she smiles and jumps out of her seat, takes my hand, and leads me out of the back door to the small garage behind the Chateau. Locating a key from underneath a stone, she unlocks the door, it's a little stiff and rusty, but with persuasion, it opens. "Voila!" she exclaims as she wheels out an old bicycle.

"But the tyres are down," I say, pointing to them dejectedly. In no time at all Sylvie takes the pump from the frame of the bike and inflates them.

"Good as new," she grins, climbing on it and

testing it out before dismounting and handing it to me.

"Do you have time to show me where the village is?" I ask hopefully.

Smiling kindly, she nods, "Yes, but it's no good going until later, they close at lunchtime for a siesta."

I push my bike, which fortunately has a large basket attached to the handlebars, around to the front of the Chateau, and lean it against Sylvie's, before heading back to the kitchen where I write out a shopping list.

"Is there anything else you want help with?" she asks kindly.

Not knowing where to start I reply, "The list is endless."

Shrugging she smiles, "Okay, fire away!"

I reel off a long list as the questions enter my head, “How do I get hold of Monsieur Bertrand? Do I need to put the hens away at night? How do I get rid of cockroaches? How do I care for goats, donkeys, hens, and a cat?

How do I access the internet and get a mobile signal? What on earth am I doing here? …sob...I want...sob...to go home!"

I only realise I'm sat crying when Sylvie gently puts her arm around my shoulder and passes me a tissue. She says nothing and kneels at my side until I stop. Wiping my eyes and feeling foolish I begin to apologise, but she makes a gentle shushing noise, smiles, and says, "There, doesn't that feel better?"

I nod, trying to compose myself, "Sorry, I just feel so isolated and out of my depth."

Sitting back in a chair, she looks at me, "I would feel the same in a strange country where I couldn't speak the language, and with such a responsibility. Let me help you with some of the questions. Firstly, Monsieur Bertrand has left the area for the summer with his family; it's his 'le grand vacance'. He will be back at the beginning of September."

I stare at her in open-mouthed shock. "What! He's left me here alone for weeks? No wonder he was in such a rush to leave yesterday! What am I going to do? Has he left someone else in charge?" Shrugging once more and shaking her head in sympathy, Sylvie goes on to say something about the hens, but I've zoned out and I'm concentrating on my breathing, as I try to fend off a panic attack.

As my breathing slows, I look over at Sylvie, who looks back at me like the school teacher that she is. "Well, you're not alone, you have me as a friend now. Come on, let's go and look at these hens, see if you have somewhere to secure them at night. But first, you need sunscreen, your shoulders are starting to burn." Now I feel like a child again when she orders me to find a long-sleeved blouse.

"I'm sorry, I used to have panic attacks when I was a child, after my parent's accident; I haven't had one for many years now, except when my gran died. It must be the stress." I say, as she helps me gather my things.

I walk with her to the farmyard, where she locates the hen hut and enclosure behind the stables, there are a few holes in the wire netting surrounding it. She quickly finds some old wooden boards and blocks them. Most of the hens seem to have already found their way inside. Sylvie gets some grain out of the shed and fills up the feed trough in the enclosure, which brings more hens scurrying inside from the undergrowth. "Just leave the door open until dusk, I think they will all be in by then, not too difficult is it?" she says. She then instructs me to fill the water bowls up. "That's all you need to do daily. And collect the eggs of course. They will need a good clean out occasionally; you can use it as fertiliser for your crops."

Again, I'm shocked, "What crops?"

Sylvie seems to find this amusing and tries hard not to laugh. "I can see you're not a country girl. You have plenty of land, you ought to be growing your own fruit and vegetables. It's too late in the year to start now; you'll have to wait until next spring. I'll bring you some; we have plenty."

Shaking my head, I firmly say, "I won't be here next spring. Anyway, I haven't got the faintest Idea how to grow anything!"

As if not hearing my reply she continues, "Don't worry, I'll show you what to do. There is an orchard, and soft fruit in a walled garden, along with a large glass house further down this lane. Some of the fruit should be ready now, probably in need of attention I should think. We'll look at it another day, time to head into the village."

Back at the house, I grab my small backpack and mount the old bike. I'm a little shaky to begin with; it's years since I last got on a bike! By the time we reach the gate posts at the end of the drive I have gained confidence, though, and pick up speed trying to keep up with Sylvie, who is ahead of me. Turning left I try to concentrate so I will be able to find the way on my own, but everything looks the same; endless fields of crops, grass verges, peppered with scarlet poppies, broken up by small areas of pines.

Sylvie stops by a narrow lane on the left and waits for me to catch up. "This is the farm where Xavier and his son Gus live, along with his elderly mother. Although I believe she's in hospital just now," she says, pointing to a group of buildings up the lane.

With my aching legs, burning lungs and numb buttocks, I only nod and smile, not wanting to lose momentum as we continue. How much further? A question I don't ask out loud, Sylvie must already think I'm a wimp. I try to concentrate on the sounds of the cicadas, still quite a novelty to me, not an unpleasant sound, but I don't think I'd like to meet one, the cockroaches are bad enough.

After what feels like an hour, but is probably only twenty minutes, the twisting road straightens and turns into a tree-lined avenue, with cottages springing up in increasing numbers. Soon, we enter the small village, and the smooth road surface turns into a cobbled square. With my sore buttocks protesting, I follow Sylvie, and we lean our bikes against an old monument. "Will they be safe here?" I ask.

Smiling she nods, "If you didn't come back for a week they would still be here."

Okay, so, not quite like the city that I come from!

Looking at my list, she suggests we start at the grocers. Entering the small dimly lit shop I look around and feel like I'm in the pages of some history book, sugar, flour, and many other dry goods are in barrels ready to be weighed out; butter is in a large slab, where you cut yourself the required amount. Tins, packets, and various boxes line the walls on wooden shelves. It's fascinating, but I can't see any cereals in the familiar boxes from home. I ask Sylvie where to look for them, but she tells me that they are too expensive, so the local shops don't stock them. I'd have to go to a supermarket in the larger town for them. Okay, that won't be happening anytime soon. Looking in a fridge, I'm about to choose some cheese, but Sylvie stops me, "We have lots of homemade cheese at home, we'll call in on the way back to get you some, along with fresh greens."

The next stop is the butcher, no pre-packed food in here. One large marble slab, the length of the shop has raw meat, while another one at the other side has cooked meats, salamis, and pates. Dead fowl, staring with unseeing eyes and hanging from hooks in the ceiling, completes the ensemble. Playing it safe, I buy some bacon, sausages, and cooked ham, only enough for a couple of days. I wonder if there's a freezer in the Chateau, I don't remember seeing one, but I haven't been back down into the cellar, it's an area I'm avoiding as much as possible.

The bakery beckons, the window is a visual delight with cakes, pastries, and croissants. I buy several of each, they look and smell divine, that's breakfasts taken care of. Last stop is the hardware store, where I buy a white powder that is guaranteed to make the pesky roaches run for the hills. Here's hoping!

Back in the small village centre, the bikes are indeed where we left them. My buttocks don't relish the return journey, but I have no alternative. Tentatively getting back on, with my purchases safely stowed in the basket, I follow Sylvie the short distance down the road to her cottage. I'm grateful to be able to dismount and wheel my bike through the small gate up the path and leave it in the shade under a large tree. Entering the cottage via the back door, I find myself in a large square kitchen, still old fashioned but newer than my sixties affair. Pulling a heavy jug of juice out of the fridge she pours us both a glass; it's cold and refreshing.

Nodding my approval, she tells me, "It's made from our own lemons."

This woman is a goddess! Is there anything she can't do? She gestures for me to sit at the scrubbed wooden table, but I tell her I'd rather stand just now, which she finds amusing. "Keep going, and you will get used to it."

Looking out of the small windows to the rear I can see that there appears to be several acres of land, with homemade sheds and an old stone outbuilding presumably housing the animals. I can see why she needs to help her parents.

Remembering my phone, I ask about the internet, she tells me that I can call in anytime to use her wifi, so I add the details to my phone.

"I'll tell my parents in case I'm not in, and you need to use it," she says kindly.

"Oh no, I would only come when you're in."

Next, Sylvie fills a carrier bag with fruit, greens, and a large block of cheese. "Please let me pay you for these," I say, but she won't hear of it. I spend the next fifteen minutes sending texts to Jenny, Claire, and Rebecca - my house mates - and checking my emails, most of which are the usual junk.

"Are you sure you can find your way back? I could come with you," she says as I climb gingerly back on the contraption that is now my only method of transport.

"I'll be fine, I've taken up enough of your time. Thank you so much for your help," I reply, and cycle off, feeling far less confident than I look.

I'm thankful that it is much cooler on the ride home. With the village and its brightly coloured window boxes behind me, I concentrate on the road ahead and think about the evening's tasks ahead of me, anything to take my mind off this suffering. My backside must be the colour of the poppies decorating the grass verges! I recognise the lane to the right as the entrance to my neighbour's farm. I keep my eyes ahead, not wanting another encounter with him. Rounding the next bend, I see the welcome sight of the Chateau gate posts. Glad to have made the journey without falling off, I dismount and walk the rest of the way up the drive with my bike, leaning it near the massive front door.

8

Fishing in my backpack, I retrieve the

oversized key, and let myself into the cool interior, flopping down on the first chair I come across to catch my breath, grateful that it has a tatty cushion on it! Once sufficiently recovered, I stow my perishables in the fridge and rush upstairs, a long soak in the bath beckons! Damn! I don't have any bubble bath, another trip to the shop doesn't appeal, shower gel will have to suffice. My sore backside and aching muscles are grateful as I relax neck-deep in the warm, soft water. Half an hour later, with skin like a prune, I force myself to get dressed and attend to my chores. Firstly, the hens need securing for the night.

Arriving at the farmyard on still wobbly legs, I take a deep breath, and tell myself I can do this. First, I peer over the stable door at the donkeys; they bray loudly at my intrusion. Do they need any more food? Gathering an armful of long grass from the edges of the paddock, I toss it over the stable door. Both donkeys rush forwards and bicker over their supper. "That will have to do until morning," I tell them and leave them to feast. The goats are still happily munching in the paddock.

Now for the hens, at least they don't intimidate me. Counting out loud, I only get to thirteen, that includes the two bigger ones that are still unhappy with each other. On closer inspection, I notice that one of them looks to be a little worse for wear, perhaps I should separate it from the others in case it has a disease? Yes, I'll let it go to take its chances outside. I'm sure the farmer billed me for fifteen, though a recount confirms I have two missing. Looking around they aren't anywhere visible. Now what? They could be anywhere on the estate, and my sore body has had enough exercise for one day. Oh well, they'll have to take their chances tonight too, maybe they'll return in the morning when they're hungry.

Looking over to the large clock above the grand outbuilding, I notice it says three-forty; that can't be right, it must be well into the evening by now. It's obviously stopped. Does it need batteries? Stupid question! It's way too big to be battery operated, another query for Sylvie then. My phone, now without signal again, tells me it's eight-twenty. My stomach agrees, and it needs feeding!

Back in the kitchen I make a bacon and egg sandwich and enjoy some of the fruits that Sylvie kindly gave me, the sweetest apricots I have ever tasted! I had intended to continue with my exploration of the Chateau today, but I'm way too tired. However, I must ring Jenny; I promised to call her. Carefully dialling her number on the old phone, an electronic voice tells me something in French that I don't understand. Frustrated I tell the voice that it's my friends' number. Trying again, I get more of the same, damn this mobile phone signal! I'm certainly not up for a walk back up the hill tonight; I'll try again in the morning.

One last job before I climb into bed. Slowly creeping into the cockroach's lair, I carefully sprinkle the mysterious white powder around the floor, paying attention to cracks and crevices as instructed, before washing my hands and collapsing into my unmade bed. Well, my first full day on my own has certainly been some initiation! I went to bed last night as a tourist and woke this morning a farmer! What will tomorrow bring?

I remember nothing until I'm brought back to reality with the loud crowing of what sounds like a cockerel, its shrill, persistent song permeates my senses and wakes me. It must belong to the farmer down the road; noise seems to travel long distances here. Looking at my phone, I see it's only five am; pulling the pillow over my head, I try to get back to sleep. Half an hour later I give up and go in search of a cup of tea, the sun is streaming through the large, full height window in the hall, as I descend the stairs; it is rather magnificent, and I try to image the house as it must have been in its glory years. What's happened to its former inhabitants, there must once have been a lord and lady with numerous children being waited on by eager servants? Where are they all now? How did this end up in my possession? Another job to add to my list, researching the history of this Chateau. I will need the internet for that task. I wonder if Sylvie knows how my great aunt became the owner? She probably does, or at least her parents might.

Taking my tea back to bed, I sit and think of my tasks for today. I need to attend to the animals; I'll make that my first job after breakfast, get it out of the way. The thought of those two donkeys is enough to accelerate my heart rate. What did the farmer say? "Y*ou 'av to be ze boss!*" Yes, I'll show them who's the boss around here!

The donkeys are pacing and braying loudly as I approach. Squaring my shoulders and appearing as tall as possible, I locate their ropes and open the stable door just wide enough to slip inside. They both approach me eagerly, but I don't flinch. I carry on walking towards them like the young boy, Gus, did yesterday. It seems to work, and they both stand still and allow me to clip on the ropes. So far so good. I step out into the yard with them. Breathing slowly, I walk over to an empty paddock and open the gate; they rush in eagerly, and the ropes slip through my fingers. I feel my hands stinging and automatically let go. Damn! Now they have got away from me, at least they're in the paddock where I wanted them. I'll leave them to settle down and come back after I've milked the goats. Examining my hands, I don't appear to have any blisters. That was lucky; it could have been much worse, next time I'll wear gloves. If there is a next time, I think they'll have to stay there. They can shelter from the sun under the big trees. I'll get them some water later.

Remembering what Gus taught me yesterday, I get five bowls of feed and the goats' line up in a sort of queue ready to be milked, obviously quite used to the routine. Despite it going smoothly, I still manage to get milk down my legs and feet, but that's probably the least of my problems. I have a fridge full of yesterday's milk, what am I going to do with it all? Sylvie makes cheese, which I've yet to try, I should give it to her, so that she can make even more. Maybe Sylvie could sell it. Finding a small bowl in the shed, I leave it full of the liquid in case the little cat comes back; the grain sacks in the shed are intact, so I guess she's working hard for me controlling the rodent population, it's the least I can do in return.

Next, the hens. Entering their enclosure, I give them fresh water and grain, looking inside a little house I see several brown eggs which I remove with a sense of satisfaction. Milk and eggs, could I become self-sufficient like Tom and Barbara from 'The Good Life'? Gran and I used to howl with laughter at their antics on the comedy channel; they don't make them like that anymore! On second thoughts, perhaps not; it would take a lot of hard work and time. As soon as Monsieur Bertrand returns from his month's holiday, I shall be leaving. I have a sensible career to go back to; I don't know how long they will hold my job open before advertising for a replacement.

Walking back to the donkey paddock, I notice they seem very occupied by the business of eating as much grass as possible. I take the opportunity to enter and try to remove their ropes. Approaching slowly, they hardly seem to notice me. I have the lines removed, and fresh drinking water sorted without them lifting their heads. Well that was easy! Looking around, I can't see the three hens that stayed out for the night, probably the victims of a fox, or some such creature by now.

Walking up the hill my phone pings to life, reminding me to ring Jenny. She answers immediately. "I've been so freaking worried about you Laura. Are you okay? When are you coming back? Is the weather nice? It’s chucking it down here!" When she eventually stops for breath, I tell her about my journey and the crumbling Chateau, the farmer and the animals, and, of course, my new friend, Sylvie. "It sounds horrific! So, you're not coming back for a whole month! Can't you come home, then return in a month to sort it out when the Solicitor returns from his jollies?" She asks hopefully.

"Wish I could, but I've got a farm full of animals to take care of."

"Well, can’t you get the mad farmer chap to look after them for you. Or take them to the market or something!"

Hmm, she has a point, I could ask Sylvie if she would like them. "I'll investigate the idea. Certainly not the farmer though, I don't know if I can even pay him what I already owe. Monsieur Bertrand hasn't left me any bank books, so I can't access the money that I've inherited yet." Saying goodbye, I promise to ring her again soon.

Reaching the faded flower meadow, I stop and sit on the grass; this is one of my favourite places so far, it's relaxing listening to the sounds of the busy insects going about life. Unlike me, they have nothing to worry about; I'll allow myself five minutes before returning to the Chateau, it's still early.

Waking up, I wonder where I am as I turn my head to the side. My eyes eventually focus, and I find myself staring into the beady eyes of a snake! Jumping up I scream, and slowly step away from the offending creature. I manage to get a picture of it as it slowly slithers away. Oh-my-God! That was close! Was it poisonous? Could it have killed me? I send the photo to Sylvie, she replies quickly telling me it's a viper and very dangerous. Having dealt with enough animals for one day, well, for a lifetime really, I head back to the relative safety of the Chateau to occupy myself indoors.

The next morning I'm woken again by the shrill sound of the telephone in the hall. Rushing down the stairs, I don't get to the phone before it stops again. Damn! This is so frustrating! If I'm to stay for another month, I must have a phone and internet signal.

Sitting in the kitchen eating one of my home-grown eggs, I see a figure in the rear courtyard; it looks like a male. Clutching my robe tightly, I walk to the window and peer out. Oh no, it's the farmer chap! I hope he hasn't come for his money, and I desperately hope he hasn't brought his ferocious dog with him! Opening the door, he strides straight in without being invited.

"Good morning, do come in," I say sarcastically.

"I am in, and I need your 'elp," he replies, the

sarcasm lost on him.

I peer back at him with raised eyebrows, "You need my help? I very much doubt that."

"Yes, it is so. I ‘av ‘erd zat you are a nurse. So yes, I do need your ‘elp," he replies, shrugging. "My muzer, she ‘as come out of ze ‘ospital - she ‘ad a stroke - I cannot leave her alone and get on wiz my work. You can ‘elp...yes?"

"Erm, what kind of help were you thinking of, exactly?"

Scratching his head, he looks away for a while then looks back at me and reels off a list, one that he's obviously practiced on the way here. "Well... She needs ze washing and dressing and ‘elp to eat ze breakfast; ze urine bag needs your ‘elp most definitely. Zen ze lunch, and ze washing and undressing at bed. You see, yes?"

“Okay, let me get dressed, and when I have sorted my animals, I will come over and meet your mother. Does she speak English?"

Heaving a sigh of relief, he points to the door,

"I will take you now. Zen go and do ze animals for you if you can elp me."

After quickly getting dressed, I get my bike, which he tosses carelessly into the back of his truck. I'm not sure which mode of transport I prefer, the uncomfortable saddle or the smelly truck.

Arriving at his farmhouse, he jumps out of the truck and shows me into the large kitchen; it resembles the small kitchen in the Chateau - same colour, and same sixties units with an equally ancient range in the fireplace. Fortunately, it also has an electric oven, like the one I'm now just getting used to at the Chateau. Looking at me, he points to a door straight ahead. Going through I find his mother laid in a small single divan bed in the lounge, and, to my horror the large dog is lying on the floor at her side. It lifts its head and bares its sharp teeth as I approach, making a low grumbling noise. I look back at Xavier who calls the dog over, and with a swish of its tail it bounds over to him, ignoring me completely. Heaving a sigh of relief, I walk over to his mother's bed, she doesn't move, and I notice her closed eyes.

"Mama," he says, gently shaking her shoulder. She opens her eyes and gives him a lopsided smile, before speaking to him. Her voice slurred due to her stroke. The poor woman, she doesn't appear to be very old either.

He begins to talk to her and, I presume introduces me. She looks at me and smiles then holds out her left hand. Realising I don't even know her name, I take her hand and introduce myself then start to explain that I'm staying at the Chateau for a few weeks.

"She az no English," the farmer interrupts, once again shrugging.

"Oh dear, how shall we be able to communicate?" I ask, perplexed.

"Gus, ee 'az no school for ze summer, he will translate. Easy!" He says as he strides out of the room, with the dog following behind.

Wait a minute, where are you going?" I ask, annoyed.

"To get ze boy and do ze animals for you...yes?" he replies, then bellows up the staircase to wake his son.

The boy arrives, looking unkempt, soon after his father has left. Yawning, he turns to me, "How do you like the donkeys and goats?"

His cheeky face breaks into a lazy grin, and I can see the resemblance to his father. Going over to his grandmother, he leans over and places a kiss on her cheek, before sauntering into the kitchen and putting the kettle on the stove.

Following him, I ask, "What is your grandmother called?"

"Nana," he replies innocently.

Okay, let me try again. "Yes, I understand that. My name is Laura, you are Gus, and your Nana is?"

Nodding, and realising his mistake, he laughs, "Alice, she's called Alice."

I continue with my questions, but getting answers is like pulling teeth - one by one. I want to ask Gus where his mother is but decide to leave that for another day. I eventually find out that Alice is only sixty-nine. She had a stroke and has been in the hospital nearly four weeks; she has only been home three days. She appears to have some control of her right arm and can weight-bear on her legs. She uses a wheelchair but can't get upstairs to the bathroom. A carer would come out to help her, they were assured, but as yet no one has turned up. Okay, that's a start.

I pull a small dining chair over and sit at her side, while Gus stands next to me. Together we tell Alice that I am going to help her to wash and dress and get her up for breakfast. She gives me a lopsided smile, waves her good left hand, and then starts to cry. After comforting her, Gus asks her why she's crying.

"Je suis tellement heureuse de pouvoir me lever et de me laver."

Gus translates for me, "I am so happy to be able to get up and have a much-needed wash." The poor woman. I hope her pressure areas are intact after lying there for days.

Taking somewhat longer than I expected, Alice is, at last clean and fresh and enjoying a bowl of porridge with her grandson. After stripping the bed, I look for a washing machine; there's nothing evident in the kitchen so I ask Gus. He points to a door in the corner that leads into a stone washhouse, where, to my horror, I see an ancient machine with two rollers on top, like the one in the cellar at the Chateau. I am clueless! Returning to the kitchen, defeated, I tell Gus I don't know how to operate it. He informs his Nana, who immediately instructs him to push her into the washhouse where through Gus, she teaches me how to use the contraption, and an hour later the bedding is blowing in the wind. Before leaving, I make a sandwich and fresh juice for Alice and Gus to eat later, promising to return in the evening.

9

The ride back home is thankfully short. Having a quick lunch followed by a much-needed shower, I decide to continue with my explorations, but where should I start? Looking into my empty coffee cup for inspiration, I decide to start at the bottom and work up. I find a torch hanging on a hook by the back door and, to my amazement, it works! The door down to the cellar creaks as I open it. Taking a big breath, I locate a dubious looking light switch on the wall, so far so good. With trepidation, I carefully descend the worn steps and reach the bottom in one piece. "Hello," I call out, my voice echoing off the damp walls. Thankfully, no one answers. Feeling braver I examine the washing machine. It looks like the one at Alice's; perhaps I will be able to wash my clothes after all.

I notice a large, old, wooden shelving unit, which looks homemade, taking up most of one wall. Had it been there when I came down here with Pedro and Monsieur Bertrand? It must have been I think I was in shock that day! On closer inspection, I see at least a dozen bottles of wine on its bottom shelf. Picking one of them up, I jump back in alarm as a colossal spider scurries out from under it, before squeezing itself through a gap in the wood. I don't know how I manage to keep a hold of the bottle! Wiping the dust off the label, I read the words 'Pinot noir', which mean nothing to me never having been much of a wine drinker. I wonder how old it is. Will it still be drinkable? I could do with a glass right now! I place the bottle at the bottom of the steps to take back up, perhaps Sylvie or the farmer will be able to tell me.

A couple of rusty tin baths hang on the wall, along with various old tools and strange items that I don't recognise. I find a weird looking chair tucked away in a dark corner. Looking more closely, I realise it's an old commode. I wonder who it belonged to; it seems like it might have been around at the same time as Florence Nightingale.

I turn my attention to the old boiler next. I expect it needs some maintenance, it still appears to be working though, so I leave it be. My gran used to say, "If it isn't broken, don't fix it." I really should make a list as I go around. I'm going to need the help of a workman of some type; perhaps the farmer will help me now in exchange for caring for his mother? What a good idea, I think to myself. I can't remember his name no matter how much I wrack my brains; then I remember he gave me a bill. Perhaps his name's on there, but where did I put it? I'll have to look for it. Glancing around, I think that's about all there is to see down here. It seems odd that the cellar isn't as big as the rest of the Chateau, perhaps part of it has been filled in at some time. Picking up the bottle of wine, I climb the steps, eager to leave this dungeon behind.

Once back in the relative safety of the kitchen, I glance at the pile of papers on the corner of the big table. I know I will have to tackle them at some point, but I need a translator; I could ask Sylvie but she's too busy. Would Gus read them to me? It would probably bore him, but he just might if I did something for him in return. I will have to give it more thought. On top of the pile, I find the bill. Xavier! Yes, that's his name. Xavier, Gus, and Alice. Turning around, I notice a new loaf of bread on the far side of the table nearest the back door. I don't think it was there earlier, who put it there? It can't have been Sylvie; she's teaching today. Well, whoever it was I'm most grateful, I finished my last one at lunch time and didn't fancy another trip to the village.

Locating a pen and paper at long last, I manage to start my list. Number one is to get advice about the boiler; two is to ask about the wine I've found; three is the tap in the sixties bathroom that doesn't work. Well, that's a start. Next, I decide to look inside all the cupboards and drawers of both kitchens. I come across lots of old pots and utensils, and I can’t begin to imagine what their use is, some are quite bizarre. One of the drawers is jammed shut in the small kitchen, and I can't open it; that goes down as four on the list.

After the kitchen, I move into the dining room, not much to explore in here except the old sideboard. I'm disappointed to find it empty, no family silver to sell. Making my way around the other rooms downstairs, I spot nothing of note in the cupboards and drawers except the remains of dead insects, anything of value must have already been sold in the past to keep the wolves from the door. A few paintings are hanging on the walls, but they don't look to be very old, or worth very much, but what do I know?

I'm distracted from my task by the shrill noise of the phone in the hall. "Hello," I say, amazed that I got to it in time.

"Mozer is needing 'elp, I will be zere in two minutes," a male voice says then the line disconnects. Xavier isn't one for small talk it seems. Before I have time to think his truck appears on the drive and he throws his door open.

“I was planning on going back to Alice when I've had my tea.”

"She ‘as toilet," he says, holding his nose and making hand gestures.

"Okay…" I don't get chance to say any more before he takes my arm and guides me out of the Chateau and into the truck. It takes a few minutes before I realise I'm sharing the passenger seat with the large dog. I jump in shock as it turns and licks my arm, "It's going to bite me!" I yell.

Xavier only shrugs and says sarcastically, "It prefers more meat on ze bone zan you ‘av."

At the farmhouse I'm out of the truck in a flash, only to find poor Alice distressed and in tears. I look around, Gus is nowhere to be seen, and Xavier makes a hasty retreat.

"Excusez-moi, pardonnez-moi!" she says repeatedly. Poor Alice, how humiliating for her living like this with her son and grandson. Looking around I can't find a commode; she definitely needs one. The hospital should have provided one for her. Then I remember the old chair in my cellar. I'll clean it up and tell Xavier to collect it, not ideal but better than nothing.

After sorting Alice out, I help her to eat her tea - another sandwich - which I notice she has difficulty swallowing. The poor woman needs a soft diet, with soups and stews; the sort of food my gran used to cook when I was young. I'm sure we can do better than this. Before leaving I help her back into bed and make her comfortable. "I'll be back in the morning," I tell her, hoping she understands.

Xavier reappears with an offer to drive me home which I accept, but insist he leaves the dog behind. I use the short journey to tell him I will need meat, potatoes, and vegetables, to make better food for his mother.

He nods saying, "I will get zem for you in ze morning."

"There's a commode in the cellar that you can take home with you. I will clean it up tomorrow."

With the commode now loaded onto his

truck, he nods, "Merci beaucoup," then climbs into his vehicle and drives away.

When he's gone, I lock the door and look for something to eat myself, it's been a hectic day, and I'm hungry and tired. Tomorrow I'll have a search of the upstairs. Falling into bed a little later, I sleep soundly, especially now that the cockroaches appear to have moved out.

In the morning, after breakfast I cycle over to see Alice. Upon entering the kitchen my eyes immediately land on a rabbit, a hen, and a pheasant; all three dead and laid on the kitchen table, complete with heads, fur, and feathers. What on earth are they doing there? Poor things!

I take a wide berth around the dead creatures, shouting, "Bonjour Alice!" Only to find Alice slumping over to the right in bed, and close to falling out. This will bed not do! There are no bed rails on her small divan; she needs a proper medical bed. I will tell Xavier to contact her GP to access the help she needs. My First job is to get her washed and dressed and into her chair for breakfast. Gus appears just as the porridge is ready. I show Alice the commode, and her face lights up as Gus translates for me. He has an old head on his young shoulders. Plucking up courage I ask what happened to his mother.

Gus shrugs, emulating his father, "She left." Feeling awkward I don't probe further. Sylvie might know. Pointing to the dead animals, I enquire as to their purpose.

"The meat you asked for," he says casually.

"What? I just wanted some minced beef or minced lamb!" Horrified, I continue, "What am I supposed to do with them? I wanted to make a shepherd's pie!"

This comment has Gus in stitches, he tells his Nana, and she too begins to laugh loudly. When Gus calms down enough he says, still giggling, "We don't have much of an appetite in France for shepherds, we prefer their sheep!"

Once the hilarious moment has passed, Alice continues to speak to Gus, and it soon becomes apparent that he has been instructed to pluck and clean the animals, ready to be cooked. I've never cooked or eaten rabbit or pheasant, and I don't much fancy the prospect, let alone know any recipes for them. Alice points to a box of fresh fruit and vegetables by the back door. That's more like it! I get to work, peeling and chopping carrots, onions, and potatoes.

As I'm putting the now prepared chicken in the oven to roast, Xavier strides through the back door and plants a kiss on his mother's head. Looking over to him, I ask if it's one of his hens. Shrugging he replies, "No, it is one of your cocks," then casually puts the kettle on the stove.

"What do you mean, one of my cocks?" I shout, standing with my hands on my hips defiantly.

"You 'ad two cocks, zey just fight to death... too good to waste, and you wanted meat. You 'av meat now. Pheasant and rabbit off your land. You 'av lots of meat to get, two male goats also - you only need ze one!" He replies, cocking his head to the left before asking,

"Do you know ‘ow to bake ze cake?"

Looking back at him defensively, I say,"I was expecting minced beef or lamb from the butcher... and of course I can make a cake."

“Smiling he replies, "You want mince, you ‘av to mince it up for yourself, and ze goat is like lamb!"

I give him a hard stare, "Don't you dare!"

Xavier speaks to Gus in French, who jumps up from his chair and takes a strange vice-like instrument off a shelf and gives it to his father, which he then clamps to the table. I look at him puzzled. "For ‘ze mince, and Mama says ‘ze cock needs to be put in a casserole wiz ‘alf a bottle of red wine and wiz ‘ze vegetables for one and a half hours. I am now returning to ze work," he finishes, walking out of the house with his cup of coffee, collecting the dog, which he thankfully left outside. That man is so ignorant and frustrating, not even a thank you for caring for his sick mother. There is no way I'm going to pay him the five hundred Euros now!

One and a half hours later and I have spruced up the old commode, made a chocolate cake, an apricot crumble, some scones and my first cock au vin. Pleased with my culinary efforts, I dish out Alice and Gus a bowlful each. Alice waves her arm gesturing for me to join them. I'm very tempted but not sure I can manage to eat my poor cockerel, so have a helping of crumble and custard instead. Perhaps I'll become a vegetarian!

As I am washing the dishes, with Gus drying, I tell him about the paperwork that I need translating. With his Nana's permission, he agrees to come back with me for an hour to look over it. A short while later, I'm about to get back on my bike when Gus points to a small lane leading out of the farmyard. "It's much quicker this way," he says, jumping on an old bike which is too small for him. Following behind, we arrive back at the Chateau in five minutes, why didn't Xavier tell me about the short cut?

10

Back in the Chateau, Gus follows me into the kitchen. Showing him the pile of letters and documents, he scratches his head and asks without hesitation, "What will you do for me in return?" This boy has clearly learnt well from his father, who appears to be devoid of emotion.

A little startled by his response, I ask, "What do you have in mind?"

Jumping up, he walks purposefully into the drawing room, apparently familiar with the place and points to the piano. "I would like to continue with my piano lessons."

Surprised once more by him, I explain, "I cannot play a single note, so wouldn't be able to help.

"I have lessons at school, but can't do my homework, we have no piano. The old

Madame used to let me practice here; she was so kind."

There is so much I don't know; in fact, it's becoming apparent that I know nothing at all, but how can I find out? I need to build on my schoolgirl French; it's a foundation, but not enough! Learn to speak French is now number five on my growing list.

Sifting through the paperwork, Gus explains that most of them are bills or receipts for bills already settled by the notaire, Monsieur Bertrand, but when he moves onto the official documents about the Chateau, which lists the out buildings and land, he abruptly stops reading and looks up at me with his mouth wide open, a little shocked.

"What's wrong?" I ask. Gus jumps up from the table and rushes out of the door to retrieve his bike. Stunned, I rush after him. "Gus? What is it that's bothering you?"

"I can't leave Nana alone for too long," he shouts back as he cycles away. How very odd! Picking up the documents, I try to make sense of them but can only translate a few of the words – voiture, meaning car, being one of them. If only I had the internet!

Instead of exploring the upstairs as I'd planned, I decide to concentrate on the 'grand' outbuilding, which I now know was the former 'carriage house' - at least I learned something today. Armed with my torch, I walk over to the building. Looking up at the old clock reminds me that it needs attention too, that's now number six. All the doors are locked. My eyes land on another large piece of masonry down the side of the building; the garage key and the shed key were both under large stones, so it's safe to assume I'll find the carriage house key under this one. It's too heavy to lift. Finding a sturdy short plank and a smaller rock, I manage with an effort to lever it up. Yes! Much to my delight, I locate the missing key! I carefully clear away the now dehydrated vegetation that's accumulated in front of the doors, not wanting another snake encounter. I then attempt to open the doors, but the locks have ceased.

Refusing to be defeated, I go back to the Chateau. Perhaps one of the old tools in the cellar will be of use. Returning triumphantly with an oil can and a hammer, I spray each lock with a liberal amount of oil, followed by a sharp tap with the hammer, but they are still unyielding. I give up for now and concentrate on the garage around the back where my bike was stored. It opens easily. With a torch in hand, I enter feeling more confident. Rummaging around in the gloom, I trip over a garden spade lying on the floor. Reaching out to save myself I knock over a stack of garden canes, which tumble down around me, taking me with them. After scrambling to my feet, I carefully lean them back up against the wall where I find a light switch. Frustratingly it doesn't work; that's number seven! Rooting around, I discover a big old lawn mower, two more bikes, an abundance of plant pots of various sizes, several jars and bottles containing liquids and powders, their labels peeling and faded. They seem to be mainly weed and pest control chemicals, as well as buckets, a hosepipe, and lots of gardening tools and implements. Very handy, not that I know anything about gardening. At the back of the building is a large chest freezer, its lid is open. I peep inside. It looks like an insect's graveyard, yuk! I don't think I'll be using that!

Time to clean up and get some tea before returning to help Alice. Back in the kitchen, the first thing I notice is that the pile of papers Gus had been reading to me earlier are now scattered on the floor. That's strange! "Hello, anybody here?" I shout. There's no reply. Looking around warily I see the back window is wide open. I had noticed that the wind had picked up today, perhaps I left it open earlier. Retrieving the windblown papers, I decide to relocate them to the desk drawer in the hall; they'll be safer there.

Back at the farmhouse, Alice is alone, Gus and Xavier are out. Oh well, Alice is familiar with the routine now, so we should be okay. I was hoping to talk to Gus, ask him what scared him away, but it will have to wait till morning. I turn Alice's bed around, with her weak side facing the wall, she should be safer this way, and leave a note for Xavier, reminding him to contact their doctor. I'd do it for them, but he probably wouldn't discuss the case with me.

The next morning is a repeat performance of yesterday, with the boys absent. Their dirty breakfast dishes are in the sink, so I know they came home last night, very odd.

With renewed optimism, I return to the carriage house with the oil and hammer. To my surprise, the key turns easily in the first door. Gingerly stepping inside, I find a small, old tractor with various farming implements surrounding it, I have no idea what they are all for; I suppose at one time, all this land was farmed. What on earth am I going to do with it?

As I near the back of the room, I see a wooden ladder fixed in place, disappearing up through a hole cut out of the ceiling. Halfway up the rickety stairs, I hear a faint buzzing noise, which gets louder as I climb. Reaching the top, I find myself in a dark loft space with a little tower that houses the clock, it's fascinating. Next to the clock is a big metal key on a chain. Picking it up, I locate the slot that it fits in, and turn it slowly, the cogs spring to life. Now I can cross number six off my list! The constant buzzing noise draws my attention. Investigating, I find a large bee's nest in the corner. I think I'd better get out of here! When I reach the bottom of the ladder, I notice a small door in the side wall. Turning the handle, I find it's not locked and opens easily. Whoever has been winding the clock has been using this door, I wonder who it was?

I leave the room and turn my attention to the other doors in the carriage house. The second door requires a little more force, but eventually opens. Inside I find a few sacks containing small white pellets, I don't know what they are, so leave them well alone. There are more farming implements and several empty wooden crates and boxes of differing sizes stored there too. Several dozen unused empty wine bottles, covered in dust, are lined up against the wall. Perhaps they made their own wine here in the past.

The third door still won't open. I tap the lock vigorously with the hammer and administer yet another dose of oil. When that doesn't help, I go in search of lunch.

After lunch, I decide that a trip to the village is necessary. I am running out of clean clothes and need laundry soap, and other provisions. I arrive to find the shops all shut. Damn! That's when I remember Sylvie telling me they close in the afternoon. Oh well, I have plenty of time. Looking around, I locate Monsieur Bertrand's office. A notice on the door states, 'Ferme jusqu' en Septembre', 'Closed until September'. Only three more weeks to wait.

I wonder if Sylvie's at home. Leaving my bike under the tree, I walk to the back door. "Hello!" I call outside after knocking, but no one answers. Turning around, I see her in the field. As I walk down through the garden, she notices me and waves for me to join her. I help her harvest beans, peas, and salad leaves. It's hard work, and we're soon in need of some cool shade.

While drinking cold lemonade in her kitchen,

I take the opportunity to use the internet and send texts home. Recounting the last few days highs and lows to her, she agrees that I need to improve my French. Sylvie directs me to a website, where I manage to buy books and CD's online to be delivered to her house. Thinking about it, I realise I've not had any post at all at the Chateau.

"The postman only delivers once a week to the outlying properties, but you can call in at 'le bureau de poste' to collect your mail if you wish," she informs me. Imagine that in Leeds!

Fishing for information about my mysterious farmer next door, Sylvie tells me that she remembers Xavier met a young woman about eleven years ago who had come down to stay at the Chateau for the summer, she was studying at university in Paris. "She unfortunately became pregnant, but only stayed a short while after the child was born. Rumour has it that she couldn't stand the isolation and 'backward ways' of the 'country folk'," she says sadly. Poor Gus, so he never really knew his mother. I wonder if she keeps in touch.

I then ask her about my great – aunt, Mary Whitehead.

"Yes, I remember her well, she was always very kind and loved children. She gave many of the village children free piano lessons. Some of the locals used to help with the harvest. She always rewarded them well and was respected by the community, despite being an 'outsider'. Unfortunately, I can't remember much more but I will ask my parents what they know."

Cycling home, I'm pleased with my afternoon's work, now back to Alice.

Another morning with Alice passes uneventfully, Gus tells me that his father has had to go out but doesn't say where. When I've finished my jobs, I again ask him why he left me in such a hurry.

"Dad doesn't like Nana to be left alone for too long," he says once more. It seems fishy to me. I think something spooked him. Xavier seems to be avoiding me too. I need to get to the bottom of this.

11

I'm determined to get inside the remaining part of the carriage house today. A swift tap with a hammer before turning the key seems to work. At last it opens to reveal its contents: an old car that looks as though it used to be red and white, now faded with patches of rust. I thought there must be one somewhere, I recognised the word 'car' on the inventory, but does it work? The driver's door opens with a loud creak, revealing a set of keys inside. Wiping the dust and cobwebs from the seat, I climb in and sit down. I think I need to have it checked by a mechanic before trying to start it, I could do some damage if it's short of oil or water... or whatever it needs. It looks very French, like one that I saw parked in the village.

Turning around to look in the back I get a shock, four tiny black and white kittens are curled up together on the back seat. They make little mewling sounds as I lean over towards them, no bigger than the palm of my hand with their eyes still shut. I'm so tempted to pick one up but think better of it. I don't want their mother to reject them. I must remember to put some food and a bowl of goat's milk down for her every day. One of the windows has been left open, that must be how she got in. Slowly climbing out I shut the door and leave them be. Tucked away behind the car is a weird looking barrel with a strange screwing implement on top, perhaps it's a press of some sort.

My list continues to grow. Now I need a

mechanic to look at the car and possibly arrange insurance. Will it require a M. O. T., do they have such a thing in France? I can't do anything though until the kittens have left. Closing the carriage house back up, I see a small hole near the bottom of the door where the wood has rotted away, that must be where mummy cat gets in. Now I have five cats to add to my inventory!

In the fridge, I find the tub of foie gras, that will have to do for mummy cat for a couple of days until I go back to the shops. I don't know what to do with all the goat's milk that I'm accumulating. It's a shame to let it go to waste. I wonder if Alice has any suggestions.

While helping Alice with her evening meal, I recount my day's activities. With Gus's help, Alice tells me that Xavier will collect the milk after he finishes work and she will teach me how to make cheese, or 'chevre' as she calls it.

Back at the Chateau, I'm about to go to bed when someone bangs on the kitchen door. Thankfully, it's not quite dark, and I can see it's Xavier, here for the milk. Why am I always wearing so little when this man turns up? Clutching my robe, I let him in and point to the two buckets of milk. One of them smells a little, and I suggest we throw it out, but he insists it will make even better chevre! Before he goes, he asks about the bottle of wine on the table.

“I found it in the cellar and don't know if it will be any good.”

After reading the label, Xavier rummages around and digs a corkscrew out from a drawer and opens the bottle with a flourish, smelling at it before he takes a gulp straight from the neck. So much for ladies first. Shrugging in his very laid-back way he offers the bottle to me.

"Is it still okay?" I ask.

Nodding enthusiastically, "It's very okay."

I'm far from an expert with wine but have a small sip. It tastes quite nice. Opening a cupboard, I find the glasses that I've already washed, and he pours us both a drink.

After consuming most of the bottle, he becomes animated and talkative; it's quite funny, so out of character for him. I take the opportunity to quiz him a little, asking how long he's lived at the farm. He instantly clams up, gathers the buckets of milk, and starts to leave. Turning back to look at me he screws his eyes up and frowns, "Zere are many secrets 'ere." What does he mean by that? His truck pulls away as I reach the door. It's only a short drive, I do hope he gets back in one piece.

Despite being tired, sleep eludes me, my mind wandering through the day's events: finding the car, complete with kittens, and Xavier's comment. What did he mean? What secrets? I finally manage to fall asleep only to be woken by the thudding noise above me again. There must be something in the roof, I will investigate tomorrow, after making the cheese!

Alice seems to be in better spirits and eager to set to work, instructing Gus which pans and utensils we'll need. There only seems to be one bucket of milk. I ask Gus what happened to the other. Laughing, he tells me it tipped over in his dads' truck. Oh well, it can't smell any worse than it already did.

Milk, lemon juice and vinegar, then boiling, stirring, and straining and we have chevre! It isn't too difficult. Alice is thrilled and instructs me to roll the cheeses in various chopped herbs. They smell delicious. Now I'll never have to purchase cheese again... Well, that is until I get home. I leave half of it at the farmhouse, before taking my share home. Well, back to the Chateau anyway. Alice seems to enjoy my company; it's almost occupational therapy for her. She would benefit from some physiotherapy too. Xavier needs to call the doctor. If he doesn't do it, then I will have to!

Arriving back home at the Chateau, I find two old bikes by the door, one of them is Sylvie's, but I don't recognise the other. A clattering noise coming from the rear courtyard diverts me, where I find Pedro extracting the beast of a lawnmower from the garage. "Bonjour

Pedro," I shout above the noise, he carries on, having not heard me. So, I call louder, he turns around and waves, then climbs off the beast and plants a fatherly kiss on both of my cheeks. A gesture I'm slowly getting used to, thanks to Alice.

Hearing my voice, Sylvie pops her head out of the garage and waves. Thrilled to see her, I go over and give her a big hug which she returns. "Your parcel has arrived, now you can start improving your French. Let's begin while Papa cuts your lawn." Glancing over at the lifeless, brown grass, burnt to a crisp by the relentless sun I have to smile as a memory comes back to me, of my dad mowing vivid green stripes onto his pristine lawn, what would he make of this?

After sharing lunch with my friends, 'chevre' salad, I have my first lesson. I'm surprised at how much I've remembered; Sylvie is impressed too and leaves me lots of homework to do. Pedro appears and asks if there's anything that needs his attention. I show Sylvie my growing list, which she uses as an opportunity to practice, helping me to translate and speak to Pedro. Pleased with my attempt, he tells me he will take care of the ceased bath tap, garage light and kitchen drawer. "I also know a local workman who will come and look at the boiler, and can recommend a mechanic for the car, once the kittens have left home."

With Sylvie's help, I tell Pedro that as soon as Monsieur Bertrand returns, and I can access some funds I will pay him back for his kind assistance. As an afterthought I add, "But for now, I hope you will accept my invitation to dinner tomorrow evening, please bring your wife too. Is seven-thirty ok?" Beaming, he nods, and with more kisses exchanged, I watch them cycle away, then remember poor Alice.

How do I get around that problem? I suppose if I go earlier, cook her meal, and help her into her nightclothes then Xavier can assist her to bed later. Yes, that's what I'll do. What about food? I could make coq au vin again, but that would mean killing one of the hens, which is not happening! I'll ask Alice when I go later, she's obviously an excellent cook.

As expected, Alice is full of ideas and suggests a French onion flan, with potatoes and vegetables, followed by apricot crumble. I require no help with that, and we have all the ingredients I need. Understanding a little of what she says, and with Gus's help, I soon have the instructions to make the flan. Leaving with my basket laden with goodies, I return to make the pastry case. An hour later and it's ready to be filled with eggs, chevre, onions and herbs. I can do that later, closer to the time. Next, the apricot crumble, which I can make in advance.

Down in the cellar, I retrieve three dusty bottles of wine. Xavier is fit and well, so it must be safe to drink, although I expect he has the constitution of a pig... and the manners to match! As I'm about to climb back out of the dank cellar, the light goes out leaving me in total darkness. Shrieking, I begin to panic and put the bottles down. How will I find my way out? I haven't got a torch with me this time! Trying to calm myself down I think of my gran, which helps me to focus. Putting my hands out in front of me, I feel for the wall then follow it around until I find the opening for the stairs. I rush back up to the safety of the hall. Groping for the old light switch on the wall, it comes back on again. Probably a loose wire, another job for Pedro! Going back down for the bottles, I leave a torch on the old shelves - just in case.

12

I don't know where the time goes, it's three-thirty already, I've been here over a week now and still haven't explored everywhere. I need to get in the loft and find the walled garden but haven't time today. I must get back to Alice soon. I've never had a dinner party before, just drunken evenings with friends as a student nurse. Sylvie and Pedro seem laid back. I hope Sylvie's mother is too - I don't even know her name! Should I set the table in the dining room, or the kitchen? I think the kitchen would be better, then we can sit in the small sitting room at the back. I hope they like chintz! The cutlery and crockery are very rustic, no fine bone china and crystal goblets, it will have to suffice. Running a duster around the place takes an age and leaves me rushing over to help Alice, glad that I prepared her evening meal earlier.

Returning with only an hour to spare, I fill the flan case and put it back in the oven, fingers crossed it will be okay while I have a quick shower and change.

Looking out of the bedroom window, I see a blue car coming down the drive. It's like the one in the carriage house but in a better condition. Reaching the hall just in time, I welcome them to my Chateau. My first guests. Sylvie introduces me to her mother, Rose, a small slim, lady with greying hair.

"Bonjour madam," I say in my best French. She replies in French too, but I only understand some of her response. Sylvie informs me that she wants me to call her Rose, and that she's pleased to meet me at last, having heard so much about my exciting time here.

I nod and smile, "Merci Rose."

Inviting them in, I take them to the kitchen and pour them each a glass of wine, then excuse myself as I finish the cooking.

Fifteen minutes later we sit at one end of the oversized kitchen table to eat. Rose seems quite chatty, and Sylvie needs to help with the bits I don't understand, though it's all good conversation practice. The flan is edible, thank goodness, and my efforts praised, but I confess to the idea being Alice's.

"How is she getting on?" asks Sylvie.

"She's improving but would do so much better with proper care."

Pedro interrupts, "I will talk to Xavier and advise him to call the doctor out." Apparently, he was a good friend of Xavier's late father.

The conversation continues mostly in French, which I'm starting to understand. Pedro tells me that the wine is an excellent one and would have been expensive, then Rose suggests I spend a day with her. "I will teach you good French cooking," she says.

If only I had time! "Once Alice gets her care sorted out, then I would love to take you up on your kind invitation," I say. These people are so friendly, and not at all like Xavier.

I'm startled by a loud bang as one of the wooden shutter's slams into the wall. Pedro goes out and secures it before checking the rest on the ground floor, the sky has changed to an angry shade of dark purple. "Yes, they have forecast storms for tonight," he tells me.

Rose stands, hugs me, and thanks me for my hospitality saying, "We must get home before the rain starts, we have left the dogs in the yard."

"Would you like me to stay with you?" Sylvie kindly asks, but I decline.

"Thank you, but I'll be fine, I've always liked

thunderstorms."

"Are you sure? They can be quite severe, especially with the heat we've had for the last few days."

"I'll be fine, but thank you," I repeat, as I wave them away.

Time to tidy up. I'm just putting the last of the dishes in the cupboard when the sky lights up spectacularly. "Wow!" I cry and start to count like my gran, and I used to do. I only get to three before a loud crack of thunder echoes off the Chateau walls. "What about the animals?" I say to no one in particular. Will they be okay? I decide to ring Sylvie for advice. She should be home now.

"Sorry to bother you but I was wondering if the animals will be okay... do I need to get them inside?" She asks Pedro who insists that they will be quite used to storms and will shelter under the trees. "Okay, thank you, and sorry to be a nuisance," I say before hanging up.

Another streak of lightening lights up the sky,

followed by a loud thunderclap. Downstairs is secured, so I venture upstairs to check the windows. Apart from my chosen bedroom and the working bathroom, I've spent very little time upstairs. It's an area I still need to explore but just haven't had time. As I reach the galleried landing, a massive fork of lightening illuminates the purple sky, followed by a loud crack. The Chateau plunges into darkness. Flicking the light switch makes no difference, the power has gone off. And my torch is in the cellar! Well, I'm certainly not going down there to retrieve it. Using the light on my phone, I search for candles. I remember seeing some in a kitchen drawer beside a box of matches. Lighting two and putting them into old brass candle sticks, I go back upstairs and look out of the bedroom window to watch the show.

It's not long before the rain starts, gently at first, pattering against the window. It almost sounds like home, but a sudden gust of wind whips it into a frenzy as the downpour begins in earnest, a welcome respite for the parched earth. Peering out into the gloom, I can almost hear my gran's voice saying, "It's coming down like stair rods." Another loud clatter gets my attention. Everything seems okay in my room. I'd best look at the other bedrooms. The first two seem okay, with nothing amiss. Moving on to the next, I find the culprit of the noise. Another wooden shutter on the outside is flapping against the wall. It's no use going outside. I can't reach it from the ground.

What should I do now? The only way I'm going to be able to reach it is if I open the window and lean out. Why didn't I think to check upstairs while my guests were still here to help me? Muttering to myself, which has become quite a habit since I arrived here, I decide to tie the long curtain around my waist. After securing it tightly, I see if it can support my weight. I wouldn't be surprised if the old metal rails pull straight out of the plaster. I'm delighted when I take my feet from the floor and find myself swinging freely, feeling invincible, like Lara Croft. Yes, this should work.

Opening the window and leaning out, I still can't reach the shutter. Damn! The rain is pouring down, and my thin nightdress is offering little protection.

Well, I'm wet now, might as well get on with it. I kick off my flip-flops and climb onto the narrow window ledge and lean out just as an impressive fork of lightening illuminates the sky. Looking up in surprise, I lose my footing and slip off the windowsill and find myself dangling in thin air, clutching the curtain. Looking down, I try not to panic. I am not destined to die like this. There are so many things I want to achieve before I meet my maker. "Help!" I shout, but I know it's futile, no one can hear me. Think Laura, think! Looking up, I force myself to let go of the curtain, praying the knot around my waist will hold. I manage to reach the window ledge with one hand, and the wayward shutter with the other. It's a struggle, but I secure the screen back onto its latch. At least I've achieved what I set out to do, now the small matter of getting back inside safely. My arms are aching, and I've grazed my hands trying to grasp the edge of the window frame, but failure isn't an option. Unexpectedly, when I don't think I can hold on any longer, I feel someone, or something grab my ankles. Screaming in terror, I lose my hold and bang my head on the stone wall. Everything goes black.

I'm freezing, and I can hear my gran's voice, "No room here for you yet lassie, get yourself back home. Alice needs you."

"Alice needs me... Alice needs me..." I repeat quietly.

I can hear words in the background - a familiar voice, and then a strange sensation on my cheek, like warm, wet sandpaper.

"You will not be much 'elp to 'er in zis state." Then a foul smell and burning taste sears my nose and mouth. Coughing and spluttering, I come to my senses. Opening my eyes, I find a familiar face staring at me – Xavier, and his dog! Why does this irritating man keep tuning up?

"What are you doing?" I snap, pushing the

glass of fiery liquid away from my face.

"What were you doing? Iz ze better question."

Looking around, I see I'm laid in a puddle of water in the bedroom, and my wet nightdress is doing very little to hide my body, or my embarrassment!

Xavier offers me a towel and turns his back while I wrap it around myself. My wet hair now plastered to my face, and a lake forming at the bottom of the soggy curtain. Slowly, it all comes back to me as I examine my stinging hands.

"You will live... but only because I got 'ere just in time. What were you doing?" he asks sharply, making me feel like a scolded child.

"I had it sorted. I would have been okay. I was nearly back inside when you made me jump and bang my head! What are you doing here anyway?" I respond defensively.

"Just as well I got 'ere when I did, or you would be spread on ze drive like ze strawberry jam. I came to see if you were okay in ze storm, but you were obviously not, as I found you dangling out of ze window! I 'ad to climb up ze pipe to ze rescue!"

Standing, I walk on shaky legs back to my bedroom to change. I notice Xavier going downstairs and a few minutes later the lights come back on. In the kitchen, he insists I drink the brandy, which I take from him. I didn't know I even had any... not that I like the stuff.

"Ze fuse box is under ze stairs by ze cellar door. Tomorrow I will show you 'ow to mend ze fuse! Will you be okay if I go now?" I look out of the window. I see that the rain has nearly stopped. Not quite knowing what to say to him I nod. He leaves, this time via the front door.

13

I wake the following morning, my aching arms and bruised face reminding me of my activities the previous night. What was I thinking? Xavier must think me a complete idiot! I can hardly blame the wine. I only had one glass. Would I have got back in if he hadn't come? Of course, I would. He's the reason I banged my head in the first place. Interfering idiot! Oh well, one of life's lessons - don't dangle out of castle windows in a storm tied to a curtain! The clock on the carriage house tells me it's already nine am. I never sleep this late, poor Alice will wonder where I am.

When I arrive, she is sat in the kitchen eating fruit in her dressing gown and tells me that Xavier helped her out of bed as he thought I might be late. She doesn't ask why, or mention my bruise, but goes on to quiz me about my dinner party. I have no idea if she knows about my idiotic adventure, but she doesn't mention it, and neither do I.

The weather is cooler and fresher today after the storm. There is a rich earthy aroma in the air. I think a long walk around the estate will do me some good. Back at the Chateau, I find the old hand-drawn map that Monsieur Bertrand left me. I've not had a chance to look at it yet. As an afterthought, I grab my hat, phone, and a bottle of water. I don't want any more mishaps!

Passing through the farmyard, I check on the animals. The donkeys are under the trees in the shade, none the worse for the storm, and at the other side of the paddock Gus is milking the goats. Waving, I continue on my way, they are in good hands. I decide to take a track that leads around the back of the paddocks, an area new to me. A splashing noise leads me to a stream gushing into a large pond, with a couple of old weeping willow trees along the edge, their branches tickling its surface. Sitting for a while on a conveniently placed boulder, I watch the swallows and sand martins skimming across the water, busy collecting food for their young. Brightly coloured dragon flies' flit amongst the vegetation, perhaps this has become my new favourite place now. Finding my phone, I take some pictures. I must remember to send some to Jenny and the girls, they're sure to be jealous. Perhaps I should invite them over, yes that would be fun! What am I thinking? In less than three weeks this will all be for sale, and I will be back at work, in the cold rain, working nights, overworked and under paid. Well, maybe I could stay on a little longer, I'd quickly get another nursing job. Yes, I could stay and show potential buyers around, only for the summer though.

After a rest and a drink, I venture further into unknown territory. Circumnavigating the pond, I can see the farmhouse in the distance. Eventually, the long dry grass gives way to a low fence, on the other side are rows of old, gnarled trees with silver leaves shining in the sunlight, they're gorgeous, and look ancient. Climbing over the fence carefully, wondering if I'm now trespassing, I find they're full of fruits, some still green, and some purple. "Wow! They must be olives," I say out loud.

Sitting under the sparse shade of an old tree, I take out my map. Geography was never my best subject, but if I'm right, this is still my land. Out of the corner of my eye, I notice something move. Squinting my eyes, and looking through my sunglasses, I see a sheep, then several others, also seeking respite from the sun. Are they mine? How many are there? Does Xavier own this land? I think not. The map suggests it belongs to the Chateau, perhaps he rents it. More research is needed.

The old olive grove ends with another fence, where rows and rows of vines begin, laden with ripe fruit - so tempting. Looking around, I can see no one. Feeling like a little girl scrumping for apples, I pop one of the small black berries in my mouth. The skin is tough and chewy, and it has seeds, but tastes extremely sweet, I don't think you could eat many of these without feeling sick. "Must be grapes for wine," I say, again thinking out loud.

I continue walking in what the map tells me is south, I eventually come to a line of shrubs and trees hiding a high stone wall, taller than me - the boundary that denotes the edge of the estate. "Wow....this place is vast!" Sitting for a moment, I look around me in all directions. Square wooden constructions are spaced evenly about twenty foot apart along the perimeter. Beehives perhaps. Their occupants have done their job here, and now appear to be flying over the wall to the neighbour's fields. Yes, I remember seeing the sunflower fields, that's where they will be going.

Thinking of honey reminds me time is marching on. I'm nearer the farmhouse than home. I think I'll invite myself for lunch, and a spot of snooping. Alice is sitting on a chair in the back garden giving orders to Gus, who appears to be picking tomatoes. Her face lights up when she sees me, and she waves me over to join them. I'm instructed to collect salad leaves and basil before entering the cool kitchen to prepare lunch.

As we are about to sit at the big, old, worn table Xavier appears, with his dog not far behind; cocking his head to one side, he says, "Glad to see you are better. But you don't usually come at ze lunch time."

I take a big bite of the course bread and chew slowly, giving me time to form a response. "I was out for a walk and ended up in the area."

His brow furrows, and he appears perplexed. "Perhaps you should 'av stayed inside to rest after banging of ze head."

Changing the subject, I remember the beehives and olive groves, "I am out of honey and olive oil and wondered if I could borrow some until I go to the village shop." Gus jumps up and goes into the pantry producing a bottle of oil and jar of honey. "Have you left enough for yourselves?" I add.

"Oh, we have loads of it, we make our own, and we sell it at the market," Gus replies with enthusiasm.

Suddenly, Alice starts spluttering and coughing as she chokes on a piece of bread. Jumping up, I stand behind her and whack her between her shoulder blades. The dog jumps up and starts growling at me, but Xavier calls him off. I repeat the process again, but she continues to choke. Reaching around her I clasp my hands beneath her ribcage and perform the Heimlich manoeuvre. Thankfully, I manage to dislodge the bread, which poor Alice spits out, then gulps for air. Xavier just stares at me in disbelief as Gus rushes up to hug his Nana. Turning to face Xavier I point my finger at him. "Either you get the doctor out here or I will!" I retort.

Rummaging around in the cupboards for a liquidiser, I have no luck and can't find one. “After you have rung the doctor, you will then get yourself into the nearest town and come back with a blender or liquidiser, so that I can make soups and smoothies!” I instruct. “What would have happened if I hadn't been here?" I say in a firm voice.

The arrogant French man only shrugs and

replies, "Ze same zat would 'av 'appened if I 'adn't turned up to save you last night."

Fuming, I turn and leave with my produce. Can't that man even say thank you? I'm going to send him a bill for the time I've spent caring for his mother. I think ten Euros an hour is fair. That's sixty Euro's a day for the last ten days! I'm already out of his debt for the animals.

Taking the short cut, I'm soon back home, still hungry, but I can at least have a honey sandwich. Spreading the golden liquid on the bread, my mouth waters. I take a bite. It really is delicious. I wonder if he extracts it himself or has someone to do it for him.. Knowing how tight he is with money he probably does it himself! A smile forms on my lips as I childishly say out loud, "I hope you get stung!" Unrolling the map, I estimate that I've only explored about a quarter of the estate this morning, but my head is starting to hurt, and I will have to go back to Alice later. Maybe a siesta would be a good idea. First, though, I'm going to have a long overdue look around the other bedrooms.

They are all sparsely furnished, like the rest of the house. One of the back bedrooms has a homemade built-in wardrobe, but the door won't open, and there doesn't appear to be a lock. It's probably stuck with years of paint. If it's anything like the other wardrobes it will be empty anyway. No, nothing of any value up here, time for a nap.

To my amazement, I sleep all afternoon. Arriving back at the farmhouse I'm pleased to find a new blender, still boxed on the table; that will make things easier, and safer for her. Alice won't have to live on porridge and eggs now. Opening the fridge, I jump back in alarm as I find five fish, their lifeless eyes staring back at me. Well, I'm certainly not giving them to Alice, she'd choke on a small bone. What is this man thinking? Shutting the door on them I turn to the vegetable box on the floor, that's more like it. Half an hour later and I've made a large batch of fresh soup, plenty to freeze for later too. Gus and Xavier have made themselves scarce again. Alice tries to tell me where they are, but I can't quite understand everything she says. I will spend the rest of the evening doing my French homework.

14

More exploring today, I think. There's a walled garden somewhere, according to the map. It's on the opposite side of the track, or rear drive as it's called on the map. Prepared with sun protection, water, food, and phone, I set off. Leaving the Chateau, and following the map through the farmyard, I find the rear drive. It's somewhat overgrown with now shrivelled vegetation and numerous potholes, but it's just about usable. Ten minutes later, I see a tall wall to my left running parallel to the drive; this must be it, I need to find a way inside. Walking all the way around takes a while, but I eventually locate the door, it's wide open, and held on by just one hinge. Peeping inside I get quite a shock. A family of foxes are playing in the overgrown garden. Keeping as still as possible, I retrieve my phone from my pocket and take some pictures before they see me. How amazing! I wonder what they find to eat. Stepping back to lean on the wall, I'm startled as a lizard scurries away. Perhaps that's what the foxes are eating. Looking back inside, they have gone. They must have seen me. There must be a den in here somewhere.

Walking into the huge space, I don't know where to look first. The wall to my left has a long greenhouse attached to it, most of the glass now broken or missing, but some tenacious bushes are still surviving inside of its skeleton. Next, a statue in the centre draws my eyes. On closer inspection, I see it's a young girl holding a sun dial, ivy now clinging to her feet and legs. Though overgrown, I can make out where the beds and paths used to be. Fruit trees dripping with fruit, scramble up the perimeter walls. Walking around, I can see ripe peaches, and plums too. Picking one and sinking my teeth into its soft, warm flesh is fantastic. I can tell the birds have had their share. I must gather the ripe ones before anymore are spoilt.

An old stone building in the corner beckons. The door is missing, its interior dark and cool. My eyes slowly adjust enough to see a big hole in the floor after removing my sunglasses, probably where the foxes are living. The building, lined with shelves holding pots, baskets, and numerous garden tools, is evidently the potting shed. Picking up a basket, I leave, not wanting to disturb the foxes. I gather the peaches that I can reach and put them in the basket, leaving the higher fruits to the garden inhabitants. My next find is an old well in the opposite corner. I can't see how deep it is or if it has water in it. Finding a small stone, I drop it down and count, I get to four before hearing a splash. Behind the well is an ancient wooden bucket lying on its side, tied to a long rope. Approaching it, I see its full of dead grass woven into an intricate nest. Another lodger, which I won't disturb.

Resting for a while, I finish my water and eat another peach. Time is marching on, and I allow myself just another hour of exploring before leaving with my basket, what a fabulous place!

"Hello! Bonjour! Anyone here?" A male voice with an English accent calls. Who on earth could that be?

"Hello!" I shout back.

Then I hear a faint, "Thank goodness."

Following the voice, I come across its owner, a middle-aged man in shorts and t-shirt coming up the drive, looking hot and bothered.

"Excusez moi, Madame - "

I interrupt him and say, "I'm English."

His face relaxes as he smiles and extends his hand. "John Burrows. Sorry to bother you but we have a puncture and can't get a phone signal, I need to contact a garage. Could you help me? My wife and children are in the car at the bottom of your drive, and we've also run out of drinking water!" After deciding he's not a mad axe man, I lead him to the top of the mound, where we both get a faint signal. First, I ring Sylvie and get the contact details for the nearest garage, which is quite a distance away. Ringing their number, we only get a voicemail service. Of course! They're closed for a couple of hours after lunch; this is rural France after all!

"Try again about four; they'll be back by then," I advise him, "Let's go and rescue your family, you can rest here until then."

Following John back to his vehicle, which is pulled in at the rear entrance, I see his car is hooked up to a large caravan. Its door is open.

"Mummy, I need a drink and a wee!" whines a little girl.

"Oh dear, I can see your problem. Do you have a spare?" I ask hopefully, looking at a rear tyre that's nearly shredded. Shaking his head, he says something about 'run flats' which I'm not sure makes sense to me, but he seems to know what he's talking about. "Well, at least it's safe here, off the road. Come home with me for a couple of hours. Your family can rest out of the sun for a while."

A little girl with long, blond wavy hair and piercing blue eyes pokes her head out of the door and stares at me. "Who are you?" she asks innocently.

Crouching down, I offer her a juicy peach, "I'm Laura, who are you?"

Taking the fruit, she greedily bites into it before looking back, " Lily Burrows ... I'm six."

Next out of the caravan is a young boy with a cheeky grin "Hi, I'm Dylan... and I'm ten."

Their mother quickly follows them and looks at me cautiously before introducing herself as Jackie. "Do you live here? Are your parents in the house? We don't want to cause any inconvenience," she says anxiously.

"I live here alone; and it's no bother, you're welcome to stay as long as you wish."

John locks the caravan door, hoists Lily onto

his shoulders and says, "It's very kind of you, but we'll be on our way shortly. We only need a new tyre. It shouldn't take long." Not wishing to curb his optimism, I only nod and smile in a typically French fashion, showing them back to the Chateau.

"Are you a princess, should I call you 'Your Majesty', like Ben and Holly?" squeaks Lily as we arrive at the Chateau.

Her mother instantly quietens her and mouths, "Sorry," in my direction, while John plants her back on her feet.

"No Lily, I'm not; and I don't know who Ben and Holly are." Lily finds this very funny and goes on to inform me about 'Princess Holly' on her favourite TV programme.

"I still need a wee," Lily chirps.

"Me too," adds Dylan.

Showing them to the ancient toilets causes more hilarity, much to Jackie's embarrassment. Sitting around the kitchen table drinking cold water and eating fruit and chevre seems to cheer the parents up a little. "Can we explore? Do you have any dungeons?" Dylan asks excitedly. His mother tells him to be quiet and sit down. Laughing, I tell him that the cellar is not quite a dungeon but still a pretty unpleasant place.

"Can I look? Pleeeaaseee," he whines.

"I think we need to get a tyre sorted for the car first, then we can carry on to the campsite," interjects John.

"But dad, I'd rather stay here... Please!" Dylan continues.

"Here... play with my tablet," Jackie says handing him her iPad.

Pleased, he takes it from her, but a minute later he announces, "But there's no signal... what's the wifi code?" Cringing, I admit there isn't any wifi either. "Oh... let's explore then. Are there any ghosts?" He asks, jumping up.

"Well, I've only been here a couple of weeks, and I haven't seen any yet, but you can go and look if you like." Pleased, Dylan rushes out into the hall before disappearing into the dining room, with Lily and their father in hot pursuit.

Jackie remains seated and looks at me apologetically. I reassure her that I don't mind in the least, and they're welcome to explore. I briefly explain how I came to find myself the owner of the Chateau. "Lily was right; it's like a fairy story. You're so fortunate," Jackie says. Rubbing her temples, she adds, "Do you have any Paracetamols? I've got such a bad head, and mine are in the caravan." Two painkillers and a glass of water later, I suggest she has a rest in one of the guest rooms, which she takes me up on and heads upstairs.

A tuneless tinkling coming from the drawing room alerts me to my guests' whereabouts, I'm just about to join them when the landline rings. Its Sylvie.

"My father has spoken to the garage, but they need the details of the damaged tyre, so they can order one." She says. I pass the message on to John, who relays the information through me to Sylvie. "I will pass this on to

my father and will ring you back shortly."
True to her word, ten minutes later she rings back. "The good news is that the tyre's ordered, but the bad news is that it will take four days for its delivery." Which is pretty much what I expected.

John's face drops with the news. "What are we going to do? The campsite is an hour away, and I have no way of getting the caravan there. I can't leave it blocking your drive for four days!"

"Perhaps I can help. There's a tractor in the carriage house, that should be able to tow, but I've never driven it before, and haven't a clue how to tow. I don't even know if it works." I say thinking out loud, then take them over to look.

"Wow, that's a beauty - Massey Ferguson. It looks to have been kept in good condition too," John says. Luckily, the keys are on the chair. With John helping me to clear the area, I climb up into the seat and turn the key. It coughs and splutters but doesn't start. After two more attempts, John comes around and fiddles with some bits. "Try again," he says hopefully. This time, the old machine jumps, coughs, then starts. Both children clap and whoop with delight. "If you drive it outside, I'll take over," John shouts above the noise.

"The handbrake won't budge!" I shout back. John comes around and gives it a sharp tap with a large hammer, which releases the brake. Before I know what's happened, I've shot backwards and knocked a small hole in the wall behind me. "Oh buggar!" I shout. Dylan starts laughing, and John rushes in.

"Are you ok?" he asks, concerned.

"Yes, I'm fine. Better than the wall," I reply, getting down to inspect the damage. Peering through the hole, I can’t see anything. It's pitch black. That's strange.

"It's a false wall," John says looking into the gloom.

"Oh well, no harm was done. Let's get this tractor out," I say. An hour later and John has brought his caravan up the drive and parked it near the carriage house as per my instructions.

"You can stay here if you wish until your tyre arrives."

Dylan whoops and claps, and Lily asks, "Can't I stay in the castle like a princess?"

Both her parents say, "No!" and Lily starts to cry.

John manages to run a wire from the caravan that he plugs into a socket in the carriage house and fills his water containers from the tap in the farmyard. I leave them to settle in while I rush back to help Alice, what a day!

15

Gus is in the kitchen when I arrive, making himself a sandwich. "Where's your dad?" I ask, but he only shrugs and eats his food. I recount the story of my crazy day to Alice, with Gus translating when needed. He asks about Dylan, and I suggest he comes around to meet him. Alice thinks it's a good idea, but again Gus shrugs.

I check on the Burrow's family before retiring for the night. The children are asleep, and they invite me to sit outside and share a drink with them. "I'm a builder," says John. "I'll mend the hole in the wall while I'm here."

"Thank you, That's kind of you."

Jackie smiles, "I'm a part-time secretary at the children's school, where we live, near Manchester."

We chat for a while longer, then I make my excuses and head to bed, I sleep well, and find it reassuring having them here.

The sound of children playing wakes me. Slowly stretching, I grab a quick shower then check on my guests. The children are running around on the front lawn and Gus is with them, playing as a young boy should. "Dad is with the animals," he shouts to me when I enquire. Waving, I walk over to the carriage house following my nose. John is cooking sausage and bacon on a barbeque.

"There's plenty for everyone," he calls, waving me over.

After breakfast, I'm back visiting Alice, who is looking off colour today. This situation can't go on indefinitely. I need to get Xavier alone for a serious talk. My chance arises as I'm about to leave.

"Who are ze English people?" he asks abruptly.

"Oh, hello Xavier, nice to see you too. How are you?" I sarcastically say, as he comes through the door. Looking at me in puzzlement, he repeats his question. "I heard you the first time. Frankly, it's none of your business who they are, but since you asked so nicely, I will tell you. They are the Burrows family. They are on holiday but got a puncture and have to wait for a replacement tyre."

Shrugging, as usual, he says, "Yes, I saw ze car," then tries to walk away.

"Not so fast sunshine! Have you rung the doctor?" I ask. Frowning, he doesn't answer, so I walk briskly to the phone and pick it up. "Do you want me to do it?" I threaten.

He reluctantly takes it from me and dials a number before having a brief conversation in French. "'E will be 'ere after ze surgery at six, are you 'appy now?"

"Would you like me to be here?" I ask, but he shrugs and leaves.

Progress!

On my return, I find Gus teaching Dylan to milk the goats; they seem to be getting on well. I invite Lily to come with me to collect the eggs, she's excited and squeals every time we find one. Back at the caravan, John asks, "Do you have any jobs that need doing?"

"If you want, you could make a start at clearing the walled garden of weeds but stay away from the foxes' den." I warn. Armed with tools, I lead the way and leave him to it. I then show Jackie where the bikes are kept, "You're welcome to use them if you want."

Then set off to the village to stock up with fresh food.

Returning to the Chateau later with the shopping done, I hear beautiful music coming from the drawing room. I wonder who's here. Putting the bags in the kitchen first, I then creep across the hall to peep through the door. Lily is sat on the piano stool by herself, giggling and looking to her left. "Hello Lily, I didn't know you could play so well," I say.

Looking at me she replies, "No silly, it was the old lady," then looks around in confusion. "Where has she gone? You've frightened her away!" she shouts, before storming out in a temper. Peering around the room, all I can see are dust motes dancing in the shafts of sunlight, filtering through the window. How strange.

I'm back at the farmhouse in time to speak to Alice's doctor, with her permission. He's a small older man, with round glasses perched on the end of his nose, like a character out of a Dickens novel. Thankfully, he speaks excellent English and listens as I recount her history since my arrival. He examines Alice and agrees she needs carers' visiting at least twice a day and leaves a pile of forms to fill in. Disappointingly, Xavier is conspicuous by his absence! Why am I not surprised? What is his problem?

Four days later, John rings the garage to find out what time the tyre will arrive. He's told that the garage has not received it yet, and they will ring back when it arrives. Jackie is upset by the news, but John and the children seem unconcerned. I quite like having them here, and the walled garden is looking good. Gus seems to be enjoying Dylan's company too. Xavier, on the other hand, remains grumpy, and the forms are still on the kitchen table, not filled in.

I find John in the carriage house, shining a torch through the hole. "There's something in here," he says. Looking through, I can see shapes but no details. "Do you want me to seal it back up?" he asks.

Thinking before I answer, I say, "Could you make a small door, so I can go in and look, like Howard Carter looking for King Tut's tomb?"

Standing back and assessing the wall he replies, "Sure. I'd need a couple of sturdy posts and a short plank."

Searching around, I manage to find everything nearby. In no time at all, I have a small entrance about three feet high to scrabble through. John follows me, and once our eyes adjust to the gloom, we can see a large shape covered in old oily sheets. "It looks like a rusty old car," I say disappointedly, pulling the ageing cloth to the side.

John stares at me, "Yes, but not any rusty old car. It looks like a Bugatti of some description." Excitedly, he starts taking pictures. "I'll send these to a friend of mine. He'll know what it is," looking at the images and frowning he continues, "a bit dark but they'll do for now. Could be worth a bob or two. You need to look for the paperwork." Staring at the old car, I rather doubt that its valuable, but I'll check anyway.

The rest of the afternoon is spent searching for the paperwork for the car, as well as its keys. John and Dylan search in the carriage house while I look in the Chateau, room by room, but by teatime, we're all frustrated and hungry having had no success. John suggests that I keep quiet about it until he hears from his friend back home, so I don't tell Alice when she asks what I've been up to today.

Two days later, and the elusive tyre arrives. Jackie is delighted, but John and the children are sorry to go. John tries to push some money in my direction, but I refuse, reminding him of all the hard work he's already done for me. Swapping numbers, they promise to keep in touch. I'm going to miss their company; it's been fun having them here.

I need to continue my search for the car keys and papers. I can't ask anyone about it, especially Xavier, he's a slippery customer, which reminds me he hasn't filled in Alice's forms yet. The attic is the only place I haven't looked, but I can't find a hatch or door to gain access, there must be one somewhere! Less than a week left now until Monsieur Bertrand returns - can I trust him? I'm not so sure I can, after all, when he left me here, he said I could phone him anytime, when in fact he disappeared the following morning for a whole month leaving me to fend for myself. No, I won't confide in him, I'll find it eventually.

Lying in bed that night I feel alone again, Jenny sent me a text earlier saying I had a letter from work asking me when I intend to return. I know I have less than a week's holiday left, but I can't go just yet... can I? I need to solve the puzzle of the car. Is it mine? Who did it belong to? Why was it hidden? Too many unanswered questions, and what about Alice? I could tell Xavier I'm leaving in less than a week, that should frighten him into doing something! Yes, I'll let him know in the morning.

As usual, he's not at home, and neither is Gus, what do they spend their time doing? With Alice comfortable, I go into the field in search of them. Soon I see them in the distance, they look to be in with the vines. Gus sees me approach and waves. Xavier on the other hand grunts and continues cutting the bunches of grapes and putting them into crates, his faithful dog forever at his side. "So, these are your vines, are they?" I ask, he doesn't answer but continues with the task. "Why haven't you completed the forms from the doctor?" I continue.

"Busy," is all I get out of him.

"Well, I'm going away next week, so you'll have to find a replacement for your mother," I announce.

"Why are you leaving?" He asks, stopping and looking at me for the first time.

Now I have his attention! Thinking on my feet, I say the first thing that comes into my head. "I have an appointment with a solicitor in Paris, recommended by the firm I use in England. I need something's clarifying which I can't find answers to here."

His brown face pales, and his eyes widen in shock. "What sort of things? Maybe I can ‘elp."

Ahh, got him, hook, line and sinker! "Let's talk when I come around later, is five-thirty suitable?" Looking at his watch he nods, and I leave them to their work.

I arrive early to make dinner, so that we can talk afterwards. Xavier and Gus appear only fifteen minutes late, result! We enjoy our simple meal, and I waste no time putting the papers in front of him. "If you translate, I will tell you what to write," I say firmly. He shrugs, and we begin.

The first two sheets are quick and straightforward. The next six sheets I help with as they are about Alice’s medical condition and abilities, I encourage Alice to participate as much as possible, and we manage quite well between us. The following two sheets seem to be the stumbling block. It requires Xavier to disclose his mother’s financial status, which he appears to be unwilling to do, saying, “Mama is private, and I don't know.” I think I'm beginning to understand. As is the case in the UK, Alice may well have to pay for her care if she has the funds. I ask Alice if she could help Xavier to complete them when I've left, and she nods in agreement.

"Now the help I require," I say.

Shrugging, he replies, "What do you need?"

"One of the documents that I require seems to be missing, but I'm not too concerned as my solicitor has requested a copy from Monsieur Bertrand, who will be back on Monday."

"'Ow can I 'elp wiz zat?" he says lazily, "it is not my fault if you leave ze windows open."

Grinning I know I have my culprit. "Xavier... I didn't tell you that the window was open. How did you know?"

Looking at me, appalled, he stutters, "It was just ze guess."

What has he got to hide? "Sunday will be my last day for a while, and you will have to make alternative arrangements for a few days," I say. My last task of the evening is to present him with the bill for seven hundred and sixty Euros - for my services as a carer, before wishing them all goodnight.

16

On Monday morning, I'm waiting outside Monsieur Bertrand's office at eight thirty - the time it states on the door that he reopens - but predictably, no one is here. I locate a bench next to the old monument and sit, keeping my eyes on his door. Ten minutes later an older woman arrives and starts to unlock the door. I'm by her side before she has time to enter the small office. "Bonjour Madam. Je suis Laura Mackley," I say, extending my hand in her direction.

"I know who you are," she says frostily in English, ignoring my proffered hand, and stepping inside. I follow her in and stand by a desk while she silently switches on the plug sockets and starts up an old desk top computer. Sitting behind the desk, she digs a pair of glasses out of her bag and stares at the screen, which is apparently taking its time.

Eventually, she looks up at me, over the top of her spectacles and asks, "Do you have an appointment?" Knowing full well that I don't, she continues, "Monsieur Bertrand is a very busy man and has a full diary today."

I want to tell her that taking four weeks holiday will do that to your diary, but I remember that I'm on a month's leave myself, and don't think she'll appreciate my sarcastic comment anyway. "I don't appear to have page seven of the documents that Monsieur Bertrand left for me... before going away on his holidays," I state.

Taking her glasses off she looks at me with her cold, grey eyes and replies, "Well, you should have checked them before he left, what do you expect me to do about it?" Trying to remain calm I ask if she could print me another copy. Sighing, she stands, straightens her tight-fitting skirt and replies, "I suppose I could, if I can find it, but that would cost fifty Euros, and you would have to come back later to collect it... with some identification!"

Open-mouthed in shock I reply, "How can it cost fifty Euros to print off one sheet of paper, and you said that you knew who I was!"

Not bothering to look at me she continues, "It's company policy. You can collect it at five this afternoon, with your passport and proof of address."

Sensing that I'm not going to get any further, until the allotted time, I leave 'Crueller De Ville' behind and visit the local shops to stock up. I hope there are no Dalmatian puppies in the vicinity.

On my way home, I call in to visit Sylvie. Rose answers the door and tells me that Sylvie is at school today but invites me in for coffee. My French is continuing to improve, and we manage quite well. I ask if I can use their internet and send an email to work informing them that I am unable to return at present and agree to them replacing me. Looking at my texts, I find one from John. The old car is a Bugatti, and he informs me that with the correct paperwork it is very valuable, as he suspected. Taking the opportunity, I ask Rose about my Great Aunt and the Chateau. She tells me that the old lady had lived there back in the sixties, when Rose herself was a small child. "But the Chateau belonged to 'the old general', injured in the war. Your great aunt was just his nurse." She says.

I ask her when my aunt arrived, but she knows no more, and her parents are dead now, so she has no one to ask. Rose suggests I ask the local priest. He may have access to old records. My quest continues but at least another piece of the puzzle is now in place, I wonder how my aunt found herself in France. Possibly the war, I think, she would have been the right age. Still, so many unanswered questions.

Feeling inspired, I continue to search for

access to the loft. Puzzled that I can't find a way up. The ceilings upstairs look intact. The unusual plaster patterns left undisturbed, apart from where they installed the additional bathroom. Taking a walk around the exterior of the Chateau, I notice a row of small windows running around the entire building, just below the roof. Why have I not seen them before? Painted matte black; they were almost invisible at first glance. Something doesn't stack up here. There must be another level up there! Probably housed the servant's quarters, I think. Feeling like 'Miss Marple', with renewed enthusiasm, I'm determined to get up there!

Around the back, I can tell that the original rear entrance has been closed off with old stones - not an exact match but quite well done - at some point. That would mean that there used to be a door, which probably led out of the back of the big hall downstairs. Puzzled, I return to the hall and examine the wall. I can find no sign of an exit in the room. The old panels have been whitewashed in the past and look shabby, with peeling paint on them. Knocking on each one, in turn, I detect a hollow sound, where the cloakroom ends, and the Formica kitchen begins. Was this once a rear lobby of some sort.

Okay, only one way to find out. After a quick trip to the cellar I take a deep breath and whack the suspicious panel with a large hammer, it splinters on the first strike. More knocks widen the crack, and eventually, I have a hole about a foot in diameter. Shining the torch into the gloom, I see a blocked-up door straight ahead, which once went outside, with a narrow set of stone steps to the left, leading upwards, hung in cobwebs. Yes! I shout punching the air! This isn't on the plan of the Chateau that I received.

Excitedly, with adrenaline flowing through my veins, I enlarge the hole until I can fit through. It smells dank and musty, most uninviting, but undeterred I walk into the chilly space. Cockroaches scurry into cracks in the masonry, making my skin creep; more white powder required in here, I think grimly. Armed with a stout stick, I carefully climb the stone stairs. The walls are plain stone, no embellishments or fancy plaster work. Forcing my way through the webs, I get to the top, only to be met by another obstacle. A narrow doorway blocked up with more large stones that prevent me from going any further. Damn! It will require more than a hammer to get through here. Feeling defeated, I retrace my steps and make some lunch. I need to contact John. Luckily for me, he's a builder, and only an hour away!

Back in the village, I'm delighted to find Sylvie at home. I tell her about the secret staircase, and she's as excited as I am. John doesn't answer his phone, so I leave him a message and suggest he rings the landline at the Chateau later.

I'm half an hour early at Monsieur Bertrand's office, passport and a letter from them in hand. His officious secretary instructs me to sit on a small chair by the door and wait. She spends the next half an hour on her mobile phone, ignoring me. At five o' clock sharp she stands, switches off her computer and instructs me to return in the morning as she hasn't had time to print my paper for me. I stare at her in outrage, unable to speak, as she ushers me out and locks the door behind her. "Bloody French!" I shout childishly but she doesn't even look back.

A letter has been pushed through my back door when I return. Opening it I find a bill from Xavier; charging me for farming at ten Euros per hour for twenty-one hours costing 210 Euros less his debt of 760 Euros, leaving a total of 550 Euros I supposedly owe him.

This man just doesn't know when to stop. I told him I was going to Paris, but he will know I'm still here, the village drums have probably sounded out my activities by now! Taking independent advice from an impartial solicitor would indeed be a good idea, but I haven't got the funds now, and I think I'm enjoying solving this puzzle for myself! Frustratingly, I don't hear from John. Like me, he may well be in an area with no signal. Everything happens at a snail's pace in these parts.

17

Back on the same bench the following morning feels like deja vu! Crueller arrives ten minutes late and lets herself in. I on the other hand, stay where I am and observe. It's not long before Xavier turns up and enters the office. How frustrating! Is he one of Monsieur Bertrand's clients too? I very much doubt it, he isn't keen to part with his money in a hurry, and these people know how to charge! Once inside I see him kiss the woman on the cheek, very informal, she must have a split personality!

I'm in luck, Monsieur Bertrand parks his car in the square and gets out. Quick as a flash, I dash over to him, and in my best French ask about his holiday. He seems surprised by my improved conversational skills and tells me he thought I would have left by now. I say, "I intend to stay for the summer," then ask if Xavier is also his client.

Laughing, he replies, "Non, my secretary, Madam Cevert, is his aunt."

How strange, why hasn't he mentioned her? I don't think she's been to visit poor Alice either.

Inside Monsieur Bertrand's office, Xavier doesn't seem surprised to see me and a nod in my direction is all I get, but Madam Cevert gives me a cold hard stare as Monsieur Bertrand motions for me to join him as he walks through a door behind the dragon's desk. Exiting half an hour later, I feel like a weight has lifted from my shoulders. I not only have the missing page, but also the bank books and documents needed to access some of the money Aunt Mary left me. I really could do with some help translating so I can understand what assets I have.

Sylvie is again at school when I call in, so I leave a message with Rose, asking her to ring me when she returns. Checking my phone,

I'm in luck. There's an email from work accepting my resignation, as well as a text from John saying he will call in this morning as they are making their way back north today. I shoot off a quick reply, telling him I'll be home shortly, and pedal back faster than is comfortable for my little legs.

Once again, I have a letter when I arrive, which is most unusual - the postie doesn't usually deliver on a Tuesday. I'm about to open it when Lily and Dylan burst into the kitchen.

"Surprise!" they exclaim in unison, followed by their tired looking parents.

Distracted, I turn to greet my most welcome guests. Jackie hugs me, which seems a little out of character and says, "I'm exhausted, it was so noisy and busy at the campsite, I wish we'd stayed here where it's peaceful."

John agrees and then says, "You should set up a small campsite here, you've got plenty of space. It wouldn't be too difficult, a couple of outside taps and electric hook up points. It would be a source of income and company for you too. I don't like the idea of you being on your own... so isolated. It's worth giving it some thought."

Hmmm, he has a point. I feel more relaxed knowing someone is here, but I'm not planning on staying permanently. So, it's probably not worth it for the couple of months left of the season, and I'm sure I'd need some type of planning permission, which many of the locals would probably object to, especially 'Crueller De Ville.'

Lily and Dylan disappear through the hole in the panels that I made yesterday, shouting," Wow... you found the dungeon!"

Jackie goes for a rest while John and I follow the children as they climb up the stone steps. Assessing the blocked door, John thinks a sledgehammer and chisels should do the job and goes down into the cellar looking for tools. Once the first block is out, the others follow quickly. Dylan helps to carry the smaller pieces outside, while John removes the larger stones.

Once, again I hear music coming from the drawing room, tiptoeing over I peep through the crack in the door. Lily is sat laughing on the stool. The music stops abruptly when I walk into the room. "You frightened her away again... where has she gone?" wails Lily, who charges into the hall. "Daddy, did you see where she went?"

John looks puzzled and puts the large stone on the floor, "Where who has gone, darling?" He asks softly.

"The old lady playing the piano!" shouts Lily, close to tears.

He looks at me and shrugs, and says, "Well, I've moved enough stone for us to get through... shall we go and explore?"

“Yes, lets!” Lily and I say together. With the old lady episode forgotten. Dylan and Lily are the first to the top of the stairs. Carefully stepping through the rubble, we find ourselves on a dark, claustrophobic landing, the small blacked out window blocking the sun's rays.

Narrow wooden stairs, not much better than a ladder lead to a hatch in the roof. John climbs slowly, testing each step before putting his full weight down. "It won't budge, can you pass the hammer?" he puffs, pushing with all his might, followed by "stand back," after I pass him the hammer when he strikes the hatch several times. The wood splinters and John sets about enlarging the crack. The children seem fearless, I would have been afraid at their age, but they seem to be enjoying their adventure.

John is first through the hole and shines the torch around. He locates a light switch, but it doesn't work. "Do you have any spare bulbs?" He calls back through the hatch. Glad that I bought a selection in the village earlier, I rush down to the kitchen and return with several different types. A few minutes later, light filters through the hatch and we excitedly scrabble up into the attic.

18

At the top of the rickety stairs, we turn left through a wooden gate into the attic. The ceilings are low, and John bends his neck to avoid banging his head on the beams. Fortunately, I can nearly stand up straight. The one bulb casts a gloomy light, but it's better than total darkness. The central area is an empty, sizeable space, except for a small built-in cupboard in the corner. The bare walls have three doors on either side. John instructs the children to stay where they are as he opens the first door. Following him, I find it sparsely furnished with an old, narrow metal bed, which looks most uncomfortable, and a small set of drawers with a wash jug and basin on top. On closer inspection, the drawers seem to be empty. The second room is a repeat of the first, it doesn't look like we're going to find much up here after all.

On opening the third door, a thud follows a flash of ginger fur, as a small mammal scurries through a hole in the roof. This room is directly above my bedroom. Now I know what's been going bump in the night, a squirrel, who has left a pile of empty nutshells on the window ledge. This lodger I think I can live with, if it doesn't cause any damage, more research needed. The squirrel's room isn't as dark as the other two. Looking up it becomes obvious why, there is a window in the roof that hasn't been painted black, and a rickety wooden ladder leaning against the wall suggesting that it may have been used as a route onto the roof in the past. I'll leave that for another day! In the corner of the room, I can see daylight coming through a hole, probably where my furry lodger gets in and out, that will need fixing before the next storm! More expense.

The rest of the room is furnished in a similar fashion, except for an old wooden chest in the corner, secured with a padlock. A search of the area doesn't reveal a key. "There's a saw in the cellar, that should cut through the lock, I'll be back in a minute," John says and leaves to find it.

"Don't leave me daddy!" wails Lily as she rushes to join him.

"Let's go and have lunch then come back later," I suggest, and everyone agrees.

Dylan excitedly tells his mother of their adventure, while Lily tells her about the 'old lady'. "Perhaps she's a ghost!" Dylan interrupts.

Lily frowns, "Ghosts don't play the piano, silly!"

"How about Daddy and Dylan help Laura to search in the attic while we go looking for your old lady friend?" says Jackie.

"Good idea, then we'll have a barbeque after," adds John.

Once again, we head up to the attic with a saw. The padlock takes some getting through, but at last, it drops to the floor with a thud. The chest lid is heavy and stiff, but soon we are inside. An old yellowing bed sheet lies on top. Removing it reveals old military uniforms, blueish grey in colour. " WOW! World War two RAF gear!" John exclaims before I even touch it. Slowly taking the garments out I think he's correct. There are several different pieces of clothing: three jackets, and several pairs of trousers, a mixture of caps and leather helmets complete with goggles. Folding them carefully and putting them back in their chest, I can't help wondering what their story is.

Crossing to the other side of the attic, we have three more rooms to explore. The first one, at the front of the house, has no furniture, but contains paintings. Looking closer, most of them are portraits of long-dead people - ladies and children in flowing gowns and portly gentlemen on horses or wearing military uniforms. There are a few landscapes, and a lovely painting of the Chateau looking splendid, before its demise, with a smart carriage outside. How fascinating! I wonder who they all were, how can I find out? I need a laptop and the internet! Lost in thought, I hear Dylan shout from the next room, "Come in here, Laura!"

The second room contains boxes and trunks piled floor to ceiling.

"Gosh! It will take me days to look through all of these, do you think the papers for the car could be amongst them?" I ask.

Shrugging, John replies, "Only one way to find out, but let's take a look in the last room before you start."

An old writing bureau with a slanted top catches my eyes, "Damn! It's locked" I announce, frustrated.

"Well, we can't break into that - it's too nice. You'll have to call a locksmith if we can't find a key," John replies.

"Look at this!" Dylan chimes, pulling a cover off two large objects behind the door. "What are they?" He asks. Jewels of light reflect from the torch beam as it catches the two crystal chandeliers that Dylan has uncovered.

Lost for words, I stare at them. Even dust-coated, the chandeliers are remarkable. "Why are all of these things locked up here? I don't understand," I muse.

"I can't be certain, but my guess is something to do with the war... that would explain the uniforms, they must have hidden these items," John says.

"From whom?" I ask naively.

"Germans," is his one-word answer.

Yes, Rose had told me of 'the old general' injured in the war; perhaps these were his things. It's going to take me ages to look through everything. Moving into the far corner of the room, my phone pings to life. "I have a signal here!" I say, punching the air in excitement. A text arrives from Sylvie.

Mama says you require my help, I'll call round at six.

I reply while I can

Fantastic, we're having a barbeque, please join us, lots to tell you.

"This can be my office... for now," I say,

thinking out loud.

"Well, the first job is to get the paint off the windows and sort out some lighting. I'll drive down to the village and pick up some things to get started, but we have to be away tomorrow - ferry to catch - the children go back to school in four days." John reminds me.

John fixes a light for me in the attic and manages to get the paint off my 'office' window, while Sylvie helps me with my documents. They are difficult to understand, being written in French 'legalese'. Good job she's a teacher! An hour later, and I have the information I need. No wonder Xavier has been avoiding me, and I now know why his aunt was so hostile towards me too.

The documents state that the Chateau, and its contents, the outbuildings, and their contents, and all the land within the perimeter wall belongs to me. Surprisingly, it also states that the farmhouse, it's outbuildings, and grounds also belongs to me. Xavier clearly knows, as I suspect he took page seven, which just so happens to be the page that mentions the farm. Well, what am I going to do with this information? Sylvie promises me that she'll tell no one, not even her parents.

John also advises me to tell no one about the contents of the attic, and the car, then helps me to move an old bookshelf out of the sitting room and position it in the hall, hiding the hole that I made in the panels. Even if I sell some of these old items, I still won't have enough money to run the estate for very long; it costs a fortune to keep a place like this running. Aunt Mary has only 48,000 Euros left in her bank. I already have two colossal bills for the French equivalent of council tax, which is due in a few weeks' time. Those, along with essential maintenance, and utility bills, will eat into that amount in no time. John reckons the car may be quite valuable, but I doubt it. It just looks like a rusty old thing to me. No, I guess I have no choice but to let the place go, but not before I enjoy the rest of the summer. I'll ring the girls tomorrow and invite them for a holiday.

John has already got the barbeque going in the rear courtyard, I have supplied bottles of wine, left from the small stash in the cellar. Jackie and Lily returned from the walled garden earlier, laden with fruits, and Sylvie brought a basket full of salad and bread. A veritable feast to see my new friends on their way. Jackie opens a plastic container by the door, looking for the sweet treats John picked up from the village. Shrieking, she jumps back and drops it on the floor, staring in disgust as two frightened lizards scurry away into the dusk. Lily follows hot on their trail shouting, "Ben, Holly... come back!" Having no luck, she returns, sobbing for her lost pets, "I was taking them home with me!"

She definitely has her dad wrapped around her little finger as I hear him whisper, "Don't tell Mummy, but we'll go and look for a lizard in the pet shop when we get home". That appears to have done the trick as Lily skips around laughing for the rest of the evening, Ben and Holly already forgotten.

19

"I don't want to go Daddy; the old lady will think I've left her!" Lily cries into her dad's shoulder, as he straps her into the back of the car.

"If Laura sees her she'll tell her where you are, and we'll be back next summer," John placates. Lily's not having any of it and asks for my address, so she can write to her. I don't disillusion her by adding that I won't be here next year, all of this will belong to someone else by then. Waving them off with a lump in my throat, I manage to paint a smile on my face. I know I'm going to miss them.

Back in the solitude of the Chateau, I re-read through the translation of the documents, knowing that I need to confront Xavier at some point. Surely, he must realise that I now know the truth, but I can't face him at the moment. I wonder how poor Alice is getting on. I should go and check on her, perhaps this afternoon. My eyes land on the letter that arrived yesterday, I'd completely forgotten about it with my guests arriving.

Sitting at the kitchen table, I pick up the weighty envelope. It was posted in Paris, as indicated by the postmark. I'm overtaken by a sense of déjà vu, as I remember the day I received a similar letter from the solicitor back home. That was only a few months ago, yet it seems like a different life now. The skin on the back of my neck prickles as I open it and start to read…

To the new owner of 'The Chateau'

First, permit me to introduce myself. I am Monsieur Phillippe Lebeau, Gus Besnard's estranged biological grandfather. I have heard that your distant relative, Miss Mary Whitehead has sadly deceased and that you have inherited the old property, which I believe to be in a state of disrepair.

I understand what a daunting prospect this must be, and expect you are eager to secure a buyer; so, you can complete the sale quickly, and return to your busy life.

With that in mind, I would like to make you a sincere offer of 500,000 Euros cash, for the whole estate and contents as it stands. I think you will find; considering its current condition that this is a fair and reasonable amount and would save you the considerable trouble of having to dispose of the contents yourself.

I look forwards to hearing your response,

Kind regards,

Monsieur Phillipe Lebeau.

Dropping the letter on the table, I sit staring at it in open-mouthed shock. I re-read it for a second time, just checking that I didn't imagine its subject matter. No, it's for real. Who is this man, besides Gus's grandfather? Has Gus ever met him? What does he want with the Chateau, and what does he know of its contents? I've told no one, and the letter arrived before I found the items in the attic. My questions, as usual, go unanswered. Just another piece to add to the bizarre puzzle.

Folding the posh paper and putting it back in its envelope, I'm at a loss as to what to do next. Do I confide in someone and ask for advice? I remember a conversation with my gran when I was back in school and had to choose which college to attend. "Sleep on it, don't make a rash decision until you're sure," she'd said. Yes, that's what I'll do, sit on it for a while and see what else transpires. I need to hide it though, can't risk it going missing.

Shaking myself out of a low mood, I try to make myself useful. Ensuring that the doors are locked, and windows firmly closed, I slide the heavy bookshelf away and go up to the attic. The first job is to invite the girls for a holiday. Sending each of them a text, I soon get my first response. Claire is revising for exams next month, as she's now specialising in midwifery, so can't take any time off. That's a shame, but I thought that might be the case.

I decide to leave my phone in the 'signal zone' for a while to give Rebecca and Jenny time to reply. Might as well make a start looking for the key for the old bureau while I'm waiting. Examining the lock, I expect the key is quite small. A search of the room reveals nothing, I guess it's going to take a while.

The next room is crammed with boxes and old trunks, but it's too dark to see clearly inside the small room. I slowly drag one of the heavy boxes out through the door into the central area where there's a light. The tape holding the top closed has long since lost its power of adhesion and peels off easily to reveal its treasures, carefully cocooned in delicate tissue paper. Unwrapping the items slowly, I start to discover a delicate tea set, elaborately decorated in gold and blue. I can vaguely make out the word 'Limoges' painted on the underside. Wrapping them back up with great care and replacing them in the box, I label it number one and make it my first entry on my new inventory list. The next three boxes reveal more of the same, this time a dinner and tea service, accompanied by matching tureens, and serving platters, quite different from the rustic crockery in use downstairs.

Box after box begins to expose their treasures: Long-stemmed wine glasses, crystal goblets, miscellaneous jugs, bowls, vases and ornaments. It seems endless, and I have hardly scratched the surface. "One more box", I tell myself, taking the lid off a sturdy wooden crate, which took all my strength to move. "Jackpot!" I shout out loud as my eyes nearly pop out of my head. I've found the family silver: elaborate candlesticks, decorated tea, and coffee pots, complete with jugs and sugar bowls, on matching trays. Underneath these, I see two boxes of silver cutlery, no wonder I could hardly move it. I'm distracted by my phone; I have a reply from Rebecca. She can't come either as she's a bridesmaid at her sister's wedding in a couple of weeks. Of course! I'd forgotten. I do hope Jenny can make it!

I'm now too hot, thirsty, and hungry. Yes, I'd better go in search of sustenance. Making sure

I replace the bookshelf to hide the hole I head to the kitchen. Feeling better after eating, I steel myself to visit Alice, not knowing if Xavier will be home. The short walk to the farmhouse feels strange, my farmhouse! How am I going to play this? Does Alice know? How long have they lived here? Have they paid any rent? The questions race around my mind and leave my guts tied in knots. Reaching the back door, I still haven't formed a plan. Alice surely must have known Aunt Mary and the old general very well. I'll have to take it as it comes.

Knocking on the back door, no one arrives so I let myself in. The kitchen is in a tip, with dirty dishes piled up and soiled sheets on the floor in the corner. It was clean and tidy when I left a few days ago, how can they live like this? I find poor Alice leaning over in her chair, with remnants of lunch all down her blouse. What a mess!

"Oh Alice, where are the boys?" I ask, rushing to her side and helping her to sit up.

"Vendange," Alice says, which I know is the

grape harvest - my grapes. Looking down, I see her catheter bag is ready to burst. Poor Alice! I ask her who has been caring for her in my absence. Her reply doesn't surprise me, "Xavier and Gus." This situation can't continue! After making her clean and comfortable I start with the mess in the kitchen, soaking the sheets and washing the dishes. As the pile on the table diminishes, I find the forms that I helped Xavier to fill in, the financial portion still incomplete. With permission from Alice, I locate her bank book and statements and complete the section, for her. She then signs it, the best she can, and I put it in my bag. Now it will be posted to the relevant authority.

I leave the farmhouse, and Alice, promising I will return later. The relief shows on her tired face. I could do with a little car, the thought of cycling to the village after a busy day doesn't appeal. With that thought in mind, I make the carriage house my first stop. Approaching quietly, I look in through the car window - the kittens have gone. Phone in hand, I walk to the top of the hill for a signal and ring the garage that supplied the new tyre for John. I'm in luck. They promise to send someone out tomorrow to look at it for me, result.

I also have a text from Jenny. She is going to check annual leave availability at work today and is optimistic, it will be amazing if she can come. I hope the car works then we can travel further afield. I've been here four weeks and gone nowhere other than the local village! I'd better get back to Alice. I hope there's some food in the fridge so that I can make her some supper.

I arrive at the farmhouse to find there's still no sign of the boys, and the fridge contains very little. Glad that I brought some juicy peaches, I make egg custard and puree some of the fruits to produce a nutritious meal for Alice. Once she's comfy and safe in bed, I leave a note for Xavier on the table, expressing my disappointment at the lack of care for his mother and that I would be back in the morning to discuss things further, then add the fridge needs stocking with food. My missive complete, I leave the farmhouse and return to the Chateau.

I'm awake at five the next morning. It's still dark, so the boys can't be out harvesting until sunrise. I have breakfast and arrive at the farmhouse a little before six. The kitchen light is on, and the boys are eating. Now I'm here I still have no clue what I'm going to say to him. They both look at me in surprise when I enter the kitchen.

"You're early," says Gus.

"I saw ze note but didn't expect you zis early," Xavier says, giving one of his usual shrugs.

Looking him in the eyes, I don't feel very confident now but know I must be assertive. My gran taught me well. Standing as tall as possible and squaring my shoulders I begin to speak, "I'm here early because I know you will be going in half an hour, but you can't pick grapes - my grapes in the dark." Xavier opens his mouth to interrupt me, but I continue, "Yes, they are my grapes, on my land. And this is my property!"

Xavier looks at me, crestfallen at first, but soon recovers. "'Ow can you be sure?" He says defiantly.

"Xavier, I have all the documents - including the one that conveniently disappeared - and I've had them translated. It quite clearly states that this is mine... all of it..."

I don't get to finish before he interrupts, waving his hands in the air. "You are wrong, ze General gifted ze farm to my grandfazer! It is mine!" The large dog is at his side in his moment of need, and I'm still not sure if I trust it.

I don't respond to his rising temper, only calmly say, "Well, if you can produce a document from an independent solicitor proving your case, I will pass it on to mine in Paris to have it verified. In the meantime, I think five hundred Euros a month would be a fair rent for the property, and the land that you have worked, with a month's deposit in hand. I will have the documents drawn up." I say, leaving him standing in the kitchen open-mouthed, while I go and tend to Alice. This belligerent man will not bully me! I have no intention of making this family homeless, but I'm going to play him at his own game.

20

Back at the Chateau by eight-thirty, I eagerly await the arrival of the mechanic. They took an age to source the tyre for John, so I expect it will be a protracted affair, as most things seem to be here. To my amazement, he arrives an hour later; a youngish man with long hair in a ponytail, the exposed parts of his body covered in tattoos, his English is excellent too. I can't help myself and ogle at his taught body, which he obviously likes to display. Looking around trying to hide his amusement he says, "Nice place."

I want to reply, “Nice body,” but manage to stop myself. He introduces himself as Jacques, and I show him into the carriage house to see the ailing car.

Slowly circumnavigating the vehicle, he cocks his head to one side, "A 2CV Dolly, 1985… if I had to guess. Tyres will have perished and will definitely need a new battery." Popping the bonnet, he leans over and looks at the engine, giving me an opportunity to admire his buttocks!

"I don't know if it will start," I say, trying to hide my blush, when he straightens and catches me staring.

He shrugs and smiles, "Not even going to try. I've brought the trailer, as some of the parts could have seized." Noticing my disappointment, he adds, "Don't worry, it's as easy to maintain as a skateboard, I'll soon have it sorted. Needs a 'Controle Technique' though." Looking at him in confusion, he explains that it's the equivalent of an English M O T. He has the car that I've now named Dolly, on the trailer in no time, suggesting I call him tomorrow to find out how much it's likely to cost.

I need to sort out car insurance too, so head back up to the attic to text Sylvie and ask her advice as I wouldn't know where to start. While I'm up here, I may as well continue with my inventory. Opening the boxes to reveal their contents is almost addictive, I have no idea what I'm going to discover next.

A couple of hours later, with the boxes now catalogued, I start on the trunks. The first one contains fine linens, tablecloths, napkins, and bedding; all embellished with beautiful embroidery. They must have taken many hours to complete. I'm ready to haul another trunk out of the small, dark room when my phone pings. It's from Jenny.

Sooooo excited! I finish on Friday. About to book a flight, which airport is nearest?

A quick call to Sylvie and I have my answer. I text Jenny back with the information she needs, and it's not long before she confirms that she will be arriving on Friday, around teatime. I only have a couple of days to prepare! I wonder if the garage can have Dolly ready for Friday afternoon. I very much doubt it, but I ring and see. I'm in luck, Jacques says they have most of the parts they need in stock, including the tyres, and promises to do his best. Wow! That's fantastic! But I go from elation to panic in an instant as the realisation dawns that I will have to drive a left-hand drive car... on the wrong side of the road... in a country I'm unfamiliar with, and I haven't driven since I passed my test several years ago! What was I thinking? The first job now though: I must go to Sylvie's house to use her wifi to purchase car insurance and register it in my name. I'll pick some provisions up in the village while I'm out.

After a late lunch with Sylvie, I venture back to check on Alice. The boys are still out harvesting, and she is again all alone. In the fridge, there is a dead rabbit, complete with head, fur, and limbs; is this Xavier's idea of shopping? Shutting the door, I notice another box of fresh vegetables on the floor. Vegetable soup it is then! I tell poor Alice that I won't be available after Friday morning as my friend is arriving for a holiday, I also leave a note for the boys saying the same. I have posted the forms off that the doctor gave her, but I assume it will take an age to be processed.

Back at the farmhouse early the following morning, the boys are still having breakfast.

"Ask her Dad," Gus says quietly to his father, who looks at me with a sheepish expression. Xavier doesn't speak, just shrugs, and averts his eyes.

"Okay, what do you want?" I ask him, expecting Xavier to request that I continue to care for his mother while Jenny is staying. I can tell he's uncomfortable, so I speak to Gus instead. "What do you want to ask me, Gus?"

Xavier exits the kitchen as Gus responds, "The grape press, we need to use it before they start to rot."

Confused, I ask, "What grape press?"

Pointing in the direction of the Chateau Gus continues, "It's in the carriage house, behind the car. We use it every year, but last year we had to pay a fortune to use one in the next village. Please can we use yours?"

Thinking back to yesterday morning, I picture the strange wooden contraption I saw and smile. "Yes, of course you can, but I haven't a clue how to operate it." Gus Jumps up and hugs me. He then rushes off in search of his father. Xavier returns and nods in my direction in thanks before disappearing once more.

This morning's task is laundry. I've been hand washing my clothes since arriving, but I'm going to have to wash bedding and towels for Jenny's stay. I have learnt how to use these old washing machines at Alice's, but don't know if mine works. A trip to the dungeon is required - my least favourite place. I prop the door open at the top of the cellar and descend the stone steps with trepidation. I take the lid off the contraption and I'm met with the usual quota of insect corpses. I jump as a giant spider scurries around in the bottom, in search of an exit. Taking an old broom from the corner, I lower it into the tub and stand back, giving the spider an exit route. Encased in rubber gloves ten minutes later, I eradicate the accumulated debris from its depths and pour in some cold water from the stone sink adjacent. It doesn't appear to leak, so I plug it in the electrical socket. Not sure if anything is happening, I go back above ground to safety - for a breather - and leave it for a while.

Half an hour later, I return to find the water is indeed hot! Turning the old dial makes the agitator spring to life. Who would believe it? After all this time it still works, they don't make things like they used to! We're already on our second washing machine back home.

The rest of the morning is taken up with washing, rinsing, and wringing. It is a mammoth task. It takes me a little while to figure out how to empty the machine. I locate a rubber hose at the bottom, which fits onto a spout, and push it on firmly, placing the end in the stone sink. I turn the dial to the right, and the pump starts whirring. I jump back and shriek, as most of the soapy water pours out of a split in the pipe - and down my legs. Panicking, I turn it off and bail out the remaining liquid with an old jug. Only a new pipe needed, not bad for a machine over fifty years old! I now have clean laundry on the creel in the big kitchen. I need to sort out a washing line outside. In the rear yard, I can see the hooks in the wall used for this purpose in the past. I only need a rope and some pegs for my next shopping list.

I can hear barking, followed by someone shouting, as I finish sorting out the wet clothes. It sounds like Gus. Following the noise, I reach the carriage house to find the boys emptying crates of grapes into the old press. It's fascinating to watch. Once it's full, Xavier lifts the heavy wooden lid into place and instructs Gus to start turning the lever attached to the screw on the top, while he lines up large glass vessels to catch the juice. It's not long before dark purple liquid starts to run out of a spout at the bottom. It could be a scene from a history book. Xavier adds a spoon full of a mystery substance, which he tells me is yeast, to each container waiting in line.

"When will it be ready?" I ask.

"It will be drinkable in a couple of ze months, but I prefer to give it ze year," he replies, not taking his eyes off the process.

Gosh, I thought it would be far more complicated than it is.

He then produces a plastic water bottle and fills it with grape juice, hands it to me and says, "But zis is for now."

I have a taste of the rich-looking juice, it's very sweet.

He fills two more plastic bottles and says, "For Mama... ze pomace is for ze goats and donkeys." Seeing my confusion, he explains that the spent grapes are called pomace, and used as animal fodder and fertiliser. Nothing goes to waste here.

With the first pressing finished, he shovels out the pomace into a wheel barrow and tells me to spread it thinly on the concrete area of the farmyard and rake it over daily until it's dry, then it will store as feed for the winter. "Also, ze meadows need cutting and drying for ze winter fodder," he adds, not even bothering to look at me.

"How will I do that?" I ask, picturing myself with an old scythe dressed in period costume.

"Ze tractor of course," he says, as if it's an everyday occurrence.

Again, caught off guard by this man I reply, "Okay, that's a job for you. I'll deduct your fee from the rent." He doesn't respond. Smiling to myself, I turn and leave them to their work. I have lots to catch up with - more chevre to make and some baking. Jenny has a big appetite.

When I go back to Alice at teatime, there is a note for me. A community nurse has visited on her doctors' instructions. She will call twice a week to check on Alice and has requested a physiotherapist to visit. "This is excellent news Alice," I say, beaming. Alice nods in agreement. "I think it's quite possible that with a lot of hard work, and physio input, you may be able to walk again." I know I'll feel less guilty about taking a week off, and, of course, I will call in when I can.

Arriving back at the Chateau, Pedro and Sylvie are waiting for me. "Dad says you need to order some more oil for the boiler, and you should also start to stock up on logs for the winter. It can get quite cold here." Sylvie says.

I find it hard to believe that it could ever be cold here, I've only seen rain once in the last four weeks, and that's an evening I won't forget in a hurry. "I will have gone by winter, but I suppose I will need oil for hot water," I say. Sylvie, with her head cocked to one side, only smiles. Pedro kindly offers to sort out the oil. "My car is ready to pick up in the morning, and I'm going to collect Jenny from the airport in the afternoon. We'll have another barbeque; you must come around… " I don't get a chance to finish before my dear friends express their concern about me driving alone for the first time. I assure them I'll be okay, sounding more positive than I feel.

"How will you get there? It's too far to cycle. I

will pick you up at nine. I'm not working tomorrow," Sylvie insists.

21

We arrive at the garage shortly before ten to find Dolly still up on a ramp with Jacques working underneath her, his lean body glistening with sweat. "Ooh, la la!" Sylvie says quietly, and we both burst out laughing. Jacques hears us and turns around, blinding us with his knowing smile.

"Come and look at the work we've done," he says, gesturing for us to go over. Cautiously moving forwards, avoiding tools and spare parts, we peer into the guts of Dolly. Jacques starts pointing out things that he's replaced, but neither of us are looking at the car. This man is too distracting! Pretending to understand, we nod and agree with what he tells us. I'm sure he could sell snow to the Inuits!

Lowering Dolly to her wheels, Jacques drives her out onto the quiet street. He then gives me the bill, and test certificate, before handing over the keys.

If you have any problems, just ring," he says, and watches as I get in.

Trying to look as though I know what I'm doing, I put the keys in the ignition and check it's not in gear. Shock number one, where is the gear leaver?

Jacques is doing a poor job of hiding his amusement, "Have you driven one of these before?" He asks.

I only shrug, and Sylvie can't help herself as she laughs out loud. What is it about this man that turns professional grown women into hormonal teenagers?

"Move over," Jacques instructs as he open the car door and jumps in the driver's seat when I've scrambled over into the passenger side. I can smell his male muskiness as he points out the controls and turns the key. He gestures for Sylvie to climb in the back. Once she's in, he engages first gear and pulls off down the street, talking me through the controls. It seems easy when he does it. Soon, he comes to a halt, and climbs out. It's my turn. It takes a few tries before I can change gear without stalling the poor car, but I eventually get the hang of it.

"Remember, we drive on the opposite side!" He shouts, before disappearing back inside the small garage with a big grin on his perfect face.

"Will you be okay?" Sylvie asks.

I nod and try to concentrate, putting all thoughts of Jacques aside, gently pulling away from the kerb, I realise I can't remember the way back. I shout through the open window to Sylvie, "I'll follow you!"

The small street ends all too soon, and I have to turn left onto the main road. Thankfully, it's quiet, and I make it out behind Sylvie. The car rolls excessively, and I'm convinced it's going to fall over. My knuckles turn white, choking the steering wheel. My heart is racing and sweat is tricking down my blouse. Why did I think this was a good idea? We could have booked a lot of taxis for the cost of getting Dolly back on the road! I don't even try to keep up with my friend as I crawl along the main street, aware of old people with sticks and mothers with toddlers. What will I be like on the autoroute this afternoon?

Pushing that thought aside, I make it through the small town and out into the countryside, where I catch up with Sylvie, who toots her horn and picks up speed. The return journey takes longer, but I make it back in one piece, and manage to park outside her cottage. "Well done!" She says, giving me a high five, then adds, "Wait a minute." She dashes inside and returns with a bundle of maps and leaflets. Handing them to me she continues, "The directions to the airport are written on a sheet for you, but it's quite an easy journey. I'll come along if you wish." Declining her kind offer, I get back in my car; this is something I need to do for myself. I can't keep relying on other people.

I have my phone as a sat-nav - for when I eventually get a signal - and a decent map, so I'm sure I'll be okay. With trepidation, I set off on my greatest adventure yet. I have only gone about a mile when a truck appears around a bend, coming towards me, the driver tooting his horn and waving his arms. That's when I realise. I'm on the wrong side of the road! I manage to swerve across onto the proper side in time to see his rude hand gesture as he passes by. Coming to an abrupt stop, I turn the engine off and sit for a moment to compose myself. Looking in the mirror, I can see the truck has stopped, and the driver is approaching me. I try my best to lock the doors and close the windows. I've seen cases of road rage in accident and emergency in Leeds, and I have no intention of becoming the next victim.

I've almost secured the windows when a voice I recognise booms out, "I should 'av known it was you! Are you trying to get yourself killed?" Of course, it would have to be Xavier.

Stumbling for words I say, "I just forgot for a moment -" I don't finish before he interrupts.

"It only takes ze moment to get killed... where are you going?" When I tell him my destination, his face pales. "You cannot drive zat far in zis wreck!" He looks at his watch and runs his hand through his messy hair, sighing in frustration before he says, "Give me half ze hour... I will take you -"

I don't let him finish. "I'm fine now, thank you, I'll be on my way." I turn the key and continue my journey watching him get smaller in my mirror. I know I'll not hear the end of this, but he has a point... I need to concentrate.

It's not long before the roads get wider and busier. My phone picks up enough signal, and the sat-nav comes to life, telling me I should arrive in forty minutes, that gives me plenty of time. Following the signs for the autoroute, I have to negotiate several roundabouts. Remembering to go around the wrong way seems totally alien, but I succeed without rolling poor Dolly over. Once through the toll booth, I manage the dizzying speed of sixty kilometres per hour, this is when I notice another of Dolly's quirks - the windows. They don't wind up and down like normal cars, no, they are strange flaps, and the faster you go, the wider they open - like little wings trying to take off. I find myself trying to go faster to see how wide I can get them. Even going as quickly as possible, everyone is still overtaking me. That's when I realise, I'm no longer terrified and quite enjoying myself. Yes, I feel liberated, and really looking forward to exploring with Jenny.

Finding my way off the autoroute to the airport isn't that easy. It's poorly sign-posted, and I'm glad of my sat-nav. There are, however, plenty for signs for Metz and Nancy, and 'toutes directions,' whatever, and wherever that might be. There is ample car parking, and I have time for a coffee while I wait. The smell of the fast food outlets turns my stomach, which is quite strange as we regularly ate such things back home, but now

I've become accustomed to fresh, local, organic produce. What's happening to me?

Jenny exits the arrivals gate with a flourish. Tossing her long, auburn hair over her shoulder, she rushes into my arms, hugging me and jumping up and down; this seems to get the attention of several natives, who look at us as though we're mad. I remember Sylvie explaining that the French are resistant to hugging, they see it as unhygienic. While kissing strangers on the cheeks - up to four times - apparently isn't!

Jenny stands and stares at Dolly. "Cool, can't believe you've got wheels!" she exclaims, pilling her luggage on the back seat. Opening a bag, Jenny pulls out the bottle of Macallan Gold that I asked her to bring for me. "I didn't know you were into the hard stuff," she says handing it over.

"It's not for me," I reply. Jenny looks at me questioningly, and I explain that my friend Sylvie, suggests I should introduce myself to the local mayor, who is rather fond of fine scotch.

"Mmm, a little bribery gets you everywhere!" she giggles and climbs in the passenger seat.

The drive home seems quicker as Jenny talks nonstop, telling me news from home and asking about the Chateau and my new friends. I tell her all about Sylvie, how kind she is, and about Xavier's frustrating behaviour. Before leaving the village and running out of phone signal, I pull over and suggest she texts home to let the girls know she's arrived. Looking at my phone I realise I have a couple of text's; one from Xavier, a rare event.

Did you arrive safely?

Frowning, I don't really know what to say. Jenny takes my phone from me and shoots off a reply before I can get it back. I'd forgotten how bossy she could be.

What's it got to do with you?

Oh dear, I can see these two not getting on very well, I'd better try to keep Jenny and Xavier apart, which shouldn't be difficult seeing as Xavier tries his best to avoid me. The other is from Jacques.

How's Dolly, did you find the airport?

Smiling as his image comes to mind, I reply.

Yes, thank you.... Dolly's a dream!

Now, Jacques is a different matter. Jenny will be all over him; she always likes the bad boys.

22

I point out Xavier's farm as we pass and tell Jenny that I'll take her to meet Alice tomorrow. Slowing down, I indicate and turn into the drive.

"Here we are," I say, not quite knowing what Jenny's reaction will be. As the Chateau comes into view, I don't have to wait long.

"Freaking hell!" she says, then turns to stare at

me open-mouthed, "Do I have to call you 'Your Highness' or something now? Girl, your minted!"

Feeling a little uncomfortable, I shrug, "It looks rather grander than it is. It's quite run down, wait till you see inside. And I'm not keeping it. It’s much more than I can possibly take on... though, I do like it here."

As soon as Dolly comes to a halt in front of the large oak door, Jenny is out of the car in a flash, pulling the bell cord.

“It doesn't work," I tell her quietly, not wanting to burst her bubble.

"Will the butler come out to take my bags to my room?" She squeals.

"Afraid not,” I say, “it's not quite like it is in the movies."

Jenny looks disappointed and gets her things out of the back of the car while I open the door. Stepping into the cool interior, the first thing she sees is the suits of armour guarding the hall. "Whoa... creepy!" She shouts. I hardly notice them now but do remember being a little disturbed when I first saw them. "Crazy floor!" Comes next, as she steps onto the black and white tiles. That I tend to agree with, they do dazzle, but you do get used to them with time.

"Let's get your bags upstairs. I don't know which bedroom you want, so haven't made any beds up... thought you might like to choose." Jenny doesn't answer but stands, looking around mesmerised. "I know it's a lot to take in. I don't think I've seen everything yet myself, and I've been here over a month now. Come on," I say, dragging a heavy case up the stairs.

Jenny follows me with the rest of her gear, and we dump it on the landing. Peering down over the full height gallery, she seems spellbound. "You could easily get rid of someone here... and make it look like an accident," she says.

"You are weird and read too many novels," I say. "Come on, lets choose a bedroom," I add, trying to get her to move.

We go into my room first, "I sleep in here, but you can have it if you prefer."

Her eyes take in the space as she looks around slowly, "Not quite the Ritz... is it?"

I have to laugh, "You get used to its charm, it's an acquired taste."

Next, we go into the two smaller bedrooms behind mine.

"Not getting any better... is it?" She states, never one for mincing her words.

After trailing around all six rooms, Jenny decides on the big front room, on the opposite side of the landing. The one where I dangled out of the window tied to a curtain, though I keep that to myself. I show her where the bathrooms are, neither of which meet with her approval. She might change her mind when she gets in the old shower. It works better than any modern one I've ever used.

With the bed now made, I acquaint her with downstairs. After she gets over the state of both kitchens, she announces, "This would be an awesome place to have a big party... fancy dress!" She's probably right, but not many folks around here would attend. It would be way past their bedtime. Mmm, Jacques might have some interesting friends. I'd better keep that one to myself too.

"I'm hungry. Please tell me you're not into frog's legs, snails... and that sort of stuff," she says, pulling a funny face.

"No, but you might have to get used to pheasant and rabbit... and lots of goats cheese," I say, finishing off the flan and putting it in the oven. I wash the salad and prepare the fruit while Jenny chooses wine, a crisp white that I got in the village. I go on to tell her about the vines and winemaking, which seems to stimulate her interest. We spend the rest of the evening exchanging news and stories. I tell her about Lily and the old lady playing the piano.

"That's freaky... do you think it's a ghost?"

I must admit it crossed my mind, but I know

it's an irrational idea. Having company for a change is refreshing. Not that I mind the peace and quiet. It's past midnight when I suggest we retire, which incites the remark, "Party pooper!" I accompany Jenny to her room then leave her to rest, and I'm asleep as soon as my head hits the pillow. I wake with a jolt, to find Jenny in my room.

"I can't sleep, keep thinking about the old lady," she whines.

"Well, I've never seen her, and Lily seemed to like her, so I don't think you have cause for concern," I reassure her.

"Can we keep the doors open, so I can shout if I need you?"

I nod and see her back to bed, leaving the doors open like we're children again. The next thing I'm aware of is someone climbing into bed next to me.

"Only me," says Jenny. There's a thudding noise coming from the ceiling."

"Yes, squirrels are living in the attic... they

won't hurt you." I add before settling back down, Jenny still sharing my bed.

"What would you like to do today?" I ask over breakfast.

"What are the options?"

I give her the pile of leaflets from Sylvie, offering an array of local tourist attractions. It takes her a while to decide before announcing she would like to hit the shops. "I don't think you'll get much in the local village. We would have to go to the nearest decent sized town. Looking at the map I think Valance would fit the bill. “It's a city about a couple of hours away, looks to have lots to see and do.” I say. Packing snacks and drinks we venture out on our first trip.

The journey takes us longer than anticipated, the roads being narrow and winding through steep-sided valleys, with me concentrating hard and driving like a tourist. And of course, I get lost more than once! Parking is a challenge, but we eventually find somewhere, and the shops are first. Jenny is like a child in a sweet shop and buys several dresses. I remind her that shorts and t-shirts will be of far more use out here, but she won't be swayed. I stock up on essentials, as I don’t want to use the old washing machine too often! Next is lunch, which becomes quite a protracted affair, there’s no fast food here, though we thoroughly enjoy the experience sat outside, watching people go about their business.

We spend the rest of the afternoon sightseeing. We visit an intriguing house in the town with fantastic architecture, adorned with numerous heads and gargoyles decorating its façade. Which is followed by an ancient church with a cool lofty interior, stunning. There’s so much to see, and the day passes by quickly. The drive home is smoother and seems to take less time as we chat about our day and plan other trips.

We're both exhausted and only need a light supper after our huge lunch. Jenny opens a bottle of red wine and we soon fall into bed - my bed - and sleep like babies.

23

The following morning is Sunday. No shops open today. I suggest we go and visit Alice who is extremely pleased to see us. Xavier is not around, but Gus tells us of a fantastic gorge, only half an hour away, that has waterfalls, rapids, and gentle pools to play in. I ask Alice if Gus would be allowed to come with us, she nods her head emphatically. I wish we could take Alice with us, but Gus tells me that the terrain isn't suitable for a wheelchair. We need to think of somewhere to visit with her next time.

The gorge is truly is magnificent. It’s just as Gus described, and we have a fantastic afternoon, swimming, and sunbathing. Gus is thrilled to find a couple of his school friends there with their families. It's lovely watching him enjoying the day as a child should, instead of being a carer. Soon the shadows lengthen, and we make our way back for supper. We help Alice wash before leaving them for the evening.

Sitting outside in the rear courtyard drinking cold beer is a pleasant way to spend the rest of the evening. Jenny can only stay for a week, so we must make the most of it. She suggests we go to the coast tomorrow. A quick call to Sylvie informs me that it takes roughly over two hours to Marseilles, quite achievable.

Up and off early, we reach Marseilles by eleven. Thankfully, most of the route was via the toll road, expensive but convenient. As luck would have it, we find ourselves in the old port just in time to hire an electric bike and join an organised tour. It takes us all around the city, visiting some of the less savoury areas as well as the regular tourist destinations. It is a multicultural destination. After an exceptionally long, late lunch, we flop down on the crowded beach for a much-needed rest.

Heading back to the car park I notice an

estate agent or 'Agent Immobilier' as they are known here. One of the shop windows advertises that they specialise in what it calls 'exclusive properties.' I observe that there are several Chateaus of differing sizes, none of them under a million Euros. My mind goes back to the letter I received, offering me only half of that for my Chateau - and its contents! I need to have it valued; I think. I tell Jenny, and she agrees. So, looking like a pair of teenage tourists, we enter the shop.

"Bonjour Mademoiselle, Puis-Je vous aider?" The smartly suited, middle-aged man asks.

"Parlez vous Anglaise?" I respond.

"But of course. I am Raymond, how can I assist you?" He asks in perfect English.

“I would like my property valuing,” I say.

He asks for the address and enters it into his computer, then looks back at me with unbelieving eyes. "Are you sure?" He asks, clearly not taking me seriously.

"Yes, definitely," I say, then take out the huge,

old key, that weighs a tonne. "My key," I continue, dangling it in my hand.

He clears his throat, looks in his diary and asks, "Will tomorrow, late morning be suitable?"

"Yes, that will be fine," I say, and leave him staring out of the window at us as we exit the shop and climb into Dolly. "I don't think he believes me, and probably won't turn up," I say, pulling out of the car parking space.

"I'm not surprised, seeing as we have dressed like this..." Jenny says waving her hands at our outfits, "and driving away in your tired, old car!" She adds with a laugh.

Raymond astounds us by turning up at eleven the following morning, and, as tactfully as he can manage, asks to see my identification and proof of ownership. All of which I had anticipated and have to hand. After satisfying himself that I do indeed own the whole estate, he looks at the plans and maps and then back at me. "Well... where to begin? I think I will have to make another appointment, probably a whole day... and bring a colleague with me." He says. It's at this point that I tell him of my offer from a potential buyer in Paris. "The value of the estate alone exceeds that amount, but I can't advise you on the contents. You would need to invite an auction house to come out and value those separately," he says, handing me his card, then adds, "I have a very respectable client who sometimes buys old Chateaus like yours and converts them into elite hotels. Would you like me to contact her to see if she might be interested?" Feeling a little dazed and confused, I agree, and he promises to return in the morning.

Feeling the need to relax and unwind, I ring Sylvie and invite her to come swimming with us to the gorge. Luckily, it's her day off, and she has no plans. We make a picnic for lunch and have a brilliant afternoon. Jenny and Sylvie seem to get on well. It's a shame Gus is back at school now though.

"Wow, where has the time gone?" asks Jenny, as we once again await the arrival of the estate agent and his colleague. They arrive earlier today and look like they mean business - striding purposefully around the exterior of the Chateau and asking numerous questions. Many of which I can't answer.

I invite them inside and offer to give them a tour. "Do you mind if we take photographs - only to use as an aid to valuation - the marketing pictures would, of course, be taken by a professional?" I permit him and suggest we start with the cellar, which ends up being quite brief. Like me, they don't seem keen to be in the dungeon.

The ground floor is next, which takes a little longer. I keep apologising for the old-fashioned fittings and fixtures, but Raymond assures me that the 'original period features' make it more desirable. Both of them marvel over the full-height hallway and galleried landing, with its magnificent window, but upstairs, they agree with me about the poor ensuite shower room. "Where are the stairs to the servant's floor?" Asks Raymond's colleague, whose name I have already forgotten. I'm not quite sure what to say to him as I remember John's words of warning. But these are professional men, and I'm going to have to tell someone at some point, especially if I sell.

"Follow me," I say, wondering if I'm doing the right thing. Back in the hall, I pull the old bookcase out of the way to reveal the hole in the panels.

Jenny looks at me in shock and exclaims, "Well! You kept that quiet!"

The two men look knowingly at each other, and Raymond says, "Lead the way."

We all squeeze through the small entrance, climb up the stairs, and go through the doorway that John opened. I point to the ladder and say, "Up there. It's easier than it looks." I go up first, then Jenny and the two men follow.

"Wow! This is freaking awesome!" Jenny shouts. I don't say anything. Observing everyone's faces is priceless. Jenny rushes in and out of the six rooms whooping, with delight.

The estate agent, whose name I have thankfully now remembered is Charles, goes straight to the cupboard at the back of the open area. "It's empty," I say, but he continues with his quest.

After some banging and cursing, he shouts, "Voila!" Then gestures for me to come and look. I move across to see what has got him so excited. There's a secret door at the back of the cupboard! I'm even more dazed and confused now.

Peering through, I can see a small, narrow set of wooden steps leading down into the darkness. "Where do you think they go?" I ask naively.

"Only one way to find out," blurts Jenny, as she takes the torch off me and slowly descends into the gloom.

"Are you okay?" I shout, as I follow her down. A muffled affirmative floats back. When I reach the bottom of the steps, I realise we are in a room, the size of a large wooden box or wardrobe. That's when it dawns on me - one of the smaller back bedrooms has a built-in wardrobe that I couldn't open. It had appeared to be sealed up with years of paint. After a few moments, we hear the voices of the men on the other side. "We'll go back to the loft," I shout. When we catch up with them, Raymond suggests we look for a sharp tool to try to open the door. Jenny volunteers to find something, disappears for a few moments, then is back with a knife and a heavy rolling pin. She has the door open in no time.

The intense sunlight filters through to reveal years of dust and cobwebs, as well as two old carpet bags stashed in the corner. I look at them, shocked, wondering what they contain. However, I decide to investigate them later when the two men have gone. This room must have been the general's secret passage up to the attic during the war.

Once back in the kitchen with strong coffee, recovering from our ordeal, the two men tell us that they have come across something similar in the past. "It's quite possibly where the resistance hid allied troops in the war," Charles says. I mention the chest with the uniforms inside, which he thinks confirms his theory. Goodness me, this building is slowly revealing its secrets to me. I wonder how many more there are?

The rest of the day is taken up with showing the two men around, the grounds, including the carriage house, outbuildings and, of course the farmhouse. Thankfully, Xavier is out, and we only look around outside, not wanting to alarm Alice.

"Alors! That was quite a day! We will contact you when we have worked out an estimated value. There is, of course, a lot of work needed – rewiring, new bathrooms, and kitchen, among other things. I would suggest you invite an auction house to value the items in the attic. It was a pleasure meeting you," Charles says, as he leaves with Raymond.

Well, I've discovered a new area of the estate today. It has ruins of the former chapel, I'd seen it on the map, but never got around to going, there was always something or someone else to attend to.

"We need to celebrate!" Jenny declares, opening a bottle of fizz that she picked up at the airport. "What are you going to do? The stuff in the attic must have some value... you could sell it and get the renovations done with the proceeds…"

I halt her before she has the rest of my life planned out, "The restoration and upkeep of this place are way over my budget. But I don't like the idea of it being turned into a hotel either," I muse. I make her promise not to share anything about the contents of the attic. Thankfully, the estate agents didn't notice the old car hidden in the carriage house.

Thursday morning dawns accompanied by a hangover, and we laze around until lunchtime when we feel a little more human. "Let's have a barbeque tonight and invite your friends. It's my last night," Jenny suggests. I agree and start preparing. We call at the farmhouse a little later, on the way to the village, to leave an invitation for the three of them, saying we will come back at seven to help get Alice in the car. As I told Jenny earlier, there's not a burger, or plain pork sausage in the butchers. We opt for steak and chicken fillets, not the pheasant that Xavier offered to bring. We'll have to be creative when it comes to Alice's food though. Sylvie and her parents are thrilled to see us as we pop in on the way back and accept our invitation.

At seven, we drive around to collect Alice and manage to get her into Dolly. Xavier follows in his truck, with Gus and her wheelchair. Everything goes well. Even Xavier is polite to me, though doesn't stay long. It's starting to get darker earlier now, and we end the evening inside. Gus plays the piano beautifully, I praise him, but he shrugs and tells me he has help. Whatever does he mean? I decide not to ask. The wine flows freely, but I don't partake, I need to drop Jenny at the airport tomorrow, and don't want another hangover anytime soon. The week has flown!

"Text when you get back," I say as Jenny checks in her luggage.

"I'm going to book some more annual leave

as soon as possible, and I'll be back. Might be a month or so. September is always popular with the older staff that don't have to stick to school holidays," she says optimistically.

"I might be home by then -" I start to say but Jenny cuts me off.

"Don't be a killjoy. You were meant to be here; this place is amazing. You'd be mad to give it up."

Sighing, I look at her and shrug, "I can't afford the upkeep, and I need a job."

Her parting comment as she disappears is, "Where there's a will, there's a way!"

24

The drive home quickly passes as I try to concentrate on the road signs. Dolly is going well, and I've realised I tend to talk to her as we advance through the parched countryside. I wonder if I can take her back to England with me? Making a detour into the nearest town, I visit a supermarket. It's fascinating looking at all the 'foreign' foods on offer. As I pass by the fish counter, I notice large lobsters still alive with their monster claws taped together. I have a notion of buying them all and rushing down to the coast to release them, but my futile actions will make little difference. Passing by quickly, I look at the next counter. I'm in luck. It's the dairy section, followed by the patisserie. I load my trolley with cakes and pastries and yoghurts, made from goats' milk. Now there's a thought!

Turning back through my grand gateposts I'm astounded by the view in front of me. "What is that helicopter doing on my front lawn?" I say to Dolly. She of course, doesn't answer me. Climbing out of the car I'm startled as a well-heeled couple arrives from behind my Chateau.

"Hello, I'm Valentina Carboni, and this is my

brother, Leo. What a lovely place you have here," says the raven-haired beauty, with only the hint of an accent. I take her offered hand, followed by her brother's. He really is rather handsome, but I notice he is wearing a wedding ring. Damn, out of bounds! "I can see you weren't expecting us. Raymond, the estate agent, gave us your details and said it would be okay to call. We were in the area on business, so dropped in on the off-chance." She explains.

Trying to compose myself, I remember the man telling me he had a client who may be interested. "Yes... err.... that's right. Sorry, you caught me off guard. Please, come in," I say, feeling like a country bumpkin at the side of these immaculately dressed people. I show them into the big kitchen and seat them at the oversized table. "Coffee?" I ask, unsure of what to say next. Putting the kettle on to boil seems inappropriate. I expect they are used to a fancy machine that turns out various options, like a skinny latte, flat white and espresso. Placing the cafetière on the table alongside the chunky mugs, I remember my shopping will be melting away inside Dolly. Excusing myself, I go outside to retrieve it.

"Let me help you," says Leo, who's at my side in an instant, who would have believed it, my very own Mellors! Who am I kidding? Not dressed to kill like that. Dragging my mind back from the gutter, I once again compose myself and graciously accept his help.

Back in the kitchen watching Leo's handsomely manicured fingers place dainty pieces of croissant into his mouth is distracting, and I force myself to look away, trying to concentrate on what they are saying. The gist of it is that they have fingers in many pies: wine, property, hotels. The list seems endless. I will have to do an internet search of them later. I tell them about the vines and the old press. They are transfixed and ask if I would be kind enough to show them. Looking down at Valentina's feet, I see they are clad in skyscraper heels. "Do you have any flats with you. It's quite a trek around the grounds." I say, wondering what size shoes she takes, though I doubt she would even consider wearing my cheap ones.

"Always carry a pair with me, I'll get my bag. Do you mind if I change into something less formal?" she asks, as though it's an everyday occurrence. It probably is. I nod, and Leo is onto it, arriving back with a designer overnight bag in each hand. I show them into the downstairs' cloakroom, anticipating what they will look like when they emerge.

The transformation is a visual delight. Valentina is wearing a red, strappy sundress, which finishes just below her knees, exposing her St Tropez tan. Her feet now nestled into a pair of nude ballet flats. Leo looks even more amazing in plain navy knee-length shorts, with a navy and white short sleeved shirt, semi-casual in style. Trying not to ogle, I manage, "That's better," and walk towards the back door. "Shall we start with the grounds, before the sun gets any stronger?" I suggest, and my eager guests agree. It's not long before I get the feeling that they were expecting a vehicle of some type to ride around on, instead of legs. They hide their disappointment well and follow me across to the vineyards. I point out various things along the way. It takes a while, but we get to our destination in one piece.

They seem genuinely interested and ask numerous questions about grape variety and production methods, which I can't answer. I explain that I have a tenant farmer who deals with the land and animals. Next, we head back across to the carriage house. Leo wants to see the old wine press. Things appear to be going well, and we spend quite a while chatting. They seem entirely down to earth, and genuinely fascinated to hear my story.

Stepping back outside, it becomes noticeable that they need a break. The sun's brightness is relentless, and the heat intolerable. "Let's get some lunch, then look around inside," I suggest, which seems to meet with their approval. Of course, it's chevre with fresh bread and salad.

"Where do you buy this cheese... it's delicious?" Gushes Valentina. She's amazed when I tell her I make it myself. "Is it for sale? I'd love to make a regular order... that's if you decide to stay, of course," she says, quickly recovering.

After lunch, we decide to start in the attic. They're eager to see the treasures I've unearthed. Leo seems intrigued by the paintings and portraits, telling me his wife and brother-in-law are artists. "Some of these are quite old, and possibly valuable, you should take advice from a professional," he says, echoing the words of the estate agent and John.

We work our way down the building, looking at all the rooms until we get to the cellar. "Nothing of interest down there, unless you're an entomologist," I say with a laugh, telling them about the big spiders that call the dungeon home.

"I like cellars... you can tell a lot about the building from its cellar," Leo says, opening the heavy door. I flick the light on, grab a torch and follow them down the steps to hell. After a couple of minutes, Leo ask, "Where's the rest of the cellar?"

I look at him in confusion. "This is it," I say.

My guests look at each other and walk over to the oversized shelving unit against the wall. With lots of heaving, Leo manages to move it forward a few inches. I jump back in alarm as several rather ugly looking beetles scurry away into the dark. "Yuk!" Valentina says in agreement, stepping back too. By this time, Leo has lodged himself behind the unit and using himself as a human lever, prises the cumbersome piece further away from the wall. He emerges from behind the shelves covered in webs and dirt, a beaming smile on his face. What possibly could have made him happy behind there?

"Come and see what I've found," he says, like a puppy with a new toy.

"I don't think I'll bother," I say, curling up my nose at the thought. Valentina, on the other hand, quickly walks through the opening in a flash. I wait for her scream, which doesn't arrive. Okay, perhaps I'll risk it, I think, and poke my head behind the shelves. I'm expecting to find a torture chamber, or something similar, but as my eyes adjust to the gloom, I can make out rows and rows of bottles and barrels lying in a dark room with a vaulted ceiling.

"It's the wine cellar... I knew there would be one somewhere," says a triumphant Leo, walking over with the torch for a closer look.

"Is it still drinkable?" I ask, thinking I'll never have to buy another bottle as long as I live.

"Yes... very, but I wouldn't recommend that you do," he answers, confusing me even more. Perhaps he thinks I have a weak constitution? After all, I am only five foot three and seven and a half stone wet through. He gets his phone out and starts taking pictures of the bottles and barrels, then says, "I need to make a call, where can I get a signal?" I tell him where to stand in the attic and leave him to it, but it does seem an odd thing to do. It could have waited a while, as we've nearly finished the tour.

I apologise to Valentina for the filthy state of her clothes and ask, "Would you like to use the bathroom to shower and change while you wait for Leo?" Taking me up on my offer, she disappears upstairs while I make afternoon tea. The siblings reappear together, chatting excitedly in the hall, both now clean and none the worse for their adventures.

"I've just spoken to a colleague who is offering 100,000 Euros, but I don't suggest you accept... it's worth way more than that," Leo says.

"Well, someone's already offered 500,000, including contents, so, I won't be accepting your offer.... but thank you for calling," I say disappointed.

Valentina looks at me, smiling, "I think you've misunderstood. The offer was only for the contents of the wine cellar, not the Chateau. Like we said earlier, you need to invite an auction house to visit, I don't think you realise just how much it's all worth... and don't accept 500,000 for the Chateau. The contents alone exceed that value." Scrolling through her contacts list in her phone, she writes down some details on the reverse of her card, then hands it to me. "Here, these are the auctioneers we use - they're very professional, and my details are on there too. Please contact me if you need any advice. It's a beautiful Chateau, and I don't think it should be spoilt and turned into a hotel. There are not many places left like this, with original period features still in place. It needs a sympathetic restoration to retain its history and charm, without having its heart ripped out."

Nodding, I think I agree with her and take the offered card. Escorting them back out to their helicopter, we say our farewells then I retreat to a safe distance and watch them lift off into the blue sky. The enormity of their advice suddenly overtakes me as they disappear from view. What am I supposed to do? I know nothing about wine, art, antiques, cars, or French Chateaus, but I do know I'm way out of my depth. These significant figures carelessly thrown around, remind me of playing Monopoly with my Gran. No wonder Monsieur Lebeau wanted the Chateau and its contents! But, how did he know what's hidden here? Well, what a day! I seem to be meeting some fascinating people on this rollercoaster ride of a journey! I sit at the table and stare at the neatly written card that Valentina gave me, exceedingly uncertain of my future.

25

I'm brought back to the present by the familiar chime of a clock and decide to check on Alice after my week off. She's happy to see me and asks where Jenny is. "Jenny's gone back home now, but hopes to visit again soon," I say.

Alice brings me up to speed with her progress with the physiotherapist, who is visiting twice a week now, and she demonstrates how well she's doing with her exercises, which is fantastic progress in just one week. I can tell she's determined to succeed. "Xavier tells me there was a helicopter on your lawn," Alice says quizzically, but I smile and tell her that some friends just called for the day. I doubt that she believes me though. I dislike lying but don't want Xavier to know anything. It's probably a vain hope. I expect the Chinese whispers will be all around the village by now.

Once home, I make my way up to the attic through the 'wardrobe route', I'm anxious to see if Jenny got back okay. I notice the two old carpet bags still sat in the corner. I keep forgetting them. Gingerly, I lift them and place them in the bedroom to investigate later. As soon as I enter the 'signal zone' I receive a text from Jenny confirming that her journey went to plan, that she's envious of my new life, and can't wait to come back again soon. Leaning on the wall, I slowly slide down to land on my bottom and sit staring around the room. My eyes fix on the old bureau. I wish I could find the key. It really is too charming to damage. With renewed enthusiasm, I make it my mission to search for it, even if it takes all night! I scour the room, but it reveals nothing. Frustratingly, it only contains the bureau and the stunning chandeliers.

Moving on, I enter the room housing the paintings. Leo liked them, but I'm not much into art, though the portraits intrigue me. Who were these well-dressed people of long ago? One lady, in particular catches my eye. She's wearing a beautiful pale blue gown, her left hand gently resting on her lap, purposefully displaying a knuckle-duster of a ring. Matching sapphire earrings and necklace complete the ostentatious demonstration of wealth. Judging by the style of her costume, the picture's at least a couple of hundred years' old. Even the heavy gilded frame continues the theme. She's not alone. There are several others from the same era, depicting possible family members, but my favourite is the painting of the Chateau. This picture is not for sale. I have every intention of seeing it hanging back in the drawing room, where it belongs.

Realising I've been side-tracked, I chastise myself and continue searching for the key.

"Think Laura, think!" I say out loud. Where would I hide a key if I was desperate to keep it from the enemy? My first thought is under the floorboards, but which room? "Certainly not in the same room, or even in the same vicinity," I again say out loud. I can't rip all the floorboards up in the Chateau. Downstairs has stone floors anyway. A loud rumble of thunder makes me jump. Leo had warned me that there was a forecast for storms this evening. I'd better batten down the hatches before it arrives in earnest. I don't want a repeat of last time. The search for the elusive key is once again halted, this time by the weather, or is this one of the ancestor's ideas of a diversion? Perhaps I'm not meant to find it, a greater force preordained life my gran believed. I'm not sure I trust in such things, but I can't explain the appearance of 'the old lady playing the piano', not that I've actually seen her, but Lily and Gus seem to have. I'm assuming it's Great-Aunt Mary, who was the previous owner. Sylvie's mother, Rose, said she used to teach the village children to play the piano, but I don't know for sure.

The storm rages on for most of the night, and I lay awake listening to the relentless drumming of the rain on the windows. Remembering the hole in the roof, I decide to check how much water it's letting in. I find a steady flow entering through the damaged roof and trickling down the hole in the floor that the squirrels use. A chamber pot lurking under one of the old abandoned beds will have to do until morning. Placing it directly under the hole, it catches most of the water. Tomorrow I will find something more significant to replace it. I need to ask Sylvie if she can recommend a roofer. If only John were still here, I could ask him to do it instead. The carpet bags beckon, and I spend the rest of the night examining their contents. Old photographs, black and white pictures, mainly of a young woman in a nurse's uniform. In some of the snaps, she's with a dashing young man in military attire, who could they be? The next bag contains more photos and a bundle of letters, but no car keys. I jump as another large flash of lightening takes out the electricity. I quickly put the bags back in the wardrobe and head for the safety of my bed.

Last night's storms have left a leaden sky behind. The atmosphere is damp and muggy. I feel the need to get out for some fresh air, but first, I must find a large receptacle to place under the hole in the roof. I remember seeing a couple of old tin baths in the cellar. Will I be able to lug one up to the attic? I don't really have many options though, as another rumble of thunder hastens my need. One of the baths is smaller than the other. Probably used by the children. I wonder when they installed the first bathroom? It must have seemed incredible to the occupants, and far less work for the servants, if only these walls could talk!

With my task at last accomplished, I wonder over to the farmhouse to find Alice sat up on the side of her bed, waiting for me. She needs less help every time I visit; hopefully, she'll be able to manage without me soon.

Turning to look at me she says, "The grape

harvest and pressing have now finished, and the olive harvest is still a few months away. So, Xavier should be around to help more."

We chat about the garden and the weather, and I tell Alice about the hole in the roof.

"There's a builder in the next village," she says, "who's my nephew. He could help." That's probably 'Crueller de Ville's' son, I don't think I want anyone so close to Xavier in the attic, so I just smile and thank her. I stay a little longer then I jump into Dolly and drive down to the village to see Sylvie.

She is with Pedro in the garden, tidying up after last night's storm. Rose comes out with coffee and croissants, and we sit for a while on the old stone patio, while I tell them about the roof. "Yes, the old roof has been patched up many times, it really is in poor condition and needs replacing. I'll get you the number of a roofer used to period properties," Pedro says as he disappears into the kitchen, returning a few minutes later with the details.

"I can't afford to replace the roof," I say in

dismay. “It will have to be patched up again I'm afraid."

Pedro also hands me another small business card saying, "Monsieur le Marie is also awaiting a visit from you. He holds permanence's at the Mairie between nine and eleven on Thursday mornings; I suggest you go and introduce yourself." I take the card from him and put it in my pocket, mentally adding the job on my 'to do' list.

I ring the roofer’s number immediately, but it goes to voicemail. I leave a rambling message, say my farewells to Pedro, Rose, and Sylvie, then carry on to the village, to pick up fresh bread for lunch. Halfway back home my phone rings, and, of course, Dolly doesn't have 'hands-free' so, I pull over onto a grass verge to answer. It's the roofer, and I'm in luck. He should have been working on a roof a few miles away, but the storm made it too dangerous to work this morning. Looking around, I notice the skies are now clearing and he agrees to come out to give me an estimate.

A couple of hours later, Gustave the roofer, arrives. He's a tall, middle-aged man with greying hair. Jumping out of his large, white van, he opens the back doors and starts to unload a sturdy ladder. "I've worked on this roof before, several years ago. It's not easy to get to. I'll probably need to set up some scaffolding," he tells me. He seems a genuine, honest guy, and Pedro recommended him, so I guess I'm going to have to trust him too. All of the doors are closed in the attic anyway, so he only needs to go in the 'squirrel room'.

"There's an easier way up. Come with me," I say. He says nothing and follows me into the hall. I take him upstairs and show him the wardrobe in the back bedroom with the secret staircase.

"Sapristi!" He declares as he follows me up the narrow steps and into the attic. "I didn't know this was here!"

"Well, neither did I until recently," I admit.

Once in the squirrel room, I show him the skylight and the hole in the roof. He positions the ladder and gradually prises the old window open. He cautiously climbs through onto the roof, and I follow him, holding on for dear life, as I pop out into the sunlight. The view is incredible. The sky has returned to azure blue, and I can see for miles, right down to the village and beyond.

I try not to look down as I take in my surroundings. There is an area about a foot wide where the parapet ends before the slope of the roof starts, creating a narrow balcony all the way around. It's fantastic! It would be wonderful to sit up here on a clear night to stargaze. I wish Jenny could see this! Holding on to the stone parapet, I slowly inch my way along, to where Gustave has placed the wooden ladder against the slope and has climbed up to examine the hole. I daren't look for more than a few seconds in case I lose my footing - I don't think I'd make a very good roofer.

Gustave climbs down and lowers the ladder back through the window. Once inside he turns and takes my hand, helping me back in.

"Wow! it's fantastic up there," I exclaim.

"Yes, it is, but promise you won't go back out there alone; it's not safe. The roof is fragile, most of the timber is rotten and needs replacing," Gustave admonishes. Back in the safety of the kitchen, he gives me the bad news, "The roof needs replacing. I can do it for 50,000 Euros."

I nearly choke on my coffee and have a major coughing session, with tears spilling down my cheeks. When I've recovered enough to speak, I say, "Unfortunately, I don't have that amount of money. Could you patch up the hole for the time being?"

"I can," he says, "but there is something I need to show you." He then takes me on a tour of the rooms where the damp is starting to encroach and damage the structure of the building. The worst area is directly below the hole - in my bedroom, where he shows me the damage that the water has done while running down the wall and into the chimney. Indeed, I can see where the mortar has started to come away from the blocks of stone inside the old fireplace.

"It's not a big job to reset these stones," he says, wiggling one and pulling it out of its ancient resting place. A metallic clinking sound gets our attention, and we both look down into the empty fire grate, to find that an insignificant looking, blackened key has landed there. Gustave looks at me, then bends down to pick it up, examining it before handing it to me. Rubbing his stubbly chin, he adds, "Looks like it fits a small lock." I take it from him and say nothing, slipping it into my pocket. My inner self is punching the air and doing a happy dance while trying to remain calm and serene on the exterior. I'm itching to bolt immediately up to the attic like Houssain, to see if it fits, but I manage to refrain myself. The next twenty minutes seem to last an eternity, while I agree a day for Gustave to return to patch the hole and repair the fireplace.

26

As soon as Gustave is back in his van, I shoot up to the attic like an Olympic sprinter. Standing in front of the bureau, I stop and take a deep breath. Will the key fit? It looks small enough. I retrieve it from my pocket and slowly place it in the lock. It fits in neatly but, to my disappointment, won't turn. I remove it and blow gently into the lock in case it's dusty; that doesn't work. What can I try next? I remember that I bought a spray can of WD40 a while ago, on Pedro's recommendation. He said that it helps to release 'stuck parts' and stops door hinges from squeaking.

Spraying it into the small hole reminds me of the time when I was trying to gain access to the carriage house. I succeeded then, and I will do so this time. I put the key back in the lock, but it won't budge; I gave the carriage house locks a sharp tap with a hammer, but this time it's too delicate an operation. I'll give it a while to soak and come back later. While I'm up here, I might as well continue with my inventory. I've only opened one trunk, plenty more to go through.

The next trunk contains more fine bed linens, and drapes, probably off some grand four-poster bed, I wonder what happened to it. Several trunks later, and I begin to find baby clothes, once white, but now yellowing with age. Holding the tiny garments up to the light, I'm awed by the fine needlework. I try to imagine a beautiful young lady sat making these small outfits in preparation for the eagerly anticipated birth of her child. Then I think about the pain she would have had to endure; an epidural wouldn't have been an option. Placing them carefully back in the trunk, I move on to the next in line.

Gasping as the contents are revealed, I stand back in disbelief. Ladies gowns, in an assortment of colours and styles. They look quite small, probably the equivalent of a modern size eight. Dare I try them on? The dresses are so delicate. Lifting out a dark green dress reveals a blue one underneath. Taking it out, I can't help but think it looks familiar. Of course! It's the gown the lady is wearing in the portrait. I can't believe my eyes! I go and stand next to the large picture and hold the dress up. Yes, a perfect match. I have to find out who she was, and what happened to her. I look carefully in the bottom of the empty trunk, but the matching jewellery isn't here, that would be too much to ask! Then again, it's all been a little too much. Why me? Some days I think it's a blessing and others a burden!

The light is starting to fade, and I'm hungry. A look at my phone informs me its past eight. I hope Gus and Xavier have helped Alice. It's too late for me to go now. Where has the time gone? I creep up to the bureau as if catching it unaware will somehow help. But, of course, it doesn't. The key still won't budge, and I don't want to break it. I'll have to wait until morning, another sleepless night ahead!

I'm up in the attic at eight the next morning, still in my nightdress, having spent the night anticipating what lies within, but the key refuses to move. I Give the lock a fresh squirt of the smelly spray before I shower, and dress then go over to Alice. She is sat in the kitchen having breakfast with the boys. They invite me to join them, but I don't much fancy the sliced meat and cheese that they are having, so only have fruit and coffee. I still miss my bowl of cereals for breakfast!

Xavier surprises me by asking, "Do you 'av ze jobs you need doing?"

I want to reply, "Yes, you can fix the roof," but I know that's not realistic.

When I tell him, I can't think of anything, he shrugs, "I will cut ze long grass for ze winter fodder, but I need ze tractor, zen I will work in ze walled garden. Apples and pears will be ready to collect."

Remembering that the old car is hidden in the carriage house makes me anxious, but he shouldn't be able to see it, John piled pallets up in front of the damaged wall.

I spend the rest of the morning out and about - helping Xavier to get the tractor out and checking on the animals. There are quite a few fluffy chicks in the hen's enclosure. They are so cute, but I'm going to be overrun if they carry on breeding. Likewise, with the cats. I need to try and catch them to have them spayed and neutered, though it's easier said than done! I'm getting better with the animals. I'm even starting to make friends with Beau, Xavier's big dog. He seems to have concluded that I'm more friend than foe.

Later in the afternoon, Xavier informs me that he has dropped a load of fruit at the farmhouse, and Alice is expecting me there for a lesson in making jam. I'm about to tell him that I have to get back to see if the lock has released but remember my slip-up just in time. Okay, jam making sounds fun!

I can smell the ripe fruits before I even enter the farmhouse kitchen. It looks like a harvest festival of biblical proportions. The table is laden with apples, pears, blackberries, and a fruit called quince, which I've never heard of before. Gus is already hard at work, peeling and chopping fruit, and I'm instructed to join in. Alice isn't idle. She's positioned herself on a stool at the sink and is washing plump blackberries with one hand. Two large copper pans are already sat on the range, their contents gently simmering. Alice teaches me how to check if the 'confiture' is ready by dropping a teaspoon of the hot mixture onto a frozen saucer. If the surface 'wrinkles' it's ready. When done, I then ladle it into the jars sterilised in the oven.

We bottle some of the poached pears, and lots of the apples are frozen. Alice instructs me to take some of the fruit home to freeze. "I haven't got a freezer," I tell her, remembering the old chest freezer in the garage full of dead insects! She chastises me and insists I get one immediately and start to stock up for the winter. She is, of course right. If I were to stay, I would need one. But I'll be gone by winter, won't I? I take some fresh fruit and a jar of 'confiture' home with me. Alice assures me that she can now manage to get into bed by herself, and Beau sleeps by her side, barking to wake the boys if she needs any help in the night. I'm starting to see Beau in a new light; now we've got used to each other.

Back home, I have a scrumptious jam sandwich for my tea, followed by fruit and chevre. Ice-cream would have been lovely. Perhaps I should get a freezer; there's plenty of room for one. After washing up my few dishes, I allow myself to go and check on the bureau. I'm no longer optimistic and feel sure I will have to call a locksmith tomorrow.

Again, I feel the need to creep up on it, take it by surprise, catch it when it's off guard, as though some strange force is trying to deny me entry. Holding my breath, I apply a little pressure. The key moves and the lock yields. I stand back and stare at the object, not quite believing my luck. Half of me wants to rush straight in to see what secrets it's been keeping, but the other half of me is reluctant. It might be empty, and then it will be a huge anti-climax, after all this anticipation.

With shaking hands, I pull down the flap

which forms the desk. Inside are various draws and shelves. The first thing I put my hands on is photographs, old, brown, sepia-toned photos. The images are of poor quality and slightly grainy, but good enough to make out the faces of long-gone people. Judging by the period of dress, they are probably Victorian, or Edwardian, though neither reigned here. Turning them over, I'm in luck. Some thoughtful person has written names and dates on the back, which will be an enormous help figuring out who's who. Mothers with children, men dressed either in suits or military uniform, one sporting an exceptional moustache! I need to take some time to study them in detail, but not now, I'm eager so discover more.

Another shelf houses more photographs, slightly more modern, possibly the 1920's. Beautiful women dressed in flapper dresses with matching hats, their partners looking dapper, in smart suits. The next batch of pictures appear to have been taken outside the Chateau. The gardens immediately in front of the old building look stunning; very formal in style, with low hedges making a symmetrical pattern filled with flowers. It's a shame it's not in colour. Another picture has an old car parked in front of the Chateau with a dapper young man standing beside it. Again, he's sporting an elaborate moustache. Could it be the same man? Probably not, wrong era. The car looks familiar though. Is it the one now secreted away in the carriage house? It seems similar. In this digital world, I usually 'zoom in' to examine photos, but this is a different time that I find myself in. Yes, it's frustrating but equally fascinating. I'm only now beginning to realise just how privileged I am to be the custodian of these artefacts. The trail is getting warmer. I have proof of the car's history. I only need to find the keys; they must be here somewhere!

The next little drawer reveals a small cloth pouch. It feels quite heavy, and I think it is probably money. Slowly tipping the contents out onto the desk I'm, once more astounded as a dozen or so gold coins nestle in a small mound. They are like the one my gran wore around her neck. It belonged to her father and now belongs to me, along with all of these. From previous research, I know they are worth about £300 each. A quick calculation tells me that I have roughly £3,600 sat in front of me. It will help but won't fund a new roof!

Pulling open the last drawer, I find a scroll of old papers. Opening them, I'm frustrated to see them handwritten in black ink, in French of course. The writing is very fancy, almost like calligraphy. I can understand some of the words. It is dated 5th December 1918, but most of it is unfamiliar, not unlike the papers from the solicitor. It mentions a Pierre Besnard. That's Xavier and Gus's surname, could this be the document he's looking for - his proof of ownership of the farmhouse? It has three different signatures on the bottom, none of them legible. I once again need the assistance of Sylvie to help me translate. Frustratingly, I know she will be at work tomorrow. It's too late to ring her now. I'll have to wait until tomorrow evening.

27

I decide to call it a day, as it's now pitch black, and the little light up here is inadequate. Should I lock the bureau? Probably not, I might not be able to get back into it, though I've emptied the drawers and shelves and still not found the car keys. I'll have another look in the morning when its light, just to be sure. Before going back down, I enter the squirrel's domain to look out through the skylight, I can see some stars, but the glass has decades of dirt encrusted on it, I really must try to clean it. Another job for tomorrow.

The next morning, I sit eating my breakfast, trying to ignore the growing stack of paperwork at my side. I know I'm procrastinating, unsure of what to do next. Sighing, I pick up the business card on top of the pile. It's for the auction house. Perhaps I need to finish emptying the trunks and complete my inventory, before inviting them to see my treasures. Yes, that would be the most sensible thing to do. And I still need to find the car keys and papers, if indeed they still exist. It's been a while since the old girl last saw daylight. If only it were a bit lighter in the attic. It's better up there at midday when the sun comes through the roof light, but the heat is stifling. That reminds me, the first job is to clean all the decades of dirt from the ancient glass. Yes, now that I have a plan, I feel a little more enthusiastic. Putting the card down, I pick up the next one. It's the details for Monsieur le Maire. Sighing, I put it back down. He doesn't have a 'clinic' until Thursday. Decision made. The attic it is. With my bucket of hot soapy water and a stiff brush, I start to cleanse the roof light of its debris. That's the inside done without any drama, dare I venture out to do the outside? I'm distracted by my phone ringing in the 'signal zone'. It's the estate agent's office.

"Bonjour," I answer.

"Good morning Mademoiselle Mackley. It's

Raymond, in Marseilles. It's been quite difficult, but we have come to an estimated value for your estate. I will, of course, send you all the details in the post but thought I would ring first."

Standing like a statue, I'm rooted to the spot where I have a signal and daren't move, despite felling jittery and wanting to pace up and down. "Oui," is the only sound that manages to escape my lips. I feel like a coiled spring about to discharge at any moment. Raymond continues his spiel, most of which I don't take in. Get to the point will you! Of course, I don't utter my thoughts, but stand still waiting for the numbers, catching the odd comment.

"It would have been worth significantly more if maintained to a better standard," he says. Yes, I get that; it's a crumbling pile that needs a fortune spending on it - 50,000 just for the roof alone - but again I keep that information to myself. When I think I can't take any more, I hear, "But there is the productive vineyards and olive groves to take into consideration...

Are you still there?"

"Oui," I manage again.

"Well, down to figures. It's worth something in the region of," Raymond pauses for a while then continues, "One million Euros." He stops talking, probably waiting for my comments, but they don't come. My brain is completely blank, and my lips don't appear to be working. No matter how hard I try to send them the appropriate signals, my neurones have blown a fuse. Probably while my brain started to shut down. ' *Due to circumstances outside our control we are unable to deal with your inquiry right now - please try again later.*'

Screwing up my eyes tight shut, followed by a vigorous shake of my head, seems to help the fog lift a little. I realise I'm sat on the floor with the phone in my lap. Putting it back to my ear informs me that Raymond is still on the line. "I realise this is a disappointment, and you were probably hoping for more... it's a lot to take in. I'll send a report out to you in the post, as I said earlier. We would, of course, be happy to assist you with the sale of the estate if you decide to proceed. If you have any further questions, please don't hesitate to contact me."

I manage to say, “Merci beaucoup,” before disconnecting the call. Time stands still while my brain runs a defrag. Here I am in a dark attic, wearing neon pink marigolds, holding on tight to a worn scrubbing brush for comfort. You couldn't make it up, this strange adventure of mine! At last, the pieces of my brain have begun communicating with each other again, as a question forms on my lips, "Does the million Euros include the contents?" It must do as my previous offer, with contents was half that amount.

On wobbly legs, I make my way to the kitchen in need of a stiff drink. Common sense kicks in though, and I make a chamomile tea instead to soothe my recovering nerves. It seems to help as my thought process slowly returns. Raymond came to do his valuation before I discovered the wine, so it can't be included. He didn't see the old car, so that can't be included either, and he said that I need to invite an auction house to value the contents. So, it all points to a no, but I should double check.

Having returned to the attic feeling a little better, I ring him back. A female voice answers, saying, "Monsieur Raymond Demonde is busy at the moment. Would you like to leave a message for him?"

"Yes, please tell him that Laura Mackley…"

Before I can continue, the woman interrupts, "Of course, Mademoiselle Mackley… I'll put you through."

"Hello again Mademoiselle Mackley... I thought you might ring back. How can I help you?" It's quickly becoming apparent that money talks.

"Does the offer include the contents?"

"Absolutely not, those are yours to dispose of how ever you see fit. But, as luck would have it, I happen to have a nephew who runs an auction house. I'll add his details to my report. My secretary is just preparing it now. I'll also send you the details of our fees, should you decide to sell. Is there anything else you need me to clarify?"

"No, thank you for your time. I'll ring back if I think of any more questions."

Unable to concentrate, I find myself wandering around the Chateau, room by room, clueless as to what to do. I feel like I'm floating, and I need to get a grip on reality. Alice comes to mind. Yes, I'll go and have lunch with Alice. She's always pleased to see me, and I can be of practical help, which will take my mind off the situation. I feel the need to off load, but I can't burden poor Alice, she has enough problems of her own. And she'd probably tell Xavier. He's the last person that needs to know! I could ring Jenny, but she'll probably be at work, like Sylvie. John would listen to me, but he'd advise me to follow my heart. What should I do?

A million Euros would set me up for life. I could buy a nursing home. On second thoughts, probably not a sensible idea. Keeping hold of staff is a nightmare. I used to work as a care assistant at a local home for extra cash when I was a student nurse. They were always desperately short staffed. Silly idea. Time to visit Alice, a distraction is what I need right now.

When I arrive at the farmhouse, the physiotherapist is with Alice, and I'm thrilled that she has her on her feet taking a few steps with a tripod walking stick. Alice beams when she sees me, which causes her to wobble a little, but she quickly recovers and continues walking around the kitchen table. I don't speak but quietly sit as I admire the progress she's making. Next, the physiotherapist works on Alice's arm, which I can see already has an improved range of movement. Before leaving, she demonstrates some more advanced exercises for Alice to perform at least twice a day.

A large pan of stew is simmering on the range. I ladle out a helping for Alice which she enjoys, but I really don't fancy any after Alice informs me its rabbit. I stick to blackberry and apple crumble with custard, which doesn't take me long to make.

“Where’s Xavier?” I ask.

“He's gone to the local town to sell his produce at the market,” Alice responds.

I expect he's selling my jam, honey, and wine! I need to find out if he really does own the farmhouse and vines. Sylvie will be out of school in a few hours. I'll take the old papers down to her cottage later.

28

Until I’ve spoken to Sylvie, I need to keep busy. Back up to the attic I go, determined to find the keys and papers for the car. The sun is still illuminating the attic, so I have another search in the bureau. I take out all of the items I've already discovered, leaving the elegant wooden interior bare. I don't appear to have missed anything. Sitting cross-legged on the floor, I lean against the wall behind me, feeling defeated. Where are the keys? Once my frustration dissipates, I relax a little, if they are here, I will eventually find them. I lean my head back against the wall, and that's when I see it! There is an area underneath the folded-down desk flap, about five or so centimetres deep, which I hadn't noticed before. Jumping up quickly, I have another search, but I'm flummoxed. There doesn't seem to be any way to get into it. I've tried pulling, pushing, sliding, and tugging. Short of taking a hammer to it, I don't know what else to do.

Sighing with frustration, I lean on the desk with my hands. I hear a mechanical clicking sound, and can't believe my eyes, when a small area between the flap and the shelves, pops up from nowhere to reveal a secret cubbyhole! I stare in disbelief for a while, before sliding my hand through the slot into a false bottom. I can feel a hard, square object. It feels like a small book. My slim fingers manage to grasp it and lever it out. Yes, I am holding a small grey notebook. When did it last see the light of day?

Opening it with great care, I soon find out – 1943 - written during the war. Now I'm torn. I want to sit and read the neat black handwriting covering the old pages, but equally, I'm eager to find what else is hiding within. Curiosity wins. I put the book down and slide my hand once more into the abyss. This action takes me back to my childhood when we used to have a lucky dip at the annual school fair; fifty pence bought you the pleasure of rummaging around in a bucket full of sawdust to try and find a tacky prize.

Feeling another object brings me back to the present. It's an odd shape, almost oval, hard, and yet soft at the same time. Sliding it through the gap, I can now see that it's a red leather case of some type. Lifting its hinged top blows my mind! I close it again quickly and put it down. Placing my hands over my face, I whisper, "Oh-my-God!" Repeating the phrase several times, I try to calm my raging thoughts. I've already discovered some beautiful things, but this really is the jackpot!

Picking the box back up, I lift the lid once more and move over to stand beneath the roof light, where the sunlight bounces off the magnificent set of sapphire jewellery. The same ones that the wealthy young woman is wearing in the portrait. I have the painting, the dress, and now the bling! Where is this going to end? Gently closing the lid, I put it in with the other objects out of the bureau and carry on feeling my way around the secret compartment.

The next object is heavy, cold, and round, attached to a chain. It reveals itself slowly; a silver pocket watch, decorated with delicate patterns, its outer cover opens to display some initials engraved inside. Squinting, I decide it reads A H D. I wonder who he was. Perhaps he was the husband of the woman in the blue dress, who owned the bling. How do I find out? They mustn't have had children as all these items would now belong to them, instead of me. I feel obliged to investigate in case there are any living relatives left. I think I ought to visit Monsieur Bertrand. Surely, he must know. That would mean another encounter with his less than pleasant secretary. Maybe she has a day off then I could avoid her. Sylvie might know.

I can't feel anything else in the secret compartment. My slender arm can't quite reach the back. Stepping away, I search for something to use instead. A wire coat hanger would be perfect, which are of course, way too modern for the Chateau. Carefully tipping the bureau forward, I peer inside with the help of my torch. I can see a scroll of paper near the back. What can I use to reach it?

A quick trip to the kitchen to search for something useful, and I'm back with a flexible palette knife; that should do the job. Sliding it to the back of the drawer, I manage to bend it around the back of the scroll. It slides forwards a little before snagging on the top of the cubbyhole. Frustratingly, I can't reach it with my hand. I try again with the bendy knife, but I hear the sound of tearing paper. I stop immediately. I can't risk damaging it, whatever it is. Possibly the documents for the old car. Wracking my brain, I decide the only person that I know with arms slimmer than mine is Gus, and I can't ask him. I don't want to risk Xavier finding anything out, at least until I'm sure of the legal status of the farmhouse. No, the scroll will have to reside in the cubbyhole a little longer. A few more days won't make much of a difference to the scheme of things. It is, after all, rural France, I'm now quite used to things moving at a snail's pace.

My phone pings. Its Sylvie, responding to my earlier text. She's home now and happy to help, I'm unsure of what to do with the valuable items. I can't risk locking them back in the cubbyhole, then finding that I can't get back into them. I still don't know what I did to release the cover over the small slot. They've been up here since the war. There's only Jenny, John, and his family, the estate agents, and Leo and Valentina who know that a route to the attic even exists. Oh, and Gustave the roofer. I decide to place the coins, pocket watch, and jewellery into the box with the family silver, then slide it to the back of the room, leaving it covered with old linen. This stuff can't stay up here indefinitely. I'm going to have to come to a decision soon.

Once I'm satisfied that the Chateau doors and windows are locked, I drive over to see Sylvie with the old documents that I need translating. She seems as excited as me as she slowly reads it, then recounts it to me in English. "It's a legal document drawn up by a solicitor called Gilles Bertrand, who I think must be Monsieur Bertrand's grandfather. It states that General Henri Augustine Deford, the owner of the Chateau, is granting Pierre Besnard - who I think was Xavier's grandfather - the right to live in the farmhouse, and use the attached land, rent free for... one hundred years."

We both look at each other with a shocked expression on our faces.

Sylvie speaks first, "So, Xavier has less than three months left... what are you going to do?"

I wasn't expecting that. I'm once again lost for words. I really have no idea what to do. My brain has had enough revelations for one day and can't process any more.

"Whose job is it to tell him?" I ask.

Sylvie looks at me and smiles, "Well, you are now the landlord, and he is your tenant, so I guess it's yours. I think you should give him a couple of months' notice though if you intend to evict him… or charge him rent," she remarks.

Evict him? I can't possibly do that. I couldn't displace Gus and poor Alice. I've already used the rent word, but we both know that I won't see any. He can't earn very much from the vines. I've seen Alice's bank statements; she hasn't got a vast amount of savings. Well, at least I've got a few weeks. I'll think of something.

29

I spend the night tossing and turning. So much has happened in such a short space of time: all the treasures in the bureau, as well as uncovering the truth about Xavier and the farmhouse. So many thoughts and ideas are whirring round in my head. How much are the contents worth? Should I sell? What would the new owner do with Xavier and his family? What would they do to the Chateau? Probably turn it into a hotel, or worse, rip it apart and make it into apartments. I'm confused and don't know what I want anymore. My first impressions of the crumbling Chateau are slowly being replaced. I've had high's and low's, but stone by stone this place is starting to get under my skin. I'm growing fond of the friends I've made here and have nothing to return to England for, not even a job!

I must have eventually dropped off to sleep, as I'm woken just before dawn by the usual thud in the attic. I'm fairly sure it's my furry friend, but I feel the need to check, with all the valuable items stored up there. I arm myself with my phone, a torch, and an old brass candlestick - just in case. I find the attic empty, with no sign of an intruder, and my furry friend has disappeared down his hole. Looking up through the window, I notice the night is losing her grip on her black velvet cloak. One by one, the stars are beginning to fade as the sun slowly makes her appearance in the east.

It looks enchanting, and I crane my neck to try and see more. In a moment of madness, I drag the rickety ladder over and push the window open. It gives easily, allowing me to climb out onto the roof. The fresh morning air kisses my bare limbs, and the view indeed takes my breath away. A fine mist hugs the ground in the dips and hollows, creating the illusion of still water. Slowly, the pink glow in the east gradually turns to orange as the illusion dissipates to reveal the earth below.

The sun dazzles as she rises above the horizon, reflecting off the silver foliage of the gnarled olive trees in the distance. Why would I ever think of leaving this magical place?

Feeling as though a heaviness is lifting from my young shoulders, I sit on the roof for a while, admiring the view. I can see the village off to my left, with its tall church spire pointing to the heavens. No doubt its inhabitants are slowly waking up to a new working day. In the far corner of my estate, the light in the farmhouse kitchen comes on as Xavier rises to wake Gus, and usher him off to school, then help Alice to get up and have breakfast. Poor man, he doesn't have an easy life. How can I even consider letting some new owner throw him out of his family home? We may not always see eye to eye, but he is a good man, and I'm going to need his help and experience if I'm to stay here. Perhaps I can make it work if I sell some of the treasures. I won't need to buy much. The locals seem to manage by living off the land and helping each other. Laughing out loud, I try to imagine that level of cooperation in inner-city Leeds - and can't.

A glance at my phone tells me it's now past seven-thirty. I've sat here long enough. A stiff breeze has picked up and starts swirling around the old chimneys, time to go back inside. Standing, I make my way carefully back towards the window. When I reach it, I turn and allow myself one last look at the vista in front of me. A loud bang makes me jump out of my skin. Luckily, I manage to grab the edge of the parapet to steady myself. What on earth was that? Looking behind me, I have the answer. The breeze has blown the window shut! With a sense of rising panic, I reach over and try to pull it open. But it won't move. "Don't panic Laura, just think," I say out loud. My brain comes up with nothing. Okay then, time to panic!

I try to calm my breathing before I begin to hyperventilate. My brain fog lifts, and my panic decreases a little. I've never been stuck on a roof in rural France before, though I have dangled out of a window in a thunderstorm! When will I learn? Okay, what resources do I have to hand? Only my phone, I left the torch and candlestick in the attic. Well, I wasn't to know that I'd need something to break the window! If only I had a suitable object to slide in-between the iron frame, like a knife. Yes, the pallet knife would have been perfect, but that too is a few feet below me, where I left it by the bureau!

I tug at a loose roof tile near the edge, and it comes away in my hand. This old roof is quite fragile. Will it survive another winter?" Laura! Now is not the time to ponder the health of the roof!" I chastise myself, as I try to force the broken tile into the window frame to lever it open, but it crumbles in my hands: that didn't work, so what's plan B? Banging my fist hard on the glass doesn't work either. What am I going to do?

Huddling up against the chimney helps to shield me from the breeze, which is more of a strong wind now, and the beautiful sky of early morning is turning ominously dark. Just what I need, another storm. I was warned that the weather could be quite changeable in

September and October, and here I am sat on the roof in my nightdress! "Well Laura, you don't have much choice. You've at least got your phone; with a signal you're going to have to use it! Who should I call? Sylvie and Pedro will be about to go to school, and I'm certainly not ringing Xavier! He would love that! He already thinks I'm a stupid, incapable, little girl; I will not give him the satisfaction. "Think, Laura!" I mutter, then exclaim, "Gustave, the roofer, of course! He has all the equipment to get me down, though I know the doors are locked and all the downstairs windows closed." Wasting no more time, I ring Gustave. It goes straight to voice mail. He might ring me back shortly; he did last time. I try again ten minutes later but have no luck. I leave a message this time, "Hello, its Laura at the Chateau... I have a problem... Please can you ring me as soon as possible."

Half an hour passes, and I'm getting very cold, at least it's not raining yet. Another fifteen minutes and I'm going numb. Is it possible to get hypothermia in the south of France? Sylvie has told me that it can get to minus ten in winter, it was hard to image this place coated with frost, but I'm starting to believe her now. I'm startled by the sound of a vehicle. Poking my head above the parapet, I can see Xavier's beaten old truck coming down the drive. Now what am I going to do? Bobbing back down quickly, I decide to lie here a little longer. Surely Gustave will ring me back in a few minutes. Xavier stops outside and knocks on the door. It's just past nine, what does he want? Xavier hardly ever calls to see me. He bangs again louder, then tries the door, but it's locked. Thankfully, I hear him walking away, he sounds to be going around the back.

I jump as my phone rings at the side of me. Oh, I do hope its Gustave! Glancing at the screen causes my stomach to lurch. Its Xavier. I quickly decline the call, but within seconds it rings again. I reject it and turn it to silent, hoping he didn't hear. That's when I hear him shout, "Laura, where are you? I 'eard your phone!" I don't answer, but he persists and continues calling for a few more minutes, before giving up and climbing back into his truck.

I stick my head back over the parapet. His truck is now halfway up the drive, when the clouds seem to part, sending an electric blue lightning streak across the purple sky. Seconds pass by as a loud thunderclap reverberates around the rooftop. How long until the rains starts? What happens when you get struck by lightning? I've done a few stints in A & E but never seen a victim. I suppose most of them go straight to the morgue. Okay, time to put my safety before my pride. Dialling his number, I think of the ways to admit my stupidity; this is not going to be pleasant.

"Ah, so you are talking to me now," he answers, in his thick accent.

"Err... yes... I'm a bit stuck," I reluctantly reply.

“Just where are you stuck zis time?" he asks sarcastically.

"Umm... On the... umm... roof" I say quietly, just as another flash of electricity illuminates the sky.

I hear a string of expletives as his truck swerves off the drive, into the long grass, and returns at speed down the drive. He jumps out shouting, as the rain begins to fall, gently at first, but soon, the large drops sting my skin with their force. I peer over the parapet to see him trying the door again.

"It's locked, as is the back... You'll need a ladder," I shout. He doesn't answer but disappears around the back. I don't remember seeing a ladder big enough in the garage. Moments later, the roof light pops open, and he climbs through, holding out his hand. I lean across and grab it. He then carefully guides me down the rickety steps into the safety of the attic.

He stands and looks at me as though I've got two heads, before shrugging and striding away. I think I've dodged his tirade, as he silently returns with a towel, and hands it to me. After I've wrapped it around my flimsy wet nightdress, he gestures to the open cupboard and says, "Go and get dried and dressed." I quickly head to my bedroom like a naughty child.

Downstairs in the kitchen, two large mugs of hot chocolate are sitting on the table.

"Drink," he orders as I sit opposite him.

Wrapping my cold hands around the mug is soothing, and I know I should have just rung him in the first place. My gran used to say, “Pride comes before a fall,” and, in this instance she would have been right.

"Well?" he says, cocking his head to the side while looking at me, waiting for an explanation. I'm embarrassed at having to be rescued once again by this pompous man.

"I'm fine; the window blew shut while I was out... checking the roof... before the rain started," I realise just how stupid it sounds the moment it leaves my lips.

"In your night cloze! In ze storm! It seems zis is ze habit you are making; can I not go out now if zere is to be a storm? In case my crazy neighbour goes for a walk on ze roof or jumps out of ze window!" he rants.

I'm determined not to lose my temper, I'm already embarrassed enough as it is, so ask calmly, "Anyway, how did you get inside? The doors are locked. And how did you know how to get into the attic?" I ask defensively.

He responds with his usual Gaelic shrug, then adds, "Ze catch on ze kitchen window is broken – 'as been since I was a boy - and you left ze doors open to ze secret stairs, which I knew were 'ere somewhere. I heard my grandfazer mention zem to my Fazer when I was little." There is a long silence, a sort of accepted truce, as we slowly finish our warm drinks.

"I came to bring you ze packet, ze postman left it wiz Mama," he says pointing to the large envelope on the table. I nod in acknowledgement, I suspect he's eager to know what it contains, but I refuse to open it in his presence. He stands and walks over to the door, then turns and says, "I will be back later zis afternoon, and don't go back on ze roof!" I open my mouth, trying to think of a reply but he strides through the door and leaves me alone with my thoughts. It's after he's gone that I remember the documents Sylvie translated for me, I'm his landlord and must decide what to do about that problem.

30

I'm restless and can't concentrate. The storm has done little to dispel the sticky, oppressive heat, which hangs in the air. What shall I do today? I could continue my work in the attic, but after this morning's fiasco, I don't fancy that idea much! I need to visit Monsieur Le Maire, but not until Thursday. I also need to see Monsieur Bertrand to double check no family members belonging to the 'old General' are still alive and to see if he knows anything about the contract drawn up by his grandfather between the old general and Xavier's grandfather. Yes, that's what I'll do today, but I'll need to be savvy.

Half an hour later, I'm sat in the square, obscured from view by the old monument. I may have to wait a while, but at some point, Crueller, alias Madam Cevert, will no doubt leave the office to run an errand of some type, even if it's to collect the croissants for morning coffee. I've seen her in the patisserie at eleven o' clock several times before. I'm in luck, as the clock on the church announces the hour, she marches down the steps and walks towards the shops.

As she disappears from view, I take my chance and cross the small square, entering the office. Monsieur Bertrand's door is open, and I knock softly to announce my presence. Peering over the top of his glasses, he waves me in. "Mademoiselle Mackley, how lovely to see you again. I trust you have settled into French life now," he says, gesturing for me to sit in the chair opposite.

"Yes, thank you, and please call me Laura," I reply, as I close the door and sit down.

"Well, what can I do for you today, Laura?" he asks. I waste no time and produce the old document drawn up by his grandfather. He reads it carefully then takes his glasses off, leans back in his creaking leather chair and looks at me. "Ah, I trust you have had this translated," I nod, and he continues, "I wasn't aware of its existence, but, yes, it remains a legally binding contract. So, you have a few weeks to decide on a course of action. It would, of course, be fair to give the tenants some notice of your intentions -" The door opens, interrupting his comment. Crueller has returned, she stands still in the doorway, with a shocked expression on her face before turning a menacing look upon me. Monsieur Bertrand stands, walks to the door, and says, "Ah, Madam Cevert, please will you bring a coffee for my client?" and closes the door, then returns to sit at his desk. He folds the document and hands it back to me saying, "This, of course, will remain confidential. I suggest you put it away before my secretary brings our coffee," he adds with a slight nod.

Moments later, Crueller enters and carelessly deposits two small cups of espresso on the desk, spilling the dark black liquid where only seconds before, the precious contract sat, slamming the door on her way out. Wincing, he continues, "I'm sure it's not personal, my dear. The family assumed that the Chateau would go to Xavier Besnard. No one knew of your existence. Is there anything else I can help you with?"

Trying hard to concentrate, I remember my next question, "Are there no surviving relatives of the old general who would have a claim on the Chateau?"

Smiling, Monsieur Bertrand reassures me that General Henri Augustine Deford left a valid will. Bequeathing the estate to his nurse, and dear friend Miss Mary Whitehead, my great-aunt. And that it now rightfully belongs to me. "I still have a copy of the original will, I dug it out for the conveyancer..." he says, taking a file out of a tall cabinet in the corner. "Here, take it, you can add it to the pile of papers that you no doubt will be amassing; it is in French though." Taking it from his hands, I stand and thank him for his time. "You haven't drunk your coffee, well, what little remains of it," he says with a laugh.

"Too bitter for me but thank you." I say. As I'm about to close the door to the square, I turn around and say, "Au revoir Madam, merci pour le cafe." But Madam Cevert doesn't bother to look up from her desk as I leave.

Feeling a little lighter, I pick up fresh bread and pastries, then make my way over to the town hall. It's not very elaborate, only a small extension on the side of the local school. The lobby has a notice board that states the time of the next 'sitting'. Sylvie is correct. Thursday, that's tomorrow morning taken care of.

I have a text message from Gustave, telling me his father is in the hospital and he can't help me today, but sends the details of a colleague who will be able to help if I have an emergency. I quickly respond, apologising for disturbing him and assure him that I no longer require his assistance, and will see him next week as planned when he comes to patch up the hole in the roof. I don't want everyone to know about my foolish foray onto the roof.

The package Xavier brought is still sitting at the end of the oversized kitchen table. Opening it reveals a detailed report from the estate agent. Thankfully, it's in English. Pages and pages of information, along with the value of one million Euros! One of the leaflets that fall out onto the table is from his nephew's auction house. I suppose I need to get the contents valued, but I think I'd prefer to use the company that Valentina and Leo recommended. They seemed like honest, decent people. There are only a few more trunks left to unpack in the attic. I should be able to get them done this afternoon.

31

Back up in the 'signal zone', I ring the number neatly written on the back of Valentina's business card.

"Bonham's, Paris," answers a posh female voice.

"Hello, sorry to bother you. I require the contents of my estate valuing, with an intention to sell some of the items," I say, and proceed to inform the posh lady of my discoveries. She's intrigued and makes an appointment for someone to come out and see me on Monday afternoon. That gives me a few days to continue the search for the car keys and papers, as well as to catalogue the last few trunks.

Only three more trunks left, then I've finished. If the car keys aren't here, I don't know where else to look. The first one contains old ledgers. It's difficult to decipher the writing, but I think they are the old accounts from the estate, dating back over two hundred years. They should make interesting reading, along with the diary from the war that I found previously.

The second is full of photograph albums, old

books, and toys. Some of the dolls are quite creepy, not what I'd consider child-friendly, and the third contains shoes and handbags. It appears that through the generations, some things don't change! I'm relieved to have finished my inventory but disappointed not to have found the documents and keys for the old car.

I decide to take the old ledgers and diary down to my bedroom. They'll give me something to do now the nights are getting longer. I'm distracted by the sound of Xavier's truck, for the second time today. He did say that he would be back later this afternoon. He drives around the side of the Chateau and out of view. Curious to know what he's doing; I pull on a pair of trainers and follow him. Soon I hear a loud squawking and honking noise, which gets louder and louder as I approach. He is parked in the farmyard, herding a gaggle of white geese into the paddock with the goats. Why does he think I want geese?

"What are you doing?" I shout above the cacophony, but he carries on with his task, heedless to the fact that I am standing next to him. I shout again, and he turns to look at me but carries on regardless. Once they are in with the goats, he closes the gate and strides across to me. "What are the geese for, exactly?" I ask again.

He only shrugs, then says, "For your protection, of course, as well as ze Christmas dinner."

I look at him in confusion then ask, "Why do I need protecting?"

He stands and looks at me for a few seconds before replying, "Just look at you, small and slight. If someone comes onto your land, ze geese will make ze big noise, and we will 'ear. Simple, yes?"

"Won't they fly away?" I ask.

"No, ze wings 'av been clipped. When zey 'ave been 'ere a few days, I will set zem free to wander around. If zey are well fed, zey will stay," he tells me.

Okay, perhaps that's not too bad an idea after

all, but I don't think I'll be eating one at Christmas, even if I am still here! Next, he opens his truck door and instructs Beau, his big dog to jump out. Beau instantly obeys his master and sits at his side.

"Now, you av ze lesson in dog handling," Xavier says, looking at me sternly.

"Why would I need to learn how to handle a dog?" I ask naively, but it suddenly dawns on me. "No way! I am not getting a dog-"

Xavier interrupts me mid-sentence, "Beau is staying wiv you for now, until I can find you ze suitable guard dog." He then hands me what appears to be a strange object on the end of a grubby piece of string. "Zis is 'is whistle. You will not be able to 'ear it, but if you use it, 'e will instantly come to you... and you will be safe. 'ere, place it around ze neck, like ze necklace, zen you will always 'av it."

I look at the dubious item and say, "That isn't going near me until it's washed!"

He shrugs, walks over to the tap and rinses the whistle, before handing it to me, "'ere, try" he instructs. I blow the whistle, but nothing seems to happen, then seconds later Beau reappears and sits at my side, awaiting a command. I'm impressed. "You will 'av speak to him in French, of course," he says and proceeds to teach me his repertoire of commands.

"What does he eat?" I ask.

"Whatever you 'av left at ze end of ze day," he says casually, walking away.

An hour later, Xavier has gone and left me with the geese and Beau. Another weird day in my crazy new life! I put Beau's dirty blanket on top of several old cushions at the bottom of the staircase, then set about searching for some supper for him. "I appear to be out of dog food; I wonder why?" I say to him, but Beau continues to ignore me; sitting to attention at the bottom of the stairs, where Xavier left him. I cook some pasta, dress it with pesto, chevre and toss in some hard-boiled eggs. I spoon a generous portion into a large bowl and take it to Beau. He looks at his food, then back at me as if waiting for something. Perhaps he's not hungry or doesn't fancy it. Leaving it by his bed with a bowl of water, I return to the kitchen to eat my share. It really is quite tasty.

32

After checking the doors and windows, I retire to my bedroom with a cup of tea for an early night. Climbing into bed, I notice the ledgers and diary. Yes, I decide, I'll read the journal. I might learn something new. I pick up the old grey notebook and begin to read.

Diary 15th August 1943.

I am writing this, sitting in the loft of what I can only assume is a large house somewhere in France. I feel the need to set the momentous events that have happened to me on paper, so all our parents and loved ones would at least know what happened if I don't make it home.

The 11th August was my twentieth Birthday, we scrounged some transport, and the whole crew took ourselves off to Thirsk to celebrate. We went to the pictures and watched 'The Gentle Sex,' a light-hearted film about Army Girls. Then got blind drunk on the local bitter, before weaving our way back home. Skipper drove as he was nearly sober. The next day, we knew ops were on again. The aerodrome was locked down, and nobody allowed out. No phone calls. The rumours were flying about, as usual, we knew the fuel load was high, so it would be a long trip. Berlin? God, I hope not.

This op would be my fourth. I have been with 408 Squadron a month now. It's odd being with the Canadian Air Force, but quite a few of us RAF bods have been seconded to make up the numbers. It could be worse; they are a good bunch, and the Halifax is a superb Kite. Our Skipper, P/O George McBride, is a little bit older than the rest of us, but still only twenty-five. He's a good pilot though and keeps a tight ship.

At the briefing, the C/O, with a typical dramatic flourish, revealed the target… Milan. The aiming point was the old car factory, now turning out engines for fighters. We took off as the light failed and formed up into a loose group heading south from Leeming. It was a cloudy night over England, and we passed over into enemy territory with no dramas. A few poorly aimed flak guns opened up as we crossed the coast, but nothing to worry about. The Navigator, PO Martin, is excellent and kept us on track towards the Alps. I looked down from my flight engineer's seat thrilled to watch the snow-capped mountains sliding 10000 ft beneath us; it seemed surreal. It didn't seem long before we could see the glow from the target; this was a maximum effort raid, and over 500 heavies were hitting Milan that night. The Pathfinders had done their job well, and we could see the coloured target indicators glowing through the cloud and smoke; the knot in my stomach grew as we got closer to the target. The flak was heavy but not as bad as the Ruhr. Fred, the bomb aimer found the aiming point from the TI's, and Skipper put us into a shallow dive. I helped him hold the throttles forward. "Hold her steady, skip… steady… steady… bombs gone," he said.

I'm not sure why he felt the need to tell us, as the plane leapt upwards as 6000lbs of heavy explosive and incendiaries fell out. Keep her steady for the photo

Skipper… steady… BANG... God, what the hell was that!... I felt a sudden gale blowing through from the front of the plane, and Skipper had reefed the plane around, tilting us forty-five degrees to the right

"Go and check up front, Harry," he shouted.

I climbed down past the wireless operator. Peter gave me the thumbs up. He's OK, tapping out a message. I could see Fred looked Ok too; he's climbed up from his aimers bench, looking a bit white. But I knew we'd taken a hit. Where? Must be the left side. Navigators compartment... had to be, the gale seemed to be blowing in from there. I looked in and found PO Martin lying on the floor, the chart table and instruments a mess, blood everywhere. Sam Martin was hit quite badly on his right side, a wound to the upper arm and face. He was still alive but looked grey and dazed. With Fred's help, we managed to get him back into the area under the astrodome and get some morphine into him.

Skipper had already turned us away from the target, and we had a debate as to the best course. It seemed logical to go back on the reciprocal bearing, but that would mean flying straight at the rest of the bomber force. We had no charts, no navigator. Heading north-

east seemed our only option. Back over the Alps the weather was clearing, and the clear sky revealed millions of stars. Framed between a stunning vista above and white capped mountains below, we flew in a black aircraft. In the distance, we could see other aircraft illuminated like us. A brilliant flash to our left marked the end of one, as it tumbled out of the sky in flames.

"Keep your eyes peeled everybody," shouted the Skipper, "the fighters are going to have a field day here."

As the Skipper finished speaking, Norman, the mid-upper gunner shouted, "Fighter on the port beam…"

The Skipper banked sharply to starboard, and I just had time to glimpse a line of tracer fire rake the underside of a Lancaster. Five minutes later, Murray Green shouted, "Corkscrew port." The plane was thrown about the sky as Murray opened fire, more tracers whipped past, and we all felt a deep thud as some of it hit the starboard wing. I glued my eyes to the instruments, checking temperatures and fuel levels.

"I think number ones been hit Skip, and we are losing fuel too," I said. The throttles were still at full

as we desperately tried to find some empty sky, but the strain was too much for the damaged engine which caught fire.

"Extinguishing number one, flight,'" shouted Skipper as he shut it off, and feathered the prop.

Another shout and a burst of fire came from Murray in the rear turret, but it was cut off abruptly by a tremendous bang, and we felt the whole airframe shake. Once again, we were thrown around the sky as we tried to evade the fighter. I decided to check the damage to the rear. I crawled back past poor Sam, who was now unconscious. I could see the whole rear of the plane was a mess. The rear turret had jammed, and I didn't need to look inside to know that Murray was dead.

Back up front, Skipper was struggling to keep us in the air. We were dropping fast, and it wouldn't fly level. We had no real idea where we were. The mountains appeared to be behind us now, but our altitude was dropping. Number two engine temps were off the scale. "What now skip?" I said.

"I think we will have to bail out Harry, get a chute on to Sam".

It was a struggle, but we managed to manoeuvre him down the lower hatch. It was not ideal, we had to tie his chord up, so it opened the chute as we pushed him out. Hopefully, he wouldn't hit what's left of the plane's tail! I helped Skipper hold the plane steady as Peter and Fred exit through the proper escape hatch. There was just Norman Poirier left. He is a good friend of the Skipper and didn't want to abandon him. With a hurried discussion, we decided there should be just enough time for us to get out of the batch before the plane inverted trapping us in. We were very low now, almost too low to jump. It was now or never. Norman jumped first. I looked forward to see if Skip was following. He was still holding the plane level, and I could see why now… Right in front of us was a village. If he let go now, the Halifax would plough straight into it. I had to go… I felt sick with guilt, but I had to jump.

There was barely time for my chute to open, but I twisted around to watch as the Bomber skimmed across the roof tops and ploughed through a small wood and into a hillside with a sickening crunch. There was only a small fire, no dramatic explosion, but I knew the Skipper was dead.

It appears I'm lucky to still be alive, as is Norman, who is with me now. We are guests of the kind French people, who, I know, are risking everything to keep us safe and free.

Sergeant Harry King (RAF), 408 Squadron RCAF.

I put the little book down and can't help wondering what happened to those two brave men, Harry, and Norman. Did they make it back home to their families? How can I find out? I have my answer when I pick the book back up to reread the account. On the next page is the name and address of his parents. They're sure to be dead now, but someone should be able to trace his family with this much information. The solicitors found me after all! Another visit to Monsieur Bertrand is required at some time.

I lay awake for ages, thinking about the two men, then my mind wanders to the inhabitants of the Chateau. The old general, he must have risked a great deal to hide the men. Now I can understand why the attic was sealed up, and the need for the secret stairs. I feel humbled by their actions and compelled to learn more.

33

Waking up with a headache, I slowly make my way downstairs in search of caffeine, that usually helps. As I near the bottom half of the stairs, an unpleasant, sulphurous odour permeates my nostrils. What can it be? I have my answer when I notice Beau, still sat on guard at the bottom of the stairs. Hasn't he slept? A glance at his bed tells me he has; the cushions are scattered, and his food bowl is empty. "Good morning Beau, no more eggs for you!" I say to him, but he continues to ignore me. Yes, I remember now, I need to speak French to him. I try greeting him again, this time in French, and he saunters over to me, giving my leg a slurp with his long rough tongue. He follows me into the kitchen, where

I give him a large bowl of milk, which he laps up greedily. He seems hungry, and I don't have any breakfast for him. I'll pick up some dog food when I go to the village this morning to see Monsieur Le Maire.

I arrive at the town hall, or 'Mairie' as it's known locally, a little before eleven to find the building empty. I recheck the notice board, which tells me I am in the right place, at the right time. Sitting down on one of the hard, uncomfortable chairs, I wait for an age before someone arrives. I look up from the magazine that I'm trying to read, which is about hunting - not my thing - but at least its good practice for my French education, and I'm horrified to find myself looking into the icy eyes of Madam Cevert. I smile, but she ignores me and makes a spectacle of removing her jacket and sitting down behind the small desk opposite. She takes her time to get a laptop and some papers out of a briefcase, puts on her ugly glasses then stares at me. "Do you have an appointment?" She asks coldly. I look at her, then back to the notice that clearly states that it's a 'drop-in clinic', no appointment necessary.

She's distracted as a short, portly man with a ruddy-faced complexion enters the small room. He looks over to Madam Cevert and nods curtly, at this point she smiles and says, "Bonjour, Monsieur Le Maire."

He then looks over to me and says, "Good morning Mademoiselle Mackley; it's nice to meet you, at last. Give me a few moments, and I'll be with you." Bobbing his shiny bald head, he nods in my direction and exits through a door on the opposite wall, so much for needing an appointment!

A short while later, he opens his door and calls me into his small office, not much bigger than a cupboard. As I approach, he makes an elaborate show of kissing me on both cheeks; not a pleasant experience, his breath is worse than Beau's flatulence! "Do sit down Mademoiselle Mackley," he says, pointing to another hard, wooden seat.

"Thank you for seeing me today. I've brought you a small gift, and please call me Laura." I respond, as he takes the bottle of Macallan Gold from me and puts it on the floor behind his desk.

"Thank you, that's very kind, I will donate it to the raffle for the old folks Christmas party," he says, producing a book of tickets out of a drawer, suggesting that I might like to buy some. "I'm also looking for kind volunteers to help," he adds, looking at me expectantly.

"Well, if I'm still here at Christmas, then I'm sure I could manage a few hours," I say to his moon-shaped face.

"Are you planning on leaving us, so soon after gracing us with your presence?"

Surprised by his question I sit for a moment, not quite knowing how to respond, before replying, "Everything is still up in the air at the moment, and I don't honestly know what I intend to do. I have grown fond of the Chateau, and the kind people I've met here, but it's been a bit of a roller coaster journey over the last two months."

Monsieur Le Maire leans forwards and puts his great weight on the creaking desk, inflicting his halitosis on me once more, and utters, "I'm glad you find our little close-knit community to your liking. We may be small, but we are quite capable of succeeding when we try. You will have already observed that we like things to continue in a traditional manner, no upsets, and nasty surprises. We work as a team and help each other." He then leans back in his chair and smiles before adding, "If there is anything, I can help you with in the future, you know where to find me." This dismissal signifies the end of our meeting, as he stands, bids me farewell and nods in the direction of the door.

The brief encounter has left me feeling a little uncomfortable. It felt more like a warning of some type, and I didn't get much chance to ask the questions I had prepared in advance. The phone signal and internet was one of them. I suppose I will just have to return another time. It appears I will need his permission to do most things. Then I remember about the idea of a campsite - if I decide to stay. Perhaps that's better left for a while. It may well come under the heading of 'nasty surprises'.

34

The shops have a minimal choice of dog food, and I get funny looks from the locals when I lug a big bag of dog biscuits over to the counter. I haven't a clue how much to feed him. The information seems to suggest that it's to do with the weight of the dog. Beau is rather large, so I guess he'll require quite a lot. I climb out of Dolly and heave the sack of biscuits to the door as Xavier walks around the corner.

"What 'av you got zere?" he asks. I don't reply as it's evident what the sack contains. Xavier opens the door for me and carries the food into the kitchen. Beau rushes over enthusiastically to greet him. Xavier scratches his furry head, then produces a dead rabbit and throws it on the floor for his dog. Beau proceeds to make short work of the poor creature, the fur and head seem to pose no problem for him.

I wince and look away as he consumes the rabbit with a crunching noise.

"Where do you zink ze meat for ze dog food comes from. 'e is ze carnivore. You will make 'im soft giving him ze dog food!" He says, ushering Beau out of the front door.

"Yes, I was just about to take him for a walk, but you didn't leave me his lead," I tell him.

Xavier looks at me then laughs, "'e doesn't 'av ze walks! Put 'im out zen blow ze whistle when you want 'im to return." I change the subject and inquire about his mother. "She continues to improve and can now do lots more things for 'erself."

"I will visit her later today and take Beau with me. I know she's fond of the big dog."

Alice is sat on a stool holding a pipe and attempting to fill the washing machine with water. I try to take over the job, but she waves me away and persists with her task. She beams at me when the tub is full and removes the pipe, slopping generous amounts of water on the floor. Oh well, the old stone flags were probably due a good wash. We chat while waiting for the water to heat up and she tells me about her progress with her physiotherapy sessions, which seem to be invaluable. Once the laundry is in, Alice makes a fuss of Beau, which he obviously enjoys. "Won't you miss him?" I ask her.

“I think you need him more than me at the moment,” she says. I'm not quite sure whether she means it's me or the treasures that need his protection but decide not to ask. She probably knows about my unfortunate 'roof incident'.

Once the laundry has finished, Alice lets me peg it outside on the washing line for her and insists that I help myself to some fresh produce from the garden. She stands in the doorway to watch as I leave with Beau. I'm thrilled with her progress, she's clearly an incredibly determined lady.

I spend the evening looking over the old ledgers. The bits that I can understand are quite fascinating. The most significant expenses were the maintenance and upkeep of the building and land, and, of course, the servant's wages. Other items were very varied, from purchasing new horses to tailors and shoemakers' bills. How the other half lived! There was a regular monthly amount, which came under the guise of 'donation'. I wonder who the recipient was?

The next few days pass quickly, with laundry and cleaning. I make a mammoth effort to have the Chateau and its contents looking ship-shape for the imminent visit from the auction house. Searching every nook and cranny in all the rooms as I go around dusting and sweeping, but I still can't find the elusive car keys and documents. They must be here somewhere!

I'm woken early on Sunday morning by the

sound of Beau barking and a commotion outside. Peering out of the window, I see some men, including Xavier and Gus, walking across from the farmhouse, shouting and waving large sticks, with several dogs running around. What on earth do they think they are doing? By the time I'm dressed and downstairs, I hear the sound of shots. Of course. They're hunting. The men must be the beaters. Well, they will need to go and shoot somewhere else. I won't allow it on my land! Those poor birds. They've done nothing wrong and don't deserve shooting.

I open the door, and Beau rushes out, eager to join the melee. I wave my arms, trying to grab their attention but Gus only waves back and continues with his task. Pulling on a fleece jacket, I stride over in their direction; two of the men turn to look at me, exchange a few words, then one walks back to meet me. I'm shocked to see that its Pedro.

"Pedro, I would prefer that you didn't hunt on my estate," I say in the best French I can manage.

He shrugs and smiles at me, before replying, " I had hoped that Xavier had already told you that we hunt on the estate, only four times in the autumn and winter. I'll let you know before the next one -"

I interrupt him, "There won't be a next time!"

He looks at me apologetically, then continues, "But Monsieur Le Maire organises it. He's one of the guns, and you will get a share of the kill."

Trying to remain calm I say, "I've managed so far to get through life without the need for game and intend to continue to do so." He apologises and suggests I tread cautiously with Monsieur Le Maire, then turns and jogs away to catch up with the others.

The sound of the gun's grates on my nerves, as I think about the poor creatures, having spent the spring and summer rearing their offspring, only to get blasted from the sky in the autumn. What a mindless activity! A while later, a group of men with guns slung over their shoulders walk passed the kitchen window and bang on the back door. I wash my hands, wet from making more cheese, and open the door to find Monsieur Le Maire standing there, holding out a hare and two pheasants.

"Laura, lovely to see you again, thank you for giving us access to your bountiful estate -"

I cut him off, "I don't remember granting you permission to kill innocent creatures in my garden-"

He doesn't let me finish. He leans forward and lowers his voice, "As I explained on Thursday, my dear, we are a small, friendly community that doesn't like change; and I'm sure there will be some things that you require help with, drop in and see me." He turns and walks away. Placing the murdered animals on the floor, I leave them in the yard for Beau and close the door, fuming. How dare he? The arrogant, short, fat, smelly man!

On Monday morning I'm up early and feeling quite anxious. I decide to take a stroll around the estate with Beau. The season is starting to change, and some of the vines are turning yellow and orange. Mornings and evenings are noticeably cooler now, a pleasant respite from the summer heat. The olives are still on the trees, Alice tells me they harvest them at the end of November. She's determined to be well enough to help. It sounds like hard work, but good fun, from the stories that she's told me. If I'm still here, I'll lend a hand. I wonder if they use the same press as they do for the grapes? I'll have to ask.

As I return to the Chateau, I notice several geese pecking around on the grass, Xavier must have been and let them out. They stop and squawk as I pass by, but I ignore them and continue to my door, where I find another dead animal on the step; a pheasant this time, minus most of its feathers! Beau immediately sits and looks to me for instruction. I kick the dead animal into the drive and let myself in, before permitting him to eat it. Yuk!

35

After lunch, I sit in the dining room and stare out of the window, waiting for my guest. At two o' clock a smart black car appears on the drive, and a tall man with salt and pepper hair steps out, wearing a dark grey suit and black tie; very solemn, perhaps he's lost and looking for the church. He rings the bell, which doesn't work but looks the part, and I wait a suitable length of time before answering; not wanting to appear desperate.

Nodding, he hands me his card and says in French, "I'm here to see Mademoiselle Mackley, she's expecting me." He obviously thinks I'm a maid or something and walks inside without permission, his eyes surveying the sparsely furnished entrance hall. Perhaps I look like a housekeeper. After all, I've dressed in navy cropped trousers and a white blouse, having made an effort, instead of my usual shorts, t-shirt and flip-flops.

I take a deep breath and say, "I am indeed the same Laura Mackley that you are here to see." Realising his faux pas, he fluently slips into polished English and apologises for his mistake. "No apology required, thank you for coming," I reassure him. He offers his hand for a firm shake, quite a refreshing change from kissing! Not that I expect him to suffer from halitosis like the mayor.

"My name is Theo Duran, my speciality is furniture," he informs me.

With formalities over I show Monsieur Durand into the drawing room and bring my prepared tray of tea and homemade biscuits from the kitchen - very English. I try to stifle a giggle as I remember Penelope Keith in the old romcom drama, 'To the Manor Born' - another one of my gran's favourites.

"Well, there isn't much in the way of furniture left," I tell him, but then remember the bureau. I recount my tale of the lost key. He appears interested, so I show him up to the attic.

"I've come across a few hidden stairs and secret doors previously in this part of France, they are fascinating. Sadly, most people just rip them out and modernise," he states on the way up.

Once in the gloom of the attic he's eager to explore my new-found treasures. I show him some of the items, which seem to excite him, especially the jewellery and dress from the painting. With permission, he takes some photos to send back to his colleagues, so they will know who best to send out to value the items.

Monsieur Durand moves swiftly to the bureau, "It's very lovely, in good condition too," he says, opening the secret compartment he continues, "Ah, there's a roll of paper stuck in here," he kneels on the floor and looks underneath. I hear a faint click, and the bottom of the bureau drops down like a flap. A large, old, brown envelope drops out, as well as the offending roll of paper. I look at him, open-mouthed. He passes me the items and smiles. "Very clever design, there's a small catch recessed into the frame. It's barely noticeable and releases the bottom, I've seen a few of these, all slightly different."

I unroll the paper and squint at it. It's a map of some sort, hand-drawn in black ink, some of the landmarks are familiar. It's an old map of the estate. There were far more trees back then. I wonder why it's locked away. I put it down and turn my attention to the large envelope. Holding my breath, I gently open the top, which has long since lost its powers of adhesion. Kneeling, I slide the contents out onto the wooden floor. Several documents and two keys drop out in front of me. Unable to speak I just stare at them, then look up to see Monsieur Durand smiling down at me. "It appears you're in luck," he says, then suggests we have another cup of tea before going to see the car.

Back in the drawing room, we look through the papers. There is an old booklet, probably the equivalent of the manual, a bill of sale, the registration document, and a photo of a dapper gentleman with slicked back hair. Its signed on the back, and I can't quite make the name out. I pass it to Monsieur Durand, who can read it. "Ettore Bugatti," he says, "and the car, if it matches the documents, is a 1935 Bugatti type 55. They are as rare as hens' teeth," he adds, raising his eyebrows.

Monsieur Durand's keen to see the vehicle. I show him to the carriage house, where he stands and whistles through his teeth before confirming that we do have the correct papers for the car. "It's a little rusty though," I say disappointedly. Again, he raises his eyebrows and assures me that it won't detract from its value, as it's rare and has provenance.

Before he leaves, Monsieur Durand excuses himself to ring his office and arrange for an expert in vintage cars to visit, as well as colleagues who specialise in art, and silver, and jewellery. Wasting no time, he assures me that a Monsieur Levant will come at ten in the morning to value the car. "Go around and put a sticker on all the items you wish to have valued," he suggests, adding, "the bureau is worth about five to six hundred pounds, should you choose to sell it. Just a word of warning, the Bugatti is a very desirable item, and collectors will no doubt contact you. Don't be tempted. We can get you the best price at auction, as these people will be trying to outbid each other."

Once Monsieur Durand leaves, I sit with my head in my hands. What am I going to do now? Do I want to sell the bureau, with its secret compartments? Surely it belongs in the Chateau? Perhaps I should bring it down and put it in the drawing room, or the library. If only I were still a little girl playing at rearranging the furniture in my pink dolls house with gran! Why is life so complicated?

Sleep eludes me once more. As I lay in bed listening to the wind whistling around the chimneys, I suddenly feel quite vulnerable. The broken latch on the kitchen window worries me; Xavier got in quickly when I was stuck on the roof. At least I have Beau; we seem to be getting on well together. I mentally add getting new locks fitted to my 'to-do' list. Eventually dropping off to sleep, I manage a few hours before my phone tells me it's eight o' clock. I have a quick breakfast, feed Beau, and let him out before beginning to label items with the small stickers that Monsieur Durand left me. I only have an hour before his colleague is supposed to arrive, so I stay downstairs and wander around the cavernous rooms.

The suits of armour at the bottom of the stairs are the first to be marked. Jenny thought they were creepy. I don't mind them too much, but don't fancy having to polish them on a regular basis. How long have they been here? Have they ever been used in battle? To whom did they belong? So many unanswered questions.

36

The sound of a man's voice brings me back to the present. I open the door to find Xavier talking to a well-dressed man, Monsieur Levant at a guess. Xavier nods in my direction before disappearing around the side of the building with Beau at his heels. Smiling, I introduce myself and invite my guest inside.

In the drawing room I serve coffee and croissants, while Monsieur Levant examines the documents for the car, he's a very talkative man, and seems passionate about his subject, he even comments about Dolly. "I learnt to drive in something similar." Monsieur Levant says with a smile. Unable to contain himself any longer he asks, "Would it be possible to see the car?" and we head over to the carriage house, where, to my dismay, I find Xavier working nearby with a strimmer, his beady eyes on us as we enter inside.

I'm careful to close the door before moving the pallets, to reveal the entrance into the hidden section. Monsieur Levant stands and stares at the sight, before slowly making his way inside. It's quite dark, but my torch is powerful. "I have some lights in my car, I'll just go and get them", he says, striding off purposefully. Back in no time, he sets them up, the bright lights illuminating the space and revealing the Bugatti in detail. "Magnifique!" He cries, and soon he's crouched down examining the car. "What a beauty, incredibly rare; in reasonable condition." I point out the rusty bits, but he appears unconcerned. After what feels like half an hour, I make a point of looking at my watch. He takes the hint and starts to take lots of photos. Packing up the lights, he follows me out of the carriage house and back to the Chateau. I notice Xavier is now absent.

"Down to business," he says over his second cup of strong black coffee, "first, we need to get her out, cleaned and stored in a secure location. Then we will enter her into the Paris auction in early spring."

My head snaps up, and I look at him, "I was hoping to sell it sooner, so I can wrap things up here and move on," I say.

"The big auction in spring attracts wealthy collectors from all over the world. Trust me my dear, the reward will be worth waiting for." He says, tapping the side of his nose. "In the meantime, we need to organise to have it moved to a safe location. I can do that for you if you wish."

"I don't have the funds for storage. Can't it stay here?"

Monsieur Levant nearly chokes on his coffee, "It won't be safe here once word gets out, prepare yourself to be bombarded by attention from collectors, the media, and of course, criminals. You mentioned that you live alone. I think a security guard, and cameras, would be a good idea at the very least!"

"I'll sleep on it and ring you back in the morning," I say. Monsieur Levant looks a little disappointed. He probably expects to walk away with a deal. As he's walking out of the door, I have a thought and blurt out, "You haven't told me how much it's worth!"

He stops in his tracks and turns to me, leaning a little closer and quietly says, "At least three million pounds."

I stare at him in shock. "What... err... mmm... "I can't form any words; my brain has blown a circuit again.

"Go and sit down with a cognac, my dear, and give it some thought. I look forwards to hearing from you tomorrow," he says as he leaves, closing the door behind him.

I've had very little to drink since Jenny left, so brandy before lunch probably isn't a good idea. My stomach feels like a cement mixer, and I don't fancy any food anyway. Looking around I notice Beau hasn't come back. I wonder if he's gone home with Xavier, he must be missing his master. Yes, I'll take a walk over to the farmhouse to see if he's there.

I'm relieved to see Beau in the kitchen. I bend

and make a fuss of him, and he wags his muscular tail, nearly knocking me over. Xavier appears from one of the outbuildings and shouts at him. The dog immediately stops and hangs his head. "We were only playing," I say sharply, but Xavier doesn't respond, and Beau lies back down. What is wrong with this man?

"'E's not ze poodle, 'e 'as to know his place," he replies without looking at me. Why did I think coming here was a good idea? Alice arrives from the sitting room and invites me to join them for lunch.

"Thank you, but I've already eaten, I was only wondering where Beau was; just checking he hadn't got lost." Xavier snorts, and Alice gives him a stern look.

Alice sits down at the table then says, "I believe Xavier has found a guard dog for you, he is going to come around after lunch and build you a kennel for him."

I look over to Xavier, who confirms this and tells me he will be round shortly. "Can't he live in the hall, as Beau does... did?" I ask cautiously.

"No, 'e lives in ze kennel; if you want ze poodle, go and get one!"

I'm getting nowhere, why did I come? What was I expecting? Realisation dawns on me as I walk home. I need someone to talk to; I need to ask someone's opinion on what I should do. Sell up and go back home, where ever that is, or stay here and make a new life. If I do decide to stay, how will I make a living? Three million pounds is a lot of money, but the Chateau needs a new roof, a new boiler and heating system, a modern kitchen and bathrooms, new windows and locks, the drive needs relaying, and I'd need help to run the place. No, I should sell. I could buy something smaller in the area. Yes, that's a good idea!

I turn back and look at the farmhouse behind me. What would happen to Alice, Gus, and Xavier? A developer would come along and evict them, do I want that on my conscience? Further down the path, a rabbit hops across and disappears into the bushes, startling me. I look up and see the sun is shining on the Chateau. Turning the old stone, a lovely honey colour, complimenting the earthy tones of the surrounding estate. Would that same developer sanitise the area, adding a swimming pool and gym complex, covering the ground with tarmac to make a car park, ripping up the vines and ancient olive groves to provide extra accommodation for the elite? Is that what I want? Arriving at the front door, I sit on the worn step and look up to the skies for inspiration. What on earth should I do?

A lone tear rolls down my cheek, putting my head in my hands, it is followed by a few more. Moments later I'm sitting alone, crying. The lyrics from a Bonnie Tyler song - 'Lost in France'-playing in my head, very appropriate. Yes, I'm lost, and out of my depth! I lose track of time and have no idea how much I've wasted, wallowing in self-pity. I gradually become aware of a warm presence at my side. I lift my head to find Beau sat on the step next to me, and Xavier sat a few feet away on a low stone wall.

He smiles, hesitates, then closes the short distance between us. And like his faithful companion, Beau, he sits at the other side of me. It feels oddly comforting seated between the two, neither of them making a sound; none of the usual sarcastic comments passing from his mouth. In a moment of madness, perhaps overcome by emotion, I begin talking. "There's a contract between the old general and your grandfather, which runs out in a few weeks. I worry for your family's future if I decide to sell. I've also received an offer from Gus's grandfather to purchase the Chateau. There are many treasures I've discovered, including an old Bugatti car, and a wine cellar full of bottles and barrels of wine." Surprisingly, he doesn't speak, only continues to sit, quietly listening, at my side. "I will need a security system too." I admit, overwhelmed by all that has happened over the last few months.

Once my outpouring is over, I turn my head to find Xavier still sat in the same position, his expression difficult to read. He continues his silence for a little while longer. At least he's not angry with me for a change. Slowly, turning to face, me he begins to speak. "Ze solution is simple. We get married, yes?"

37

"What planet is he on?" I say out loud, once more lying wide awake in bed. We must be the two most incompatible people, ever! Does he have no feelings? I could never consider a life with him. He would drive me crazy; we're polar opposites! A business proposition, he called it, a marriage of convenience. It might be convenient to him - a caring stepmother, and daughter-in-law for his family - but I would become his skivvy and his meal ticket. I don't know where he gets the audacity!

On the other hand, I have come to rely on him. Perhaps we could work out some sort of business arrangement, but certainly not marriage. I'd rather eat my own spleen! Yes, I'll ask Monsieur Bertrand to draw up another contract, it will have to be fair. Maybe he could run the estate and live rent-free, but he would have to sell the farm produce and make a profit. I need something to live on after all. Valentina appeared interested in buying my chevre. We could set up a small business, selling cheese, eggs, honey, wine, and olive oil. We'd have to expand, of course. There's enough space. Yes, that might work. John also suggested opening a small camp site; that would be fun.

The morning sun illuminating my bedroom wakes me. Sitting up, I remember Xavier's proposal, was it a dream? More like a nightmare. I still haven't forgiven him. I think the best thing to do is forget it ever happened and carry on as usual, whatever that is. Gustave is coming today to patch up the roof, that will provide me with a distraction for now. Shall I instruct him to replace it in the spring? Possibly not, I need to wait until the car is sold. It might not go for the amount Monsieur Levant suggested. That reminds me,

I need to ring him and give him the green light. The car has to go. It feels like a liability now.

After breakfast, I ring him, and he's delighted with my wise decision. "I will personally attend with a builder and transport to take the car away to a secure location before the end of the week," he says. I feel lighter for making my first major decision, but I'm still not sure what to do about Xavier. My wonderful ideas formed in the small hours seem like pipe dreams in the cold light of day.

Could we make it work? Who do I ask? Who can I trust? Again, I'm transported back to my youth, when I used to have a dilemma as a teenager, usually about a boy. My gran always said, "Trust my own instincts." Yes, the long and short of it is that I have to make life decisions for myself. No one can tell me what to do. I suppose people can advise, but ultimately, it's down to me. But whose advice do I trust? In my mind, I can see John's face. He appears a level-headed guy. I think I'll ring him. He texts regularly to see how I'm getting on. Yes, I'll ring him this evening. He'll be at work just now.

Gustave arrives and sets about making the roof watertight for the coming winter, which takes him most of the day. He also orders new locks for the downstairs windows and doors, which he hopes to fit before the weekend. Xavier arrives with a truck full of logs. I don't go out to him, only watch from an upstairs window as he piles them neatly in a shed in the back yard. He then continues building the kennel for my new arrival, of which I've yet to learn. I'm curious but decide to refrain from communicating with him for now, not wanting to encourage any further advances from him. I've grown fond of Beau and will miss his company.

A long evening alone looms ahead of me. I need something to do, and decide to continue working through the rooms, putting stickers on the items to be valued. In the library I stand and stare at the shelves laden with old books, I know nothing about them. Could some of them be valuable? It would take an age to look through them all. I go out of the room and quietly close the door behind me. I'll sift through them in the winter if I'm still here. Continuing through the halls, I enter the back bedroom and see the carpet bags where I hastily left them in the storm.

38

I carry the carpet bags down to the kitchen and put their contents on the table, spreading the photos out in what I think could be their time order. Turning them over, I'm thrilled to see that some of them have dates and names on the back. Some are quite faint but readable. The nurse in the photos, it seems is Aunt Mary as a young woman during the war. And the dapper young man in uniform is called Henri. Her boyfriend perhaps? Eager to learn more I continue searching through the bags. A large bundle of envelopes, neatly held together with a ribbon, is the last item in the bag. They are all addressed to Miss Mary Whitehead, my great aunt! With shaking hands, I open the first one, written in 1944, and I begin reading.

September 8th

Dear Mary,

We were all so relieved to get your letter telling us of your safe arrival in France. We're all well here and understand that you can't tell us very much. We appreciate your short notes, so we know you're OK. I've sent you a small parcel, hope it gets to you. It's not much but all we can spare - food is still rationed here. Flo sends her love and says to tell you that she misses you, as do we all.

Much love, mum and dad. xx

So, she came over to France in the war. I wonder why gran never mentioned her!

November 12th

Dear Mary,

We haven't had a letter from you for some time now. I

know you must be very busy, but just a few lines to put our minds at rest would be a relief. Old Mrs Booth has passed away, a heart attack they say, we're going to her funeral tomorrow. Not much else has happened here. Thankfully, we're not getting the doodle bugs, like the cities in the south.

Write soon.

Much love, mum and dad. Xx

I place the letter back in its envelope and open the next one.

December 6th

Dear Mary,

It's been over two months since we last heard from you, we hope and pray that you are safe and well. Flo is beside herself with worry, as we all are. Please write, just a line to put us out of this misery.

Much love, mum and dad. Xx

Again, I place the letter back and continue reading from the pile.

January 17th

Mary,

We were very disturbed by your news; it spoilt our Christmas. It is with a very heavy heart that I have to tell you that your father insists that you cannot return home in your condition. He doesn't want you to write again. You will always be in my thoughts and prayers.

Mum. x

I put the letter down in shock. She must have been pregnant! What happened to the baby? Poor Aunt Mary! How could her father abandon her like that! Intrigued, I carry on.

February 2nd

Dear Mary,

Mum won't tell me what's wrong, only that we can't write to you anymore. I'm so worried about you. Please write to me. Send it to my friend Hilda at number 26. She'll pass it on to me.

Missing you so much! Flo. xxx

Flo was my gran, Mary's younger sister, why did she keep her a secret from me? I have to carry on reading. I need to know more.

March 2nd

Dearest Mary,

Henri sounds like a good man, and I'm so thrilled he's proposed to you! Fancy, soon you'll be called Madam Mary De Ford! His father sounds lovely and I'm glad he's taken you in until Henri comes back for his next leave. Sorry I won't be there at your wedding. Don't worry about dad; once you're married into a respectable family, he'll see sense and come around, and if not it's his loss. Mum is finding it difficult, but I know she still loves you dearly, as do I.

All my love Flo xx

Eagerly, I place the letter back and pick up the next one.

April 10th

My dearest Mary,

I was *devastated to hear the dreadful news about poor Henri! God works in mysterious ways. It's kindly of his father to let you stay on; I do so wish I could be there to comfort you at this terrible time. Stay strong and think of the baby.*

Please let me know when I become an aunt. This terrible war will soon be over. I promise to visit.

All my love, Flo. xx

Oh no, poor Henri! What happened to him? He was in the services; the old general must have been his father.

June 6th

Dear Mary,

I don't know how to respond; your news has left me feeling cold and empty. I am so very sorry to hear of your loss. It must have been dreadful for you enduring so much then losing your baby son, perhaps the shock of Henri's death brought about his premature birth. I hope you have recovered from the delivery, stay strong. God must have other plans for you. You mentioned that you were going to stay at the Chateau to care for

Henri's father, I didn't know that he was injured in the great war. Please take care and keep in touch.

Your loving sister. Flo xx

I put the letters down. I can't bear more of this terrible saga! Poor Aunt Mary, what a sad life she had, if only the baby had survived. This Chateau would have been his, and I would have been his niece.

39

I sink into bed with a heavy heart. Poor Aunt Mary, I can't get her out of my head. Did she enjoy living alone in these ancient walls after the death of the old general, or was she lonely? Alice has told me snippets about her life, as she used to help her clean the Chateau, and she donated her clothes and personal effects to the local convent following her death. In her younger days, Mary was heavily involved in village life and used to volunteer at the school helping with music, which was her passion, but seemed to keep herself shut away in the Chateau as she became old and frail. I wish that I'd known of her existence, I would have loved to have been able to visit and get to know and help her; it's too late now; there are so many unanswered questions.

It's frustrating, as every time I bring up the subject of the war, I'm shut down by some throw away remark or subtle change of subject. It seems to be a subject that no one wants to discuss. I don't know how I'm going to learn more. As I'm dropping off to sleep, I remember that I was going to ring John for his advice. I always seem to have so much to do and think about and not enough time!

A whimpering noise awakens me. It's quite faint. It can't be Beau as he stayed at the farmhouse. As I turn over and try to go back to sleep, it starts again. Curious, I pull on my robe and look out into the early morning light. It's drizzling and quite windy, the leaves on the treetops are blowing about fiercely. Peering into the gloom I can vaguely make out the shape of a dog. It doesn't look as big as Beau. Quickly making my way downstairs, I open the front door to see the dog disappear around the corner. I head back inside, through the kitchen and out of the back door to find the creature cowering down in the corner under a slight overhang. Xavier must have left me the new guard dog. Well, he could have told me; it's escaped out of the kennel.

Should I approach it? Is it vicious? I grab a handful of dog biscuits and pick up one of the walking sticks by the door to protect myself, and slowly walk in its direction. It seems skittish and slinks away into the shadows, holding one leg up off the ground. It must be injured. I put the stick down and walk towards it, placing the dog food a few meters away, before retreating to the kitchen door. After a few minutes, it gets braver, and crawls low to the ground towards the food, gobbling it down in seconds. It's starving! Feeling more optimistic, I lay a trail towards the kennel and open the door, placing a bowl of food and water inside, and wait near the back door. It has the desired effect, and the dog heads into the kennel. Once its safely inside, I secure the kennel door and go back inside to dry off. At least it has food and water, as well as somewhere dry to spend the night. Some guard dog! What on earth is Xavier thinking? It's clearly not going to be much of a deterrent!

Following an early breakfast, I march over to the farmhouse to confront Xavier. He's in the kitchen, making coffee. Storming in, I begin my tirade, "You have a very warped idea of what constitutes a good guard dog!" Xavier doesn't even bother to look up from his task and continues spooning sugar into a mug. "Did you hear me?" I add, getting more irritated.

When he eventually acknowledges my presence, he shrugs and replies, "I ‘av no idea about what you are saying."

Frustrated, I walk over and stand in front of him, "The dog. The starving, emaciated, injured dog that you left for me -"

He interrupts my outburst, "I ‘av not left you ze dog yet. I'm picking ‘im up today." He looks at me with indifference and continues, "Do you mean ze skinny ‘ound zat ‘as been sniffing around for a few days? He is ze stray." He stops talking and disappears upstairs, returning with his gun.

"Just what do you think you're going to do with that?" I shout.

He only shrugs once again, then thinks before replying, "I am going to ‘elp ze animal."

I hold my hand up and protest, "I don't think so, not with that! It needs a vet!"

Sighing, he says, "It needs putting out of ze misery."

That does it! I turn around and, on my way out of the door I shout, "Don't you dare come near that dog with your gun!"

I rush back to the Chateau and head up to the attic to get a signal and ring Sylvie. She gives me the number for the nearest vet but tells me they won't be open for another half an hour. This is so frustrating! I need a phone signal lower to the ground! I decide the safest thing is to go and sit outside near the kennel until the vet opens, in case my stupid tenant comes around to "'elp ze dog'.

Half an hour later, with thankfully no sign of Xavier, I ring the vet. They take my details and tell me that they will send Enzo out to see me when he does his morning rounds. I hope he speaks English, or French, I can't converse in Italian! Without an exact time, I don't know what to do. Should I sit out here in the rain in case Xavier arrives? I open the kennel door, and the dog looks up at me with limpid brown eyes. I crouch down and offer him more food. He continues to look at me warily before limping over and taking the biscuits from me. The poor thing, he used to belong to someone. Perhaps he's microchipped. Is it mandatory to have the dog's microchipped here?

Having decided that Xavier probably won't come, I go back inside to wait for the vet. It's not long before a dirty Land Rover trundles slowly down the drive and stops outside. An attractive young man with short, sandy coloured hair gets out and strides over to the door. Holding out his hand, he says with a weird accent, "Bonjour. Je suis Enzo, le vet." I accept his firm handshake and try to explain to him about the dog, apologising for my limited French. "Are you English?" He asks surprised, in a strong Scottish accent. I stare at him for a moment before laughing. Who would believe it, a Scottish vet called Enzo in the south of France!

I take the vet to the kennel and show him the poor dog. He puts gloves on then assesses the dog carefully, saying, "It has an abscess in its paw; is severely malnourished and has mange." He gives the dog a cocktail of injections to kill the mites and relive the itching, as well as antibiotics and cream, along with instructions on how to care for him.

"Is he microchipped?" I ask, Enzo runs his code reader over the dog but finds no microchip. "What shall I do with him?"

"Don't let him inside until his infection is clear and keep him away from other animals; a couple of weeks should suffice. Avoid skin contact with him until he gets the all clear, I don't want you catching anything." I invite him in for coffee, and he tells me that he'll ask about and put a notice up at the surgery to see if he can locate its owner, and suggests I put some fliers up in the village too.

"What if no one claims him?" I ask.

"Let's worry about that after my next visit, in about two weeks' time. If you have any problems in between, just ring," he says, before climbing back into his vehicle and moving off to his next client. After he's gone, I realise I didn't pay for the treatment, I know vet bills are expensive in England; I guess they are here too, probably why Xavier wanted to shoot the poor thing.

I take a quick photo of the dog and drive down to Sylvie's to print out a few posters to pin up in the locality. She says she'll take one to school with her tomorrow. On the way back, I call in at the farmhouse, Xavier is out, so I tell Alice about my new-found lodger and his skin condition, suggesting Beau stays away for a while. I also ring Xavier to postpone the guard dog, but it goes to voicemail, so I leave him a message.

40

The days fly past. Gustave replaces the locks, and I continue deciding on what to have valued. I manage to speak to John, and he suggests I have a chat with some ex-pats in the area to hear about their experiences and views on the locality, as well as having a conversation with the mayor about my idea of running a campsite. I suppose it's all sensible advice, although I don't relish another encounter with that man.

Monsieur Levant rings to tell me he will be arriving in the morning with a builder to safely take down the remains of the wall and take the Bugatti away to be cleaned and stored until spring. He will also be bringing two colleagues with him to start the process of valuing the other items. I will feel safer when the car has gone. I don't think I'll be needing Xavier's guard dog, after all, and he hasn't even bothered to return my call!

The builder arrives at eight-thirty, shortly followed by Monsieur Levant and his colleagues. They get to work immediately, and seem very efficient, going through one room at a time, keeping notes on a tablet as they proceed. By early afternoon, the wall is down, and the car is slowly winched into a pristine white trailer, similar to a streamlined horse box. I have to sign several documents before the vehicle is taken away up the drive and disappears out of view. I hope I'm doing the right thing!

When Monsieur Levant and his busy co-workers reach the attic and start appraising the art, they call me over to show me some of their discoveries. One is an old map, showing the Chateau and estate, and the other is a family tree, beautifully handwritten, which goes back to 1828 finishing in 1945.

"Wow! I hadn't seen these," I say.

"Well, they were hidden behind the stack of portraits and paintings, which we've got an estimated value for now. These two, however only have sentimental value, "Monsieur Levant tells me. I'm thrilled; the family tree will help with my quest for information. Monsieur Levant goes on to say that they do have a modest value, but as local artists painted most of the portraits, they would be put to better use adorning the walls of the Chateau. His colleague, however, goes on to tell me that the jewellery is worth several thousand pounds alone. He says, "I do know of a collector that would pay considerably more if you would consider selling the dress, jewellery and portrait of the lady wearing them, as one lot."

"The Chateau needs a new roof, so I have to raise a serious amount of money if I'm to stay here," I tell them.

"Well, it's your good fortune that we have found one painting by a sought-after artist, a landscape, worth about 20,000 Euros," Monsieur Levant says.

Having completed their valuations, they head back downstairs. Climbing into their vehicle, Monsieur Levant says, "It's been a long day, we will compile a report and send it to you by post. Have a pleasant evening; perhaps have a glass of champagne."

I suddenly remember all the wine in the cellar and blurt out, "Oh, yes! I forgot! There's a secret room in the cellar full of vintage wine and things!" The trio looks at me in shock, climb back out, and follow me down into the dungeon.

Once down there, Monsieur Levant volunteers one of his male colleagues to squeeze behind the old wooden shelving and into the void beyond. We hear a string of expletives before he returns wide-eyed to report his findings. The three converse in hushed tones before deciding that they need to send out their wine expert. I offer the poor man a towel to wipe away the dust and cobwebs from his clothes and bid them farewell. They look exhausted but come to think of it, so am I!

The following morning at nine o' clock, the shrill tone of the landline in the hall surprises me: it hardly ever rings. "Bonjour," I answer, the male voice on the other end introduces himself as Paul Boscoe, the wine specialist, and arranges to visit tomorrow afternoon. He seems so eager!

Next on my list is the stray dog. Sadly, no one has come forward to claim the dog yet. As I near the kennel, the dog stands and stretches, then slowly comes to the bars to greet me. Wearing my pink rubber gloves, I scratch the dog on the head then enter the kennel, and carefully pour warm water on him, before massaging in his special shampoo. He loves the process and willingly stands still for his ministrations. He's no longer limping, and his skin is much improved too. Enzo will be back in a few days. I do hope he's found his owners or knows of someone that would give him a new home.

I have a busy day ahead. I need to write a list for my visit with Le Maire tomorrow morning. I do hope he's in a good mood.

I suppose I need to talk to Xavier and Alice about the future too; I need to hear their views. Alice is doing so well now; I don't see her as the type of woman that enjoys being idle. I'm sure she'll want a small role in the running of the estate, along with Gus. Yes, I need to call a meeting. No time like the present, so my gran used to say. Xavier's phone goes to voicemail, as always. I leave him a brief message, asking for a meeting with him and Alice, and suggest this evening at his place.

41

I arrive at seven o' clock. The family are

finishing their evening meal and I accept a glass of 'our' homemade wine, which is surprisingly palatable. I sit at the table while the boys clear a space; it looks like they mean business, pen, and paper at the ready. The boys return, and Xavier asks, "'Ow can we be of assistance?"

I look at him for a moment then back to Alice, who seems concerned. "I think it's more about being in a symbiotic relationship, rather than you assisting me," I say. Gus translates for Alice, and she jots everything down, nodding in agreement at my reply.

I clear my throat and start my rehearsed speech, trying to remain as professional as possible, "As you are aware, your previous agreed tenancy contract is about to expire, which puts you in a vulnerable position... " Xavier tries to interrupt me in his usual belligerent fashion, but I soldier on "... I do not wish to make you homeless, but, as you can understand, this puts me in a difficult situation." Alice nods in agreement as Gus continues with his translation. "I have carefully considered my options, which are: One, selling up and going back to England, but I suspect a developer would probably purchase the Chateau and turn it into a hotel. They'll probably evict you in the process. As you may be aware, such a person has approached me already, but it wasn't to their taste. Two, selling up and buying a smaller property in the area, but that would likely result in the same situation for yourselves. Or, three, Keeping the Chateau, making it my home and trying to turn it into a viable business. Then, if you were willing to work for me, you could stay in the farmhouse. Financial details would, of course, have to be worked out, but you have my word that I would keep the 'contract' as fair as possible for both parties."

I sit back, indicating that I have finished and wait for his tirade, but it doesn't come. Instead he looks at me blankly, then looks over to his smiling mother. I want to go to over and hug her, but restrain myself, as I wish to keep the meeting formal. To my surprise, Alice speaks first, with Gus translating, although I do understand most of what she says, "Thank you for sharing your options with us; what sort of business did you have in mind?"

"I'm thinking of expanding and selling more produce, not only locally, but to high-end hotels that are looking for local, organic, artisan produce," I explain, then continue, "I've already had an enquiry from a potential client. I've also been thinking of adding a campsite, and bed and breakfast, or auberge type of accommodation to help bring in income."

Alice thinks this is a fantastic idea. She also comes up with some ideas of her own, "When the Chateau had dinners and functions, I used to do the catering; making large amounts of food, pastries and cakes for the guests, perhaps you could consider looking into using the Chateau for events and celebrations like weddings and birthdays." This idea is something I hadn't thought of! She goes on to say, "I'm regaining my strength, and will be able to help you."

"Of course, all of this depends on getting the legal permits to stay and work in France, along with the necessary planning regulations for a campsite. I intend to visit Monsieur Le Maire in the morning," I add, wincing.

Alice stands and walks over to me. Putting her hand on my shoulder, she quietly says, "He and I are good friends, would you like me to come with you?" I nod in gratitude. Well, I never saw that coming!

With arrangements made I stand to leave.

"Let me walk you back; it's dark now," Xavier says, surprising me.

"No, thank you," I decline his offer, fishing a torch out of my bag, "I'll be quite alright," but Alice insists and pushes him out of the door. We walk back through the half-light without speaking.

As we reach the Chateau he asks about the stray dog. I give him an update, admitting that as yet, no one has come forward to take him home. I'm expecting a sarcastic comment, but again he remains quiet. Turning to leave, he says, "Good luck with your meeting in the morning." I must admit I feel less daunted now, knowing that Alice is coming with me.

The next morning, I collect Alice and drive down to the village, she seems thrilled. I don't know if it's because she's getting out and about again, or the prospect of the meeting with 'her good friend'. On the way she points out various places, telling me some of her memories from her younger days. I mention the war and tell her about the diary that I've found. However, she says she knows very little about the war, as she was born a few years after it finished, and her parents refused to talk about it. She goes on to say, "There's a memorial in the village, erected in honour of a pilot who crashed locally. He stayed in the stricken plane, sacrificing his own life to prevent it from landing on the village."

Oh, my God! That would probably have been George McBride, the pilot that Sergeant Harry King wrote about in his diary. I have to find out more, but how? Alice suggests I broach the subject with Monsieur Le Maire, "It would be considered courteous to ask his permission to research such a difficult subject." So, I add 'research war years' to my list.

We enter the small waiting room to find Madam Cevert already in situ, and not at all surprised to see us. Standing, she walks over and greets Alice warmly, then gives me a curt nod in acknowledgement. Well, at least its progress, I don't suppose we're ever going to be best friends though!

Monsieur Le Maire makes his entrance, nodding first to his secretary, before approaching us." Madam Besnard, how wonderful to see you again," he says, kissing her warmly on both cheeks, then holding her at arm's length and continuing, "you look so well, I'm delighted to see that you have made such a speedy recovery."

She smiles affectionately, looks into his eyes and replies, "Yes, I'm progressing well; thanks to the tender care of my neighbour, and great friend, Laura." A little embarrassed, I remind Alice that most of her recovery was down to her determination, but she waves me away, "I would never have recovered so well without your help."

Monsieur Le Maire smiles politely and says, "Well Laura, it appears we have much to thank you for; Madam Besnard is a fine upstanding member of our community. Come into my office and tell me what I can do to help you."

42

Monsieur Le Maire is intrigued when Alice informs him of our ideas to make the Chateau earn it's keep.

"I've meant to ask you how I can get a mobile phone booster and internet connection put into the Chateau," I say. Monsieur Le Maire passes on the details; and it's not as difficult as I thought.

We continue chatting, and when I enquire about other immigrants to the village from elsewhere, Monsieur Le Maire says, "There are, however, no other ex-pats in our village. Though I do know of a group in town, who have a monthly meeting. I'm sure you'd be welcome to attend."

I ask him about the war years, but he is unwilling to discuss them, saying, "You should do research online if you wish to learn more about it."

The meeting goes better than I expect, and I leave with numerous forms to take away and fill in to apply to live and set up a small business in France. Feeling optimistic, I drop Alice back home and join her for lunch, before returning home to await the arrival of Paul Boscoe, the wine specialist.

The man in question arrives with a young assistant, and they quickly change into overalls, before disappearing into the dungeon with a lighting rig and make short work of moving the old shelving unit. A myriad of crawling critters scurry into the dark corners, sending me back up the steps to safety, leaving the pair to their task.

Two hours pass, which I put to good use in the kitchen by trying out a few of the cake recipes that Alice gave me. I really do need a large new oven, especially if I'm going to sell homemade produce. When the men return, they share their findings with me over tea and cake. Most of the details lost on me. Nevertheless, the bottom line is that I have a fortune in the cellar. "I will come back with transport to have the stock taken away to be carefully cleaned and stored until the next auction," Paul tells me, as they both say their farewells, "I will ring as soon as I have organised things."

With the men gone, I sit and think about the things that need replacing, the roof, the kitchen, and bathrooms - guests will expect en-suite shower rooms at the very least. A loud knock on the back door brings me back to reality. Its Enzo, back to check on the dog. "Something smells good," he says as I open the door. Smiling, I tell him I've been trying out new recipes. We make our way to the kennel where he examines his patient and declares him fit and well, saying "I'm sorry, I've had no luck finding him a new owner. I have contacted the SPA, but they have too many stray dogs at the moment."

I bend down and stroke the poor dog, he stares back at me with big brown eyes, and I already know that I'm going to keep him. "Can I take him in the house now?" I ask.

Enzo looks back at me with a broad grin on his face, and says, "I knew you'd keep him; most or our British clients end up with several strays, we're just too soft. I suggest you have him neutered when he's settled down to his new routine."

Enzo and my new dog follow me back into the kitchen. We sit at the table for yet more cake, and the dog sits at my side; only moving when I stand to get milk out of the fridge. "It looks like you've got yourself a new best friend, what are you going to call him?" Enzo asks, between mouthfuls of clafoutis, with icing sugar clinging to his top lip like a fine dusting of snow. I have to stop myself reaching over to brush it off. Shaking my head and trying to concentrate, instead of fantasising about my new vet, I shrug and admit that I haven't thought of a name yet, hoping my face isn't too red from my blush. When did I last think about the opposite sex? I ask myself. That would have been Jacques the mechanic; not really my type though, he's too much of a player!

After lingering longer than necessary, Enzo leaves with a generous chunk of chocolate cake for his supper, reminding me to ring and arrange a date to have the dog neutered. I wave him off, feeling much better about the world. Turning around, I nearly trip over the dog; scratching his head, I say, "You're like my shadow... Yes, that's it, I'll call you Shadow!" Looking back at me, Shadow wags his tail and barks. He seems to agree with his new name. I continue talking to him as I go about my activities; retrieving the blanket and cushions that Beau had slept on, now freshly laundered. I put them under the stairs in the hall with a bowl of water and food and say

"Stay," but Shadow follows me as I walk away. I try again in French, and he immediately reacts and sits in his new bed. How could anyone abandon him? Sadly, Enzo told me that strays are a huge problem in France, and they destroy most of them.

43

Shadow remains in his bed until early evening, when I decide to take him out for a walk. I don't have a lead or collar for him, should I improvise with some rope? The grounds are vast, and it will be dark soon. I can't risk losing him. Opening the front door, I turn to call him. He trots up to me and waits for his next instruction; this dog has obviously been well trained. I decide to risk it and walk out of the door with Shadow following me. Once outside he gets playful and excited and runs off into the trees. I run after him, shouting, but he appears to be following a scent. He suddenly stops and starts digging a hole. When I catch up with him, he rolls a black knobbly thing out of the hole and sits at the side of it, wagging his tail and looking incredibly pleased with himself. "Come on Shadow!" I shout, but he refuses to move and barks louder. He then rolls the object with his paw in my direction, "I see, you want me to throw it," I say, picking the lumpy thing up and throwing it. Shadow looks at me with his head cocked to one side then runs after it and brings it back. "I'll go out and buy you a ball tomorrow, so that we can play fetch," I tell him. Back in the Chateau, he drops the object by his bed and settles down for the night. I pick it up and put it on the windowsill, not wanting him to eat it. It could be poisonous.

The following morning, the same thing happens again. After breakfast, I walk in the garden with Shadow. He rushes back over to the hazel grove and finds himself another small knobbly ball and brings it back home. I place it on the windowsill next to the other one, somewhat puzzled. "Right, I'm going down to the village to get you a collar, lead, and a ball, then you can play in the back yard."

As I'm leaving Xavier arrives to tend to the animals, "Where is ze dog? 'es not in ze kennel."

I show him into the hall where Shadow is sleeping in his bed and say, "I'm nipping to the village to get him a ball, so he will stop digging strange root things out from under the trees."

"What strange root zings?" He asks, his eyebrows shooting skywards. I show him the two objects that Shadow found, and he stares at me as though I've got two heads. "Where did 'e get zees?" He asks excitedly.

"In the hazel grove. Why, are they poisonous?" I ask.

"Zees are black gold!" He shouts, causing Shadow to bark.

"Shhh... you're frightening him," I admonish, then ask what black gold is.

"Truffles! Worth zere weight in gold. But zey

are not quite ready yet, need ze few more weeks. Don't let 'im dig anymore just yet and tell no one. Zis is our first business...yes?" Confused at his intensity, I only nod then head to the shops.

I rush back from the village with a collar, lead, long rope, and a selection of dog toys. How am I going to be able to keep Shadow out of the trees? By late afternoon, Xavier has built a fence around the hazel grove and instructed me to hammer a peg into the ground everywhere that Shadow attempts to dig.

"'Av you ever ate ze truffle?" He asks.

"No, I haven't, and I don't think they look very appetizing."

He shrugs, picks up the two truffles on his way out of the door. "Come to ze farmhouse for supper at seven." I'm tempted to take Shadow with me but think it might be better if he met Beau outside, rather than on his patch; something that needs to happen soon.

I arrive at the farmhouse to a delicious, earthy, musky aroma, and find Alice stood at the cooker, watching over a sizeable simmering pan. The kitchen is looking much tidier, and the table set with pretty floral cloth, napkins, and flowers. Such a transformation from only a few months ago. Xavier enters the kitchen, having showered, and changed out of his work clothes. A rare event, I suspect. He insists his mother takes her place next to me at the table, while he and Gus serve our meal. "So, exactly what are we eating?" I ask as I look down at the food on my plate. Alice beams as she explains that its truffle risotto, with duck breast in a truffle sauce, telling me it's such a luxury.

I'm a little reluctant to eat the duck, a first for me, but Alice has achieved so much, and I don't want to hurt her feelings. I start with the risotto, which contains various mushrooms as well as the truffle. I'm pleasantly surprised; it's very palatable. Realising I can't put off the inevitable, I tentatively put a small piece of duck in my mouth. I'm expecting it to be rubbery, but again, I'm proved wrong. The skin is light and crispy, while the meat is juicy. When I look up, I'm shocked to see that all three of my companions are looking at me smiling, as if sharing a secret joke. As I'm leaving, Xavier hands me a bag with the remains of the duck for Shadow, "'is reward for finding ze truffles."

44

A few days later, I'm in the process of making a quiche for lunch, as Sylvie is coming to help me fill in all the complicated forms from the mayor when Xavier arrives in a large beaten up old van with another man, who he introduces as his cousin Bert. They waste no time and haul a large chest freezer into the kitchen, depositing it in the back porch. "Where did you get that, how much do I owe you?" I ask.

Bert winks and says, "It's an unwanted item from a house that I'm refurbishing for a friend, but I would gladly accept a bottle of homemade wine, and perhaps one of your cakes, too." I hand over the goods, feeling a little bemused; this appears to be how business is conducted around here, but I'm not complaining.

Shadow comes over to investigate the new item, and Xavier strokes him, most unusual. I suggest he brings Beau around later, to introduce him to Shadow.

"Okay, I'll be back late afternoon," he says, then disappears with his cousin.

Sylvie arrives to help me with the forms. I need my passport, birth certificate, and various documents proving I own the Chateau, which, fortunately, I have already. The form filling process is long and complicated but finished at last. Sylvie advises me again to stock up for the winter, especially now I have a freezer, as it can get very cold and occasionally blocked off by snow. I find it terribly hard to imagine after the long hot summer that it ever snows here!

Xavier arrives and sits outside on the low wall with Beau beside him. I make a show of fussing with the big dog, and covering myself with his scent, before going back inside and sitting next to Shadow, who seems quite interested and sniffs around me. I then put him on a lead and walk him outside. Beau stands when he sees us, Xavier remains perched on the low wall. The dogs stare at each other, with Shadow looking away first. He then turns and runs off into the garden, pulling me with him racing down the drive. He stops abruptly and starts to scratch the ground under the trees flanking the drive. Xavier pounces on him and pulls him away, placing a large stone over the area. He looks at me beaming. More truffles I expect. Meanwhile, Beau has decided to join us and walks at Xavier's side, paying no attention to Shadow's antics. I don't quite know what I expected, but it undoubtedly wasn't indifference.

Over the next week, Paul and his team take the vintage wine, champagne, and spirits away to be cleaned and auctioned, and some of the other treasures that I've discovered in the Chateau too. Some of which I'm sorry to part with, like the dress and jewellery, and others, namely the suits of armour, that I'm glad to sell. I have mixed feelings as I watch the items loaded into pristine vans but know it's necessary to raise the capital to live and work here. The bureau now has pride of place in the drawing room as I couldn't possibly part with it. I also intend to have some of the paintings, and the chandeliers hung back in their rightful place in the Chateau, and display some of the historical artefacts, which, hopefully, will attract visitors when I get up and running.

However, today's task is the installation of the mobile phone booster and internet connection. Two men are already here sorting it out. It's amazing what you can achieve with Monsieur Le Maire on your side! I'm also hoping it won't take too long for my planning and applications to be approved, having submitted my business plan with the help of Monsieur Le Maire and Monsieur Bertrand, and Xavier's input, of course. Once I have things in place, I can start some of the work; converting one of the outbuildings into toilet and shower facilities, laying hard standing for the caravans and water, drainage and electricity points, though I need to raise some capital first. The first auction is next week. I have the glossy catalogue, but I've declined the invitation to attend. It was hard enough watching the items being taken away.

I have my first function booked too; a bit of a practice run. I'm hosting the Christmas party in a few weeks for the older people of the village. Alice, Sylvie, and Rose have volunteered to help. I know I won't make much of a profit from the event as I'm only charging for the food, not the venue but, as I've learned, good will gestures go along way here. Jenny is hoping to come over too, to lend a hand. The men arrive to fill up my oil tank; the second time since I arrived. I must conserve as much as possible for the winter now the mistral is blowing, temperatures are dropping. Xavier is coming around to show me how to light a fire once he's cleared the chimneys of birds' nests, but today he's gone out with Shadow on their debut truffle hunt. The area is holding its first truffle market of the season at the weekend, and we've booked a stall. I do hope they find some!

Xavier arrives back with Shadow and scratches the dog on the head before producing a rabbit for him, which I insist he devours outside. Beaming, Xavier empties his backpack onto the kitchen table, asking for the scales and sorting his harvest into two piles. "Zis dog is good!" He exclaims as he weighs his bounty. There's a little over four kilograms in total, but some are a lighter colour and will have a lower value, so he tells me, adding, "Tomorrow I take 'im into ze forest; zere will be more!"

I shake my head, "Shadow is booked in with the vets, they are neutering him tomorrow."

Looking at me aghast he continues, "You cannot chop off ze balls! When 'e az built up ze reputation, we will breed from 'im. Ze offspring will be valuable!" I can't believe that this is the same man that called him ze skinny 'ound zat needed putting out of ze misery!'

We arrive early, but the market square is already a hive of activity. After setting up our stall, I walk around with Xavier to view the competition - the air heavy with the now familiar musky aroma of truffles. Approaching one of the booths, we overhear a heated conversation. Two men disagree about the best methods of truffle hunting; one prefers hogs and the other dogs. The one who prefers dogs goes on to tell the sad tale of his dear friend who, alas, isn't here today as his dog ran away in the spring; adding that he doesn't blame the poor hound as its owner ill-treated it. Xavier looks at me knowingly and ushers me past quickly. When we arrive back to the safety of our stall, he whispers, "We ‘av to get ‘im microchipped, and you must not let ‘im outside alone." I agree with Xavier, and it’s another good excuse to invite Enzo to the Chateau.

We have a good day and sell most of our stock, making a reasonable profit. Returning home cold, tired, hungry but optimistic. Alice takes the remaining truffles to turn into truffle oil to sell at the next market, though insisting that she leaves a few for me and giving me instructions on how to make scrambled eggs with truffles, and other simple recipes with which to experiment. I ring Enzo and ask him if I can have Shadow microchipped; he thinks it a good idea and agrees to come out to do it in exchange for supper.

45

I search through my meagre wardrobe, looking for something suitable to wear to entertain my dinner guest. It's a cold evening, so I opt for trousers and a fleece jumper. If I'm going to host functions and have paying guests I will have to invest in some smarter clothes, but these will have to do for tonight. Shadow barks as Enzo's Land Rover stops outside.

"Mmm," he says, sniffing the air, "it always

smells delicious here," he hands me a bunch of flowers. "Let's get business out of the way first," he continues as he brings out his equipment to microchip Shadow.

"Poor Shadow, will it hurt?"

"No more than an injection," he replies, as he performs the task. Shadow doesn't even whimper and Enzo rewards him with a chew stick. Once the paperwork is completed, Enzo checks the chip is working with his scanner before putting his gear back in his vehicle.

I serve my truffle and wild mushroom fettuccine, which gets Enzo's seal of approval, followed by honey truffle sponge pudding with, you guessed it, truffle crème anglaise. "Wow, they'll be queuing to stay here with food like this," Enzo says grinning between mouthfuls.

"I have booked myself onto a health and safety and kitchen hygiene course, and, of course, first aid. It's one of the stipulations before setting up in business, and it will all be in French," I tell him worriedly.

Sensing my self-doubt, he reassures me that I'll be a natural. "I doubted myself when I decided to come and gain my first years' experience in France, leaving my family and friends behind. I've only been here four months, but it's flown by quickly. My family live in Glasgow and have an ice-cream business. My great-grandfather came over from Italy as a young man, seeking a new life, hence my Italian name. Why don't you make ice-cream with the goats' milk? I'll come and help you, as I used to work in the factory during the school holidays."

The evening passes all too quickly, and he leaves, promising to email me his family's recipes while suggesting a day to come and start production. Something to look forward to.

I wake to a white landscape, the first frosts of winter. I think back to last night, and the thought of cold ice-cream doesn't appeal, time for soups and stews! A text from Xavier informs me that he's on his way to clear the chimneys and show me how to light the fires.

Not before time, I'm hosting the old folks party in two weeks. I need the Chateau to be warm and looking festive. We have our work cut out. The soup is already made and in the freezer. The meat will hopefully be wild boar, or whatever the men catch that week, and the vegetables will be collected from the local market a couple of days in advance. Sylvie is busy wrapping each guest a small gift, and I've decided to make the same pudding I tried out on Enzo, quite simple but delicious. Alice and Rose will be operating the old range. I haven't got the confidence to order the industrial cooker that I've seen online. I need my applications approving first, as it's a rather expensive piece of kit. However, I've allowed myself the luxury of a modern washing machine!

Xavier uses the old twigs and sticks out of the chimneys as kindling and shows me how to light a fire, starting in the kitchen. "That looks simple enough," I tell him. He smiles and tells me it's now my turn to light one in the small sitting room at the back of the house. I follow his instructions but somehow don't seem to have the knack, I have several more attempts without success. I can't seem to get the logs to burn. "Don't you have any firelighters?" I ask.

Xavier gives me his usual shrug saying, "You could use firelighters, but shouldn't rely on zem," shrugging again he adds, "You never know when you might need to light ze fire in ze emergency." He gives me a firelighter, and I soon have a decent fire going. Back in the kitchen, I add firelighters to my shopping list.

Shadow continues to go truffle hunting with Xavier twice a week, which is helping with my bank balance. And I feel happier now that I've paid Pedro the money, I owed him for all his previous hard work. "Out of debt, out of danger," my gran used to say.

A couple of days later, as I'm setting off to the airport to collect Jenny, I'm stopped by the postman as I turn out of the gate. He hands me two letters, which I drop on the seat next to me, carrying on with my journey. The sky is a menacing dark grey, and the distant hills obscured by low cloud. I do hope Jenny has packed some warm clothes. As I drive along through the barren countryside, I feel like I'm in a different country - gone are the bright yellow heads of giant sunflowers following the sun, and the scarlet poppies bobbing in the breeze - such a transformation. The rain starts as I hit the autoroute, hammering on the roof of my little car. The wipers are struggling to keep up with the deluge, but I soldier on slowly, trying to keep out of the spay from the lorries, not so different from home.

I enter the small terminal, now familiar with the routine. Jenny soon appears in the arrivals area with lots of luggage. I had paid for her excess baggage to bring some of my winter clothes from home, cheaper than buying new. After numerous hugs, and the cases safely stowed in the back of Dolly, we take a detour to the supermarket for essentials; toiletries and cleaning products that cost a fortune in the village, and, of course boxes of cereals, crisps, beer, and cider.

Jenny can't quite get used to the change in climate, but at least she's brought some warm clothes. She's going to need them as we're helping with the olive harvest, which is now in full swing. Thankfully, the sky has changed to a watery-blue, and the heavy rain had missed our commune, allowing the harvest to continue.

46

With little time to waste we join the others in the groves, where they're already at work with their simple tools. It looks a bit like a garden fork with a power supply, which gently flicks up and down, persuading the ripe fruits to drop into the waiting nets below. Those without tools are shaking the younger trees by hand in the traditional method. After stripping each tree, the nets are gathered up and emptied into a wooden crate, which, when full, is loaded into a truck ready to take to the press in town. We need to work quickly, as tomorrow is our day to rent the olive press. In return for their hard work, I am expected to throw a party for the volunteers on Saturday night. It seems like a fair exchange. Enzo stands out from the crowd with his sandy hair and pale complexion, causing butterflies to take flight in my tummy. He waves and continues shaking his tree while Gus gathers up the nets. Luckily, it's a school holiday again.

"He doesn't look very French," Jenny says, pointing to Enzo. I tell her he's Scottish, and only here for a year's work experience before starting at his local vet's practice next summer. "Not my type; almost a ginger nut like me. I much preferred the mechanic," she adds, winking. When she's distracted, I look in my contacts and find Jacques number, sending him a quick text and inviting him to our party on Saturday night. That should be a pleasant surprise for her! We carry on working until after dark with the aid of a light rig and eventually finish in time for a late supper. Then falling into bed, exhausted, well after midnight.

I get a reply from Jacques the following morning, accepting my invitation and saying he'll bring his guitar to provide some live music. Sounds like a plan, but I keep it to myself. During brunch, Jenny hands me the letters that I left in the car yesterday. I toss them onto the table with the rest of the paperwork to deal with later. "Aren't you going to open them?" She asks.

"They're probably just bills," I reply with a mouthful of toast, and I'm suddenly transported back in time. To the morning that I got home from work to find Jenny excitedly waving a letter in front of my eyes. The letter. The one that led me on the long journey here. Sighing, I pick the first one up and slit the top open with my knife. It's from the planning office! Sitting up straight, I read the writing on the paper.

I carefully re-read the letter for a second time, not believing the good news. It's granting me permission for fifteen hard standing pitches, not the twenty that I requested, though it doesn't stipulate how many tents I can have.

It sets out where each pitch must go, with the required distance between them, and makes changes to the location of the sceptic tank. Well, that's good news. I had prior warning that they would probably be granting less than I requested. It appears its standard practice, but Le Maire had assured me that after proving myself for about a year, I would then probably be allowed to expand. Well, I can live with that. The second letter is from the auction house, listing the items that have sold. Enclosed is a cheque with a large amount on it, enough to set the ball rolling. Time to prepare for the party, celebrations all round!

I try to contain the party to the kitchen and dining room, with the music in the drawing room. Jacques is exceptionally good with his guitar, and Gus plays the piano beautifully. I wonder when this Chateau last hosted a party! Thankfully, Shadow is staying at the farmhouse for the night with Beau. The older residents depart early, leaving the younger ones to party on and, like all great parties, we end up gathered around the big kitchen table, drinking, and finishing off the food. Jenny had helped me make up all the beds earlier, in anticipation of people being unable to drive home. Once everyone's gone upstairs, Enzo helps me lock the doors and windows, and follows me up. As I'm climbing into bed, there's a knock on my door. Wrapping myself in a robe, I open it a crack to see Enzo stood alone. "All the rooms appear taken so I'll crash out here in the hall; if that's okay," he says.

"No, you won't. Have my room, and I'll share with Jenny," I reply.

He laughs and says, "I don't think so; unless you're into threesomes!"

I settle him on the old sofa in the sitting room with blankets and cushions, "It has to be better than the floor."

"I've slept in worse places in my student days."

The following morning, I make my way downstairs to the aftermath, seeing bottles, cans, glasses, and plates strewn around. With a strong black coffee inside me, I set to work, sorting the rubbish into various recycling bins. It's not long before Enzo joins me and lends a hand. By the time my guests' surface, the kitchen looks almost back to normal. I offer everyone coffee and croissants before they leave. Jacques lingers in the hall with Jenny, arranging to meet her again, before kissing her passionately and waving with a goofy grin on his face as he leaves. She, on the other hand, has the look of a woman that had a good time. Enzo hugs me warmly before leaving and thanking me for a super evening – quite the gentleman.

"Well, that was lame. Wasn't Enzo good in the sack?" Asks Jenny nonchalantly, while nursing a black coffee.

I look back at her messy hair and pink cheeks, and reply, "Unlike some people, I don't jump into bed with men at every convenient opportunity."

She snorts and pokes out her tongue, before saying, "Loosen up and enjoy your youth while you still have it. You're likely to become a little old spinster with lots of cats."

47

The following week is taken up with preparing the Chateau for the Christmas party for the 'old folks'. Xavier and Gus spend time in the woods with Shadow, returning with holly, ivy, a large tree, as well as truffles, while Jenny and I scour the local Christmas markets for inexpensive decorations, as well as getting inspiration for making our own.

The big day arrives with a frenzy of activity. We prepared most of the vegetables yesterday, so they're ready to cook, and the dining room table is extended and decorated with festive touches. Alice is busy at the range, slowly roasting the poor boar that happened to be in the wrong place at the wrong time, and Rose is stuffing an unfortunate goose with garlic, leeks, potatoes, and herbs. And Jenny? Well, she's just floating around looking pretty. My jobs include warming the soup, cooking the vegetables, and making the pudding. The sponge only needs to be warmed up, and the crème anglaise not made until required. Pedro is the wine waiter, and Sylvie should be arriving soon with the school choir. Enzo has kindly volunteered to drive the minibus, delivering our elderly guests.

With everyone in their seats, the feast commences and is well received. My honey truffle sponge and crème anglaise go down a treat; it's a good job I made enough for seconds! After lunch, the guests are assisted into the drawing room to listen to Sylvie play the piano, while the children sing traditional carols. The raffle is drawn by Monsieur Le Maire, with not a bottle of Macallan Gold in sight! After the event, the elderly guests are given a gift before being ushered back into their waiting bus, declaring the party a huge success. Most of the children are in the kitchen finishing off the left over's when I hear the piano playing in the drawing room. A chill runs down my spine. Oblivious, Sylvie continues handing out gingerbread men to the children in the kitchen. I creep into the hall and peep through a crack in the door to see a young boy sat, laughing on the piano stool. He appears happy, so I tiptoe away, not wanting to disturb the moment, whatever it may be. I hope Aunt Mary enjoyed the party too!

After clearing up the aftermath, I'm exhausted and head upstairs for a long soak and an early night. Jenny, on the other hand, is getting ready to go out with Jacques. I give her a key and tell her to be careful, but doubt she'll be back tonight. As expected, its lunchtime the following day before Jenny returns. She's cutting it fine as usual; her plane leaves at six this evening.

The following week, I get my first enquiry for a small wedding reception. Philip Balaux is marrying for the second time in early March, and only immediate family and a few close friends will attend. His elderly mother, who is paying for the reception, was a guest at the old folks Christmas party and wants the same menu serving. I'm both excited and nervous at the same time as I make an appointment for the happy couple to come out and see the venue. Philip and Joelle, who live and work in Paris, though have a second home in the Ardèche, seem happy and relaxed and not too bothered by the details. According to them, it's just a small party to appease his wealthy mother, who objects to them living in sin. I hope all my clients will be as easy to please.

I have an appointment in town with the printers this afternoon, who are supplying my new stationery, but the weather forecast is grim. Jacques has fitted winter tyres to Dolly, so I should be okay. As I climb out of the valley bottom, the rain quickly turns to sleet and a few miles higher it turns to snow, truly festive, and only a week to Christmas. A little snow will be pleasant. Shadow, as his name suggests is sat in the passenger seat, peering out into the winter wonderland. Dolly doesn't have in-flight entertainment, not even a radio, so I sing Christmas carols to Shadow as we wind our way up the valley side. The snow is getting heavier, and I'm starting to feel a little anxious, as I've never driven in the white stuff before. I try to remember my quick 'You Tube' lesson on - 'how-to-drive-in-snow' - keep in low gear, - keep moving, - don't brake on bends. Yes, I'm doing all of that. I've brought a shovel too; in case I get stuck. Easy. What could possibly go wrong?

The pine forests around me are stunning, exactly like a scene from a Christmas card. Looking at the view reminds me that I will have to go around the village with my newly printed cards advertising my... The thought shatters as I slam my brakes on as I round the next bend into a dip. A fox, or is it a young boar, is crossing the road? Time stands still as I slide slowly, diagonally down the road in almost slow motion. The brakes, and steering are useless. They don't respond as I continue to glide. I'm only a passenger, going wherever fate chooses. I see the hill side approaching. At least it's not the side with the steep drop, I think, strangely calm. I feel a bang. Then everything goes dark.

When I regain consciousness, it's starting to get dark, I slowly try to pull myself upright, then realise I'm still wearing my seatbelt. Looking around, I can see that I'm at an angle, but not completely on my side. Dolly seems to be propped up by a sturdy pine tree. The side window is broken and, on the floor, with a severed branch lying inches from my head. Talk about a lucky escape! Unclipping myself carefully, I check that all my limbs are working, then assess for bleeding. Nope, not anywhere visible at least. Shadow! Oh No! Where's Shadow? Forgetting about myself, I drag my body out of the car and look around. The snow has stopped, and I can make out tracks leading back the way we came. Poor Shadow, I hope he's okay. I can't see any blood in the snow, so hopefully, he's not injured, but he won't know where he is. Lost in this deep snow, how will he find food? He'll be so cold, possibly hypothermic by now! Starting to panic, I locate my phone, Xavier will know what to do. No signal! Damn this stupid country! What am I going to do?

Trying to calm myself, I go into professional mode. I've worked in A&E, seen much worse than this. Think Laura! I wrap myself in the blanket that I put on the back seat and pull my wellies and gloves on, then assess the car. Apart from the broken window and a small dent on the side of the roof, Dolly seems to be okay; If only I can get her back on her wheels. Pushing and heaving have little impact. I'm getting nowhere and using up my reserves. Should I start to walk? It's about ten kilometres back to civilisation. It will be dark soon, and I don't have a torch. I could end up in more trouble. No, my best chance is to stay by my car. Surely someone will pass by soon. Yes, that's my plan. I open the car boot and find my red warning triangle, placing it in the middle of the road. Dolly's lights are still working, so I leave them on, clearing the snow from the lenses. I lean against a tree and wait. Half an hour passes and I'm starting to get cold, extremely cold. The Mistral has picked up and is blowing the snow around, and the light is fading fast. I need to find shelter. Should I risk getting back into the car?

It's far enough off the road and there's no other traffic, but what if someone else skids on the same spot and crashes into me? It's unlikely, lightening never strikes in the same place twice – so the saying goes. An icy wind whips more snow into my cold face; it feels like a hundred little needles piercing my skin. I'll have to take the risk. I can't stay out here any longer.

I decide to sit in the back. Then I can prop myself up. Looking in my bag, I find a wrapped biscuit and a small bottle of water, which have probably been in there for ages. I'll save them until I get desperate. I can always eat snow. I smile to myself remembering the old joke, 'never eat yellow snow'. Perhaps I shouldn't have scoffed at Xavier when he was trying to teach me how to light a fire. As I lie back my head starts to pound. I lean over to look in Dolly's little mirror. Damn, I have a small cut above my left eye. Nothing that a few Steristrips won't fix. Lying back down, I try to relax my body and stop thinking about the intense cold. Poor Shadow. I do hope he finds somewhere to shelter out of this bitter wind.

I feel like I'm floating. Yes, I'm in the fresh sparking water in the gorge, bobbing about below the waterfall. I can feel the warm rays from the sun on my face, but it's wet... and rough.

I slowly open my eyes to see Shadow standing over me with his warm rough tongue licking my face. But I know I'm still dreaming, poor Shadow. Lost. I'll probably never see him again. He wasn't truly mine anyway; he's a nomad, wandering from place to place, lost. A bit like me, he doesn't belong anywhere. I do hope he finds someone special with whom to share his next adventure. I close my eyes and slowly drift once more.

I'm floating again, moving slowly downstream. I feel the occasional jolt, but it's just the rapids swirling between the rocks. It's so peaceful and serene.

Ouch, that stings, I think groggily. I try to bat away the evil wasp causing me pain.

I'm out of the water now, wrapped in a big warm towel. I can hear voices... a man with a familiar accent. Who is he? What does he want? Go away, I want to sleep; I'm so tired...!

I awaken slowly, feeling warm for the first time in a while. "Welcome back. How are you feeling?" Asks the familiar voice with piercing blue eyes, I push him away and sit bolt upright. "Hey, it's okay, you're safe now, take it easy ..." he says.

I feel like I'm hungover. Was I at a party? Have I slept with this guy? Slowly, the pieces of the jigsaw click into place. Dolly in the snow, and Shadow, "I've got to go and look for Shadow. He's lost in the snow!" I shout, pushing back the duvet and attempting to get up. The man gently takes my hand from the duvet and places it on the warm furry thing sat at my side, instantly stilling my movements. My eyes focus, and I look down to see Shadow snuggled at my side, keeping me warm. I peer back up into the kind blue eyes in front of me to see Enzo looking concerned. Perhaps I've died and gone to heaven.

"Shhh, everything's alright." He says quietly, "Shadow is safe and well. You've probably got a bit of concussion, but I didn't want to risk the long trip to the hospital in the snow. There's a wee cut on your forehead, but I've patched it up. You'll be good as new in no time. Now you need to rest."

I glance around. I appear to be in a log cabin, with a wood burner in the centre of the room. "Where am I?" I ask, lying back into the comfortable sofa.

"This is where I'm staying; it's in the grounds of the vets' practice where I work," he replies softly.

I lean forward to thank him, but no words pass from my mouth. Instead I kiss him gently on his soft, warm lips and whisper, "I've wanted to do that ever since you sat at my kitchen table, eating clafoutis."

End of book one

Read on for a sneak preview of book two…

If you have enjoyed my first novel, I would be incredibly grateful if you would consider leaving a review. Thank you.

You can contact me at –

info@emma-sharp-author.com

www.emma-sharp-author.com

SWEET PEA

Book 2 of The Chateau Series

1

I wake the next morning in the middle of a big double bed; wrapped in a warm duvet. Alone. Its eerily quiet. Where's Enzo? No creaking doors, thudding in the attic or clanking pipes. Carefully, I untangle myself from the bedding and look out of the small window; the land is huddled under a blanket of fresh snow, at least a foot deep. How am I going to get home? Just as I start to look for my clothes Enzo arrives with a breakfast tray.

"Hey, you should be in bed," he says, as he puts the tray down. Realising I'm only in my underwear, I take his advice and make a dash for the bed; my head instantly throbbing as it hits the pillow. Looking at me sympathetically he continues, "You need to take it easy for a few days, here, get this down you."

I look at him over my bowl of porridge, and say, "I don't remember going to bed, in fact, there's quite a lot I don't remember."

"Well, I'm not surprised; you took a nasty knock on the head when you lost control in the snow, but the only thing that matters now is that you're here, safe."

Finishing my breakfast, I look up, "Where did you find Shadow?"

Taking the tray from me he replies, "Well, I got a call from Xavier, he was worried that you'd set off and the forecast was bad; apparently he tried to talk you out of going but… Well, you went anyway, and ended up in a ditch. I was on my way to look for you when I came across Shadow - running back towards the village. All's well that ends well."

I sigh and touch my head to feel a neat row of Steristrips above my eye, which feels swollen.

"Have I got a black eye?" I ask, wincing.

"You look like you've had a round with

Rocky," he replies, as his phone rings. Looking at me he apologises and takes the call. "Sorry, I have to go, there's a horse down in the snow that can't get back up, it doesn't sound good, but I'll try my best. Don't do anything. I'll be back as soon as I can."

I climb out of bed and watch his Land Rover disappear behind the trees; I do hope he'll be ok. Locating the bathroom, I manage a quick shower. Not wanting to wear the same pants, I borrow a pair of Enzo's; too big but my jeans will hold them up.

With Enzo absent I examine his temporary home. I notice the cabin is small but snug, one open plan living-kitchen, with a bedroom and bathroom. Not much to explore, no photographs of family or friends, and very few personal effects. Eventually, glancing at my phone I see I have several missed calls and texts from Xavier. I really don't fancy a lecture from him right now, so I send him a quick text.

Sorry to scare you, I'm safe and well at Enzo's, back soon.

"There, that's as much as he's getting!" I tell Shadow, who barks in agreement.

Flopping onto the sofa I turn the TV on, but can't concentrate, pressing the off button I lean my head back and close my eyes. The last few months of my life are projected onto the inside of my eyelids like a film, starting with the letter from the solicitor; informing me that I'd inherited a Chateau in France. But they omitted some important information - like its state of disrepair, and the secret staircase hiding treasures in the attic, the false wall concealing an old Bugatti, the hidden wine cellar, battling with red tape, and much more. The highs, making new friends, and the lows as some people just want to be enemies.

Then there's Enzo the Scottish vet with Italian ancestry, working in the south of France. I know I'm falling for him; but does he feel the same? He's going back to Glasgow in the summer to work at his local practice, while I've just committed to making a new life in the Ardeche. Is there much point perusing this burgeoning romance? A disturbing thought pops into my head – has he already got a girlfriend? He hasn't mentioned anyone, and I haven't found a photograph at the side of his bed. Surely, he wouldn't have let me kiss him if he were currently in a relationship. He doesn't seem like a player. Hey, what would I know? I have a poor track record when it comes to men.

I wish I could be more like my good friend Jenny, 'enjoy every day as if it's your last,' that's her motto; perhaps she's right. I've just had a lucky escape. This is my one and only life. It's not a practice. So, what if he goes back home? It's not the end of the world - as my gran so often used to say. Yes, take the bull by the horns, make hay while the sun shines, strike while the irons hot, if the cap fits, wear it. She had some funny sayings, but I do miss her words of wisdom. I'm brought back to the present by my phone, a text from Xavier.

Stay where you are for now, ze electricity supply is off, zey are trying to fix it, will let you know when its back on.

What am I supposed to do now? I can't stay here, there's only one bed for a start. I can manage without electricity for a day or too, can't I? I've got oil and logs. I won't tell Enzo; I'll just ask him to take me home when he returns.

I'm woken by a kiss on the top of my head. "How are you feeling? Sorry I was longer than I'd hoped; there's a tree down on the road, it's taken the power out. You'll have to stay here until they get it back on."

Sighing I ask, "How's the horse?" Enzo just shakes his head and walks over to feed the log burner. I know my protests will fall on deaf ears, but I'll try anyway. "I'll be fine at home; I've got logs and oil…"

"Non-negotiable. You're staying here where I can keep an eye on you." He says, without looking in my direction.

Okay, I didn't think I'd win that battle. My phone rings, it's the insurance company asking where I want Dolly recovering to. I instruct them to take her to Jacques, he'll repair her for me.

"You need a 4 x 4, something like mine, I know you're attached to Dolly but she's not practical, or very safe," Enzo lectures.

Nodding I concede, "If this is a taste of winter here then you're right, but I'm not getting rid of her."

After supper I know I need to address the elephant in the room, "I'll sleep on the sofa, it's quite comfortable…"

I don't manage to finish before Enzo interrupts. "I don't think so, not with concussion, you use the bathroom first while I grab a pillow and blanket."

When I wake the following morning, Enzo is nowhere to be seen; just a note by the kettle, 'called out to an emergency, will ring'. After breakfast I get another text from Xavier.

Ze power is back on

I quickly reply

Great, can you pick me up?

I feel bad bailing on Enzo, just leaving a note saying Xavier called and I scrounged a lift home, but I'm still confused and unsure of what to do about him. I never was particularly good at making the first move, and I've got so much to do; only a few days to Christmas. I'm making Christmas lunch at the Chateau for Alice, Gus and Xavier; Enzo is on call but said he'd come if he's available. I've never liked Christmas since my parent's accident, gran always tried her absolute best, but it was never the same. I've worked for the last three Christmas days; always volunteered, it helps to keep busy. Stops me from dwelling on the past.

Xavier stares at me as I climb into his truck. "It looks worse than it feels" I say, as I fasten the seatbelt. Thankfully, he has the good grace to keep quiet on the journey home.

Alice is in the kitchen at the Chateau with hot soup bubbling in a pan, she kisses me, then chastises me for going out alone in the snow. Before they leave Alice announces that Christmas lunch will be at the farmhouse, and that I'm to do nothing. I accept graciously, not really feeling up to cooking a goose and all the trimmings. The events of the last twenty-four hours are creeping up on me, and I know I ought to rest. Yes, practice what you preach Laura.

www.emma-sharp-author.com

ABOUT THE AUTHOR

Emma Sharp is the author of The Chateau Trilogy comprising of: The Letter, Sweet Pea and Secrets and Surprises. She is currently working on her latest novel, Innocence in Provence, which will be available in late 2020.

Emma, a former nurse was born and raised in Yorkshire. She has two grown up daughters, a grand-daughter and a much-loved French Bulldog, Nellie. She loves to travel and finds that she writes her best work when she's at her caravan amidst the stunning scenery of the Yorkshire Dales.

She has also appeared on local radio reading her short stories and is as a member of a writing group, who meet regularly to review and appraise each other's work.

I hope you enjoy reading her novels.

Printed in Great Britain
by Amazon